THE REGENCY LORDS & LADIES COLLECTION

Glittering Regency Love Affairs
from your favourite historical authors.

THE REGENCY LORDS & LADIES COLLECTION

Available from the
Regency Lords & Ladies Large Print Collection

LADY CLAIRVAL'S MARRIAGE

Paula Marshall

First published in Great Britain 1997
Large Print Edition 2009
Harlequin Mills & Boon Limited,
Eton House, 18-24 Paradise Road, Richmond, Surrey TW9 1SR

© Paula Marshall 1997

ISBN: 978 0 263 21031 6

Set in Times Roman 16 on 17¾ pt.
083-0209-84691

Printed and bound in Great Britain
by CPI Antony Rowe, Chippenham, Wiltshire

Prologue

There was no reasoning with him. The steward panted up the tower stairs after his master.

'M'lord, I beg of you. Do not be overhasty. M'lady…'

He got no further. The face the Marquess of Clairval turned on him was a baleful one, suffused with so much anger that it was no longer purple, but almost black. He flourished the whip in his right hand at his overbold servant.

'Be silent!' he roared. 'Or I'll use this about *your* sides instead of on hers. She will obey me today, or the worst will befall her.'

The Marquess possessed a turn of phrase which would not have disgraced a Drury Lane melodrama, but this was no play but real life; the blows he intended for his abused wife were real ones, not the acrobatic tricks of an actor—as the steward well knew. But he had never used a horsewhip on her before…

The man fell silent. He followed his master up the stairs with a sinking heart, condemned to witness whatever cruelty Clairval decided to inflict on his helpless wife. The steward had watched her turn from a pretty young bride into a gaunt shivering wraith, unrecognisable to anyone who had known her before she became Clairval's lady.

Best to be silent. The monster in front of him would doubtless double the punishment he intended for her simply because a servant had been foolish enough to plead on her behalf.

They were past the turn of the steep stone staircase: an oak door strengthened with great iron hinges stood before them.

'Unlock it!' snarled the Marquess, standing back.

The steward put the key in the massive lock, and threw the door open. Clairval strode by him, cracking his whip. The room he entered was small, with a curtained recess in one corner which held a rude bed. It contained a deal table, two chairs, a candlestick, a shelf on which a few books stood, a washstand and an iron pail. A chest for clothes stood in another corner. The only daylight came from a slit in the massive walls.

There was no sign of the woman held prisoner in this grim cell.

'In bed, one supposes, the idle bitch,' sneered the Marquess. 'Come out, madam. I would speak with you. Delay can only make matters worse.'

There was no answer. The steward coughed nervously, and his master turned on him. 'Be quiet, damn you. I would have her answer me, not listen to your rantings and snivellings.'

He raised his voice. 'Come out, madam, or I will drag you out to give you the punishment you deserve for disobedience,' and he cracked the whip again.

Still no answer.

With a muttered oath Clairval strode over to the recess, pulled back the curtain to find...nothing.

Both recess and bed were empty.

The bed had been carefully made. A ragged cotton nightgown was folded neatly on the pillow. But of its maltreated owner there was no sign.

'No!' This came out as an animal howl as Clairval staggered back into the room to stare round it, to gaze at the low ceiling as though his wife might somehow be hanging there. He even strode over to the bookcase to pull it from the wall lest she had found a way to conceal herself in the small space behind it.

Common sense told him that there was nowhere

that she could hide; that his wife had, by some means he had yet to discover, escaped from the prison he had made for her these past two years.

Someone would pay for this, by God! and that someone was cowering behind him, as apparently shocked and surprised as his master. But no matter, in lieu of anyone else, his back would serve as well as hers to bear the brunt of Clairval's anger on discovering that his bird had flown.

Not only did he use his whip to beat his steward senseless, but at the end, he threw him, unconscious, down the stone stairs, where he lay unmoving, before he descended them himself, roaring vengeance on those who had helped her to escape. For sure, she could not have found her way out of her prison alone.

Nor had she; but how she had done so, and with whose help, Clairval was never to discover, only to suspect—and if any of his vast staff of servants knew who it was who had risked everything by rescuing his unfortunate wife, they never betrayed him by word or deed.

All Clairval's bellowings and threats were in vain. They could not make his servants tell him what they professed not to know. No one had seen his missing wife for at least two days, and although he organised a search immediately, no trace of her could be found.

'For,' said his secretary, a cowed man of middle age who could not hope to find new employment if Clairval dismissed him, 'the turnpike road from York runs south not far from here. She may have taken the coach for London—and if she has it would be difficult to trace her. But that, of course, is merely my supposition.'

'To hell with your suppositions, man! You know no more than I do. A madwoman is loose, and that madwoman is my wife. Have bills printed, offering a reward for her return. See to it. At once.'

'Yes, m'lord. At once, m'lord.'

His secretary knew better than to do other than to try to placate him. That the bills would be lies, and that the mad person was the Marquess of Clairval, not his unfortunate wife, was a truth that no one, in that part of Yorkshire which Clairval owned and controlled, dare utter. His excuse for imprisoning her had been that she was mad, and the law in 1827 said that a man might do as he pleased with his wife without let or hindrance. She had no separate existence but was his to do with as he wished. He might imprison her, or turn her out of the house, penniless. All this the law allowed.

And now his wife had disappeared from Clairval Castle, and the law gave him the right to drag her back to the prison from whence she had fled—particularly since he had branded her as a madwoman.

But although the Marquess of Clairval might be the Lord of all around him, the months dragged by, and still the Marchioness remained lost…and daily he grew more grimly determined to find her.

And if he ever found her…what then?

Chapter One

'I must say, Luke,' remarked Cressy, Lady Lyndale, carefully laying a flawless blue wash of sky on the water colour painting before her, 'that I never thought that you would still be unmarried at nearly thirty.'

'Nor did I,' replied Luke Harcourt cheerfully. He, too, was busy painting the same beautiful scene. It was a fine day in a spring which had arrived early that year. They were both sitting on the terrace overlooking the park at Haven's End, the Lyndales' home in Wiltshire. Behind them was the great house from which the estate took its name. Before them the ground fell away towards open country, lush and wooded.

There seemed little useful to reply to that, so—remarkably—Cressy said nothing, although she was used to expressing herself freely and forcibly.

She merely frowned, and gazed into the middle distance where her husband, James, Earl of Lyndale, sat propped against a tree, reading.

Beyond him, at the point where the parkland ended and the open country began, two of his small sons were flying a kite with the help of their tutor. His daughter, demure and well-behaved, sat beside her governess sewing a fine seam, not far from Cressy and Luke.

Five minutes later Cressy tried another ploy.

'You have met no one who really interests you, perhaps?'

Luke, intrigued by her persistence, for she had never spoken to him on such a subject before, looked across at her and said slowly, 'I believe that to be a correct description of the matter.'

He thought that to speak so baldly and shortly might be thought of as a snub, so he added, carelessly, 'I like my freedom, you know, and would not lightly surrender it to the claims of domesticity.'

Now this, Cressy knew, was a surprisingly pompous statement from Luke, who despite his immense learning, always avoided any appearance of pedantry. Cressy also knew that he was not speaking the exact truth, but she did not like to say so.

Instead she continued painting, and willed herself to wait for any further comment on the subject to come from him—if he wished to make any, that was. She knew that she had been treading on forbidden ground, but Luke's continuing refusal to commit himself to anyone was beginning to worry her—not the least because she feared that she might in part be responsible for it.

She also felt responsible for *him*—and his refusal to marry.

Luke's surname might be Harcourt, and it was generally and politely assumed that he was a distant relative of the Lyndale family, but he was actually her husband's illegitimate son, who happened to be exactly the same age as Cressy was. The politeness consisted in everyone in society accepting the distant-relative explanation of his existence.

Luke had never given any sign that he was hurt by his dubious status or that he resented the fact that he would never inherit his father's title or the beautiful house which had always been his home. Nor had he ever reproached his father for his illegitimacy. He knew that James had been forcibly prevented from marrying his mother, and that when his mother had died in childbirth James had adopted and educated him.

More, once his father had succeeded to the earldom he had settled enough money on Luke to give him an annual competence, large enough to keep him in comfort. He had also been given one of the Lyndale family's many surnames. His wit and charm had made him popular, and he was accepted everywhere in good society.

So far however, he had not chosen to marry, something which worried his father because he felt that his son's consciousness of his illegitimacy was responsible for his remaining single.

He had recently told Cressy so. His wife had looked thoughtfully at him—and did not tell her husband what she knew was the real reason. She had first met Luke when they were both eighteen, when she was already in love with his father despite the difference in their ages.

Luke had fallen passionately in love with Cressy from the very first moment that he had met her— but he had also seen that her love was given, once and for all, to his father. He had behaved impeccably towards them both, but Cressy, wise beyond her years, had rapidly divined the secrets of Luke's heart. Now she was beginning to suspect that his never-to-be-fulfilled passion for his father's wife had rendered all other women pale beside her.

This she deeply regretted.

Luke ought to marry. He was everything a good husband and father should be—but she could not tell him so. Nor could she tell James Luke's secret.

What she *could* do was to try to turn Luke's thoughts towards marriage. Now this, she knew, was meddling, and something which she normally avoided, but she could not resist saying, 'There must be some young woman somewhere, Luke, who could possibly…' She paused for a moment, not knowing how to finish the sentence. Luke finished it for her.

'Prevent me from turning into a crusty old bachelor.'

'Exactly.' Cressy was relieved that Luke had done her work for her. 'That is the point.'

Luke turned his head in her direction and gave her his infectious grin. 'James thinks that I am that already. Or rather, a crusty young one. You know what his nickname for me is?'

Cressy's smile was rueful. 'Oh yes, the "Man of Letters"!'

'No "Man of Letters" ought ever to have a wife. Bachelorhood, a tortoiseshell cat, a faithful and elderly housekeeper, and a band of bachelor friends are all he deserves.'

'You deserve more than that,' was Cressy's quiet response, and the pair of them fell silent again, concentrating on their painting until the arrival of Cressy's elder son, Robert.

'Mama, Luke! What are you doing? Oh, please

let me look,' he exclaimed as he reached them. He was dragging his kite behind him, and Will, his younger brother, was panting in his rear. Their tutor was engaged in conversation with James who, having finished reading, was walking towards the little group on the terrace.

He arrived in time to hear Robert say excitedly, 'Oh, Mama, you should see what Luke has done. It is most remarkably like.'

'More like than mine?' questioned Cressy, lazily waving her brush.

'Oh, but he has not painted the same picture as you, Mama. Do show her, Luke.'

Luke thus urged, turned his painting round for the whole party to view it. There, caught for all time, was Cressy, her head bent over her work, an expression of still and utter concentration on her face. It was an expression that all three men had seen many times before: it was the other side of her usual lively vivacity.

But the portrait was something more than that. It was a revelation of the painter's feelings for his subject. Each delicate stroke was a witness to Luke's love for Cressy. His talent for drawing was not the equal of hers, but as with his writing he was able to translate on to paper the deepest feelings of his heart.

Looking at it, James knew at last why his son had never married. Cressy merely said, rather feebly as she afterwards thought, 'I had supposed that you were painting the scene before us.'

'And so I was,' replied Luke, deliberately misunderstanding her. 'Here, it is yours,' and he handed it to her.

James said quietly, 'I paid Lawrence a small fortune for an oil which never showed the truth of my dear wife half so well.'

Something in his voice moved Luke, who said, 'A fluke, sir. I could not do such a thing again.'

Afterwards he was to think that the small painting was in some way a farewell to an impossible dream. He was never to know that he had betrayed himself to his father—although Cressy did.

That evening, as they sat alone in her room, James asked Cressy a question. 'How long have you known, my dear?'

'That Luke is in love with me? Since I first met him, James. But he has never said a wrong word to me. Luke is a man of honour—like yourself.'

'I know. That he is a man of honour, I mean. And that is why he does not marry?'

Cressy rose and strode restlessly about the room. 'That, too. Oh, James, I pray that he will find someone to love, and who will love him. I do so want him to be happy—as we are.'

James put out a hand. 'Sit by me, my dear, and do not fret. The matter is not for us to settle.'

'No, I know that. He is a grown man.'

'And a good one. The only thing which worries me is whether he has enough steel in his character.'

'Oh, as to that,' replied Cressy, and her answer was in her dominant mode, 'we none of us know that until we are tested, I suppose. I don't think that Luke has been tested yet.'

This was what Luke always called a Cressyism. Something so obvious, and yet so profound that it came out almost like a hammer blow. James remembered what she had said some years ago when he had unexpectedly told her that he wished to resume his Parliamentary career, 'I always knew that one day you would wish to be more than a simple squire on your acres. I think that I would make a good hostess for you, don't you?'

He had been fearful that she would argue with him, or object—and all the time she had been waiting for him to make such a decision. And now she had summed up Luke.

He rose, 'To bed,' he said, 'and before that we will pray for our son. That all will be well with him when he returns to London tomorrow.'

'Or offer a libation to the gods for him,' responded Cressy, who, like her late father, was something of a heathen. 'Between us we ought to secure him a happy future!'

Luke arrived at his London lodgings in a downpour. The warm and verdant spring of Haven's End seemed far away; even his landlady's cheerful greeting hardly lifted his depressed spirits.

'Come in, Mr Harcourt, come in, out of the rain! Your journey has not been too troublesome, I hope. You must allow me to put the kettle on. A cup of tea always works wonders for the weary traveller.'

Luke put down his bags and smiled gratefully at her. Mrs Britten was more than his landlady—she was his friend. A middle-aged widow whose parson husband had died early, leaving her only a small annuity, she let the first floor of her comfortable home to a respectable gentleman in order to supplement her income. For the last five years that gentleman had been Mr Luke Harcourt.

Mrs Britten sometimes thought that it had almost been worth coming down in the world to have him in the house. He never caused her any trouble—unlike some of her earlier lodgers. The parties and dinners he gave were always discreet.

He showed no signs of wishing to marry, and it was to be hoped that he never would. She thought that she would never be so lucky again as to have someone in her home who was so charming and so considerate.

Luke followed her into her pretty drawing-room. She had obviously been expecting him, for a tea tray was laid out on a small gate-legged table before the fire. He did not, at first, notice that there were three cups, saucers and plates waiting, not two, nor that on his entrance a young woman rose from the big armchair by the fire.

So quiet, indeed, was she, that afterwards he was to think that his first meeting with her was almost symbolic in nature, in that she was a woman who improved with knowing—unlike some who, after a first splendid impression, grew less and less attractive.

On seeing her, Luke bowed in her direction, and Mrs Britten, before picking up the silver tea-pot, introduced them to one another.

Mrs Cowper, a widow and now her parlour boarder, Luke was rapidly informed, sat down again quickly, allowing him to do so.

She was young, for a widow, with a delicate oval face, dark hair neatly dressed, and the appearance of one who had been recently ill. Her pallor was extreme and she was painfully thin. Her blue eyes were fine, but strangely shadowed. Her clothing was plain and shabby. Her gown was grey, with a wide white linen collar like that of a Quakeress. She had a small piece of fine sewing in her hand.

Luke was later to discover that Mrs Cowper earned a living as a sempstress, making the most exquisite garments. Baby linen, small girls' frocks and little boys' frilled shirts were among her specialities.

'Mrs Cowper is a distant relative of mine,' Mrs Britten explained, handing Luke his tea. 'After her sad loss she fell ill, and I am only too happy to give her a home for as long as she wishes.'

'Mrs Britten has been very good to me,' remarked Mrs Cowper quietly. 'I am deeply grateful to her. She also tells me that you have lodged here for some years, Mr Harcourt, and that you are a famous writer.' Her voice was low and pretty.

'A writer, but hardly famous,' he replied, 'one day, perhaps, but not yet.'

'He is too modest, my dear Anne,' interjected Mrs Britten robustly. 'He is responsible for a remarkable tome on politics which I understand caused quite a stir when it was published, and now he writes for all the best magazines. He had a piece in Blackwood's recently.'

She could not have gazed more proudly at Luke

if he had been her own son. She and Mr Britten had been childless: a great grief to them both.

Luke waved a hand as a mild disclaimer. The fine eyes, he saw, never looked directly at him—which piqued him a little. It was not that he was vain, but it would have been dishonest for him to pretend that he was unaware of his good looks. With his dark, lightly waving hair, amber eyes, a sensitive shapely mouth, and a physique which was notable for its strength, he was accustomed to draw all feminine eyes—but not, apparently, Mrs Cowper's.

Her gravity, too, was extreme, as became plain when the conversation continued. 'This book you wrote, Mr Harcourt? May I ask what its subject was?'

'A philosopher who has been greatly neglected,' he told her. 'An Italian, Niccolo Machiavelli, whom I consider understood the practical art of government better than anyone else whose works I have ever read.'

'Old Nick,' she said suddenly. 'The devil was nicknamed after him, I believe—or he was nicknamed after the devil!'

This surprised Luke so much that he said without thinking, 'Now that *is* truly remarkable, Mrs Cowper. Not many with whom I have spoken have known that.'

For the first time she looked straight at him: not at her work, or the opposite wall, or the fire.

'My father gave me a good education, but he also believed that I should acquire what he called the womanly arts—which was prescient of him, because a lady who wants bread may earn it by sewing, not by an understanding of political philosophy!'

'Very true,' remarked Luke, 'if unfortunate—for the lady, I mean. Our society does not much consider what a gentlewoman is to do to keep herself alive if she has no husband or father to look after her.'

Mrs Britten, surprised a little by the animation of her friend—but not completely so, because she privately thought that Mr Luke Harcourt could charm birds off trees if he so wished—made her contribution to the discussion.

'You may well say that, Mr Harcourt. I do not know what I should have done if Mr Britten had not left me this house and a small competence. They have enabled me to live in comfort, rather than merely existing. Gentlewomen are not supposed to speak of these things, I know. I also know that you, Mr Harcourt, will not think us wrong to do so.'

'Gentlewomen are not supposed to think of many things,' said Mrs Cowper equably, examin-

ing her beautiful stitching. 'But we have to eat—
just like gentlemen. And there are so many things
that we may not do to earn our daily bread.'

She paused and stitched on for a moment without looking up. Then still in that gentle voice, she
said, 'I am surprised, Mr Harcourt, that you did not
choose to become an MP. Mrs Britten tells me that
your patron, Lord Lyndale, controls several seats,
any one of which you might have chosen to grace.'

'Despite the fact that Mr Pitt was Prime Minis-
ter at four and twenty,' riposted Luke with a smile,
'I feel that I am still too young to grace the
House—later, perhaps.'

'You have no wish to put your Machiavellian notions into practice, Mr Harcourt?'

He thought there was just a touch of criticism in
her tone, and, indeed, after saying this she avoided
Luke's eyes completely.

He gave a light laugh and replied, a slight melancholy in his voice, 'I think that perhaps you do
not judge me to be sufficiently serious.'

Her fine brows rose. 'On such a short acquaintance, Mr Harcourt, I have no right to judge you
at all.'

Luke had no answer to that. Mrs Britten, apparently unaware of any odd undercurrents running
between her two protégés, offered happily, 'I am

sure, Mr Harcourt, that if ever you do become an MP you will make a splendid one.'

Whether or not Mrs Cowper agreed with her was not revealed. She stitched on for a few moments before rising to her feet, saying, 'You will both excuse me, I know, but I must complete this little garment for tomorrow, and although I have enjoyed Mr Harcourt's conversation I must absent myself from it in order to concentrate on my work.'

Luke stood up immediately and watched her walk to the door.

He thought that she limped slightly but not enough to mar the air of contained grace which sat so much at odds with her humble occupation and her dowdy dress. He had the uncomfortable impression that if he had not been present she would have been content to remain and chat with Mrs Britten.

How he knew this was a mystery to him—as much a mystery as Mrs Cowper was. She turned at the door, gave a little bow, saying as she rose from it, 'It has been very pleasant to meet you, Mr Harcourt. I wish that I could say that I had read your book.'

'Oh, if you would like to do so, Mrs Cowper, then I have a copy in my room which you may borrow. We could have a little chat about it later.'

For a moment he hoped that she was going to

smile, but she thought better of it. 'If so, Mr Harcourt—' was her parting shot '—you must be kind to me when you do. Mrs Britten has already told me that you were expected to be a great scholar at Oxford, once you gained your degree there, but disappointed everyone when you decided to live in the world and be a writer instead. I have no guns as large as that to counter you with.'

She had surprised him again. There was a delicate edge to everything she said. If only she would look at him! But she was gone, the door closing behind her, and he was left with tea, cakes, and Mrs Britten.

'Come on, Harcourt, old fellow! You must be tired. I've not known you so quiet since Examination Day at Oxford! Surely a couple of months in the country haven't ruined your appetite for fun.'

Luke looked up at his friend and fellow scribbler, Patrick O'Hare. Pat had a pretty opera dancer on his knee and was tenderly feeding her brandy from the glass in his hand. They were in a dubious hell off the Haymarket, and Pat's destination for the evening was obvious. For some unknown reason, or perhaps the memory of a pair of blue eyes, Luke had no taste for amorous adventure that night.

He had spent the first part of it listening to Mrs Britten telling him that Mrs Cowper's life had been a sad one. 'I believe that her marriage was an arranged one and not too happy. She was left virtually penniless as a result of her late husband's lack of consideration for her in making his will. After his death she became ill, and is only just recovering. She deserves our utmost sympathy.'

Mrs Britten spoke with such passion and feeling that Luke felt that she considered that he had been a little rough in his treatment of Mrs Cowper, and if so, he reproached himself. It had not been his intention to disturb her.

He would take more care in future—although he doubted whether in his busy life he would run across her very often. After all, she was Mrs Britten's friend, not his.

Feeling a little lonely after leaving the loving cocoon of Haven's End, he had gone on to The Coal Hole where Renton Nicholson kept open house. There he had met Pat, who had a fine tenor voice, and had entertained the company with songs both sentimental and bawdy. Half-cut before he met Luke, Pat had insisted that the pair of them seek livelier entertainment than even Nicholson provided.

Luke had demurred a little and then agreed. It

was not his habit to go trawling for loose women, or barques of frailty. Until his recent visit to Wiltshire, he had had a long-term relationship with a pretty milliner who called herself Josette.

He had wined and dined her at Cremorne Gardens the night before he had left London for the country, but when the meal was over, she had put a hand over his, and had said earnestly, 'Luke, there is something I have to tell you.'

What a simple-minded ass he had been!

'Can't it wait until we go home?' he had asked, home being the two rooms he had rented for her in a house off the Haymarket.

She had shaken her head, and had said, 'Oh, no, Luke. We must say goodbye here. It would be kinder to both of us.'

'Goodbye?'

He remembered how puzzled he had been. Nothing had been said between them to suggest that she was about to end their happy arrangement.

'Yes, goodbye.'

He remembered her unaccustomed firmness. 'I shall shortly be going back home, Luke, to Kent, to marry my childhood sweetheart, now that I have saved enough to help us to start married life together.'

Luke was a kind young man, but his life had always been easy. The only hard thing in it had occurred when he had fallen deeply in love with Cressy, so deeply that he had resigned himself to remaining unmarried.

Nevertheless, the loving relationship which he had enjoyed with Josette LeClerc—her real name was Jean Clarke—had come to mean a great deal to him. He had found it impossible not to say what would hurt her, although afterwards he had cursed himself for his cruelty.

'And does this young man know how you have earned the money which you have saved?' he had asked her coldly.

Josette had flushed and had pulled her hand away from his. She had hung her head a little and had said in a low voice, 'No, and I hope that he never does. He thinks that I saved it out of my pay for working in Madam's shop.'

She had paused before continuing. 'I had not thought that you would be unkind, Luke, because you have always been so good to me. But you and I both know that you would never have married me. I want a real home of my own, and babies, and Nat will give me both of them.'

He had not been able to contradict her, for it had been nothing less than the truth. But something important was going out of his life, and when he returned to London it would not be to Josette's welcoming arms.

Was it that which was haunting him? He had taken Josette's hand in his again, had stroked it, and had said, as lovingly as he could, 'Forgive me, my dear, but I was shocked at the thought of losing you.'

And that had been the truth. He had not been lying to please her.

'Yes,' she had told him steadily, 'for you had all the pleasures of marriage, did you not? And none of the pains.'

Luke had not thought her to be so shrewd. Then he remembered how quickly she had learned the manners and carriage of a lady. She had persuaded him to teach her how to read and write, and had asked him for advice on dress. Would she unlearn it all for Nat—or use just enough of it to help him in her new life?

They had parted kindly enough at the end, though the parting had been bittersweet and had pained them both. He had pulled out his purse and had tipped a pile of golden sovereigns into her hand. 'For you,' he had said, kissing her on the cheek. 'For your new life.'

'Oh, no, Luke, no need for that. You must know that it was never just the money with you.'

He would not let her say him nay. 'I am not trying to pay you off, Josette. What I give you is in gratitude for the happiness we have shared. Try to think of me occasionally—but not if it spoils your new life.'

'And that is how I wish to remember you, Luke. You were always kind to me. Not like many.'

So it had ended…

'Still silent, Harcourt? It's not like you.' It was Pat again, reproaching him cheerfully for his moodiness. Luke acknowledged that it *was* unlike him, and called for another drink. Remembering how he had lost Josette had quenched whatever appetite for 'fun' which he had arrived with.

'You're right, Pat,' he said. 'I *am* tired. Forgive me. I'll call a cab and try to get a good night's sleep.'

It was not so very late, after all, but opening the door into Mrs Britten's, he was as quiet as he could be, tip-toeing up the stairs so as not to disturb the sleeping house.

Not quiet enough perhaps, for the door of the small library-cum-study on the first floor was opened as he passed it—and there was Mrs Britten's new lodger.

She was still in her day dress, although it was just past midnight, and her dark hair was in a cloud about her shoulders. She had a candle in her hand.

'Oh, it's you, Mr Harcourt. I thought it might be a burglar. Indeed, I do not know what I thought.'

'I am sorry to disturb you,' he said. 'Although I see that you were not asleep.'

'Not in the library, no.' She was looking away from him again. 'I fear that I often find sleep difficult. I will try not to disturb you if the need to arise and find something to entertain me in the night's watches should occur again.'

He could not prevent himself from a pleasantry—if only to find out how she reacted to it. 'I see that I must lend you my book as quickly as possible. It is sure to send you to sleep!'

This sally brought the shadow of a smile to her pale face.

'Nothing about Old Nick could possibly send me to sleep, Mr Harcourt. Indeed, I would consider that it is sure to keep me awake.'

They had been conversing in whispers in order to avoid waking those already asleep. Luke was suddenly conscious that to be found on the first landing with Mrs Cowper after midnight could scarcely help her reputation.

'I will bid you goodnight, Mrs Cowper. It would not do for us to be found alone together in the dark.'

She looked him straight in the eye for the first time. 'Oh, Mr Harcourt, think nothing of *that*. So much worse things might befall a lady than talking to a perfect gentleman such as yourself after hours.'

Luke was not sure by her words or her manner whether she was funning or not—or reproaching him. There was something fey about her dry manner, and the tilt of her head when she had finished speaking. It was as though she was making an arcane joke impossible for him to understand.

His only response was to bow, bid her goodnight again, and leave her. From something Mrs Britten had said earlier, he gathered that Mrs Cowper had two rooms on the second landing. Whether or no she was repairing to them immediately was no business of his.

On the other hand, she had succeeded in driving his lost Josette from his mind. Instead, he was puzzling over what was so strange about Mrs Cowper because, for all the slight acerbity of her speech to him, he had gained the impression that he frightened her.

Which was not the usual effect Mr Luke Harcourt had on ladies, married, single or widowed!

Chapter Two

Luke saw little of Mrs Cowper for the next two weeks. Like the man and woman moving in and out of a weather house, she was never in the drawing-room when he was there, and presumably always inhabited it when he was out. They never even passed on the stairs. It was difficult not to believe that she was avoiding him. To his surprise, Luke found himself looking out for her. Perhaps it was because her manner to him was so enigmatic that he had come to think of her as a puzzle to be solved.

Luke loved puzzles, both in life and in literature, and he was good at solving them, which was what his new employer found useful in his writing. He had recently been trying to sell the series of articles which he had written whilst he had been staying at Haven's End. They were analyses of the various programmes for electoral reform that had been proposed over the last few years, and he had finally succeeded in placing them with Pomfret Bayes, who edited *The Pall Mall Gazette*.

Bayes had suggested that he might write short stories, political satires or sketches of high life for him. 'You bein' so acquainted with society, Mr Harcourt, would make you just the feller to have a go. I could get young Cruikshank to do the draw-ins for you, so I could. There's money, there, Mr Harcourt. Not, I understand, that you're short of tin, but a young gent like yourself could always do with more, I'll be bound.'

Luke was thinking over this offer all the way back to Islington. He was beginning to dislike being so dependent on his father, and the idea of making himself less so had its appeal. Mrs Britten put her head round her drawing-room door when he came in.

'Oh, there you are, Mr Harcourt. I was hoping that you might arrive early. I've just laid out tea and a little something to eat for Mrs Cowper and myself, but, alas, I've been called out. Why don't you take it with her? She'll be down in a moment.'

Is it possible that the old dear is matchmaking? was Luke's amused thought. And what if she were? It would be an act of charity to take pity on a lonely widow woman, would it not? After all, they could always engage in small talk about his book which he had left with Mrs Britten some days earlier for her to pass on to her protégée, who was so intent on avoiding him.

He was examining the small china ornaments on the mantelpiece with apparently passionate interest when Mrs Cowper arrived. She took one look at him, and stood back—again as though his mere presence disconcerted her. To reassure her, he bowed and indicated the seat in front of the tea table.

'Mrs Britten has been called away, and has asked me to keep you company. If that is not what you wish, then I will leave—but I must say that I would find it exceedingly pleasant to take tea with you.'

He noticed how graceful she was when, a little hesitantly, she sat down: she possessed the manners and speech of a perfect lady. She had brought her work basket with her, so he assumed that she would have spent the rest of the day keeping Mrs Britten company.

For the first time Luke appreciated how lonely life must be for the two women. He had his work, his friends in the world of journalism, his club, his visits to the gym and fencing academy where he kept himself in trim, and the entree into high society where he was frequently asked to dine, or to attend receptions. His life was so busy that finding time to work was his problem, play consumed so much of it! Not so with Mrs Cowper. Her work was her life.

Because he was silent, she was silent too. She seemed to find speaking difficult, and only did so when she thanked the maid, Mary, who came in with the hot water for the tea, and a plate of muffins, already split and oozing butter.

'Pray offer the muffins to Mr Harcourt first, Mary,' she ordered. 'I am sure that Cook would like him to eat them whilst they are still hot.'

Luke took a muffin, thanking both women, and then bit into it. Alas, it was so well filled that it almost exploded, showering him with butter. Mary could not resist a giggle at the spectacle of him trying to do two things at once: mop himself clean with his spotless table napkin, and try to prevent his muffin from landing on the carpet.

Quite deliberately Luke made a little pantomime of his misfortune before looking up to see that, for once, Mrs Cowper was showing some genuine animation. She was trying hard not to laugh.

His napkin in the air, his muffin in pieces at his feet, he smiled and murmured reproachfully, a twinkle in his eye, 'My dear Mrs Cowper, if you wish amusement you should visit the theatre to watch a genuine *farceur* who is paid to entertain you. My efforts are poor by comparison.'

Her dark eyes shone as she replied to this feeble attempt at wit. 'But yours are so much more spontaneous, Mr Harcourt, do admit. And spontaneity, like brevity, is surely the soul of wit.'

'Now how do you know that I had not planned that little contretemps simply to see you smile, Mrs Cowper? It becomes you, you should do it more often.'

No one was more surprised than Luke when this shot out of him.

'One must have something to smile at, Mr Harcourt. Besides, you could not have known that you were about to be provided with the means of causing me amusement. On the stage, now, you would have practised that little turn for several days before you dared to delight an audience with it.'

Luke's own amusement was unfeigned. Neither was his admiration of what her pleasure at this exchange was doing to her face. She looked years younger than the pale and gaunt drudge whom he had met a fortnight ago. For the first time he wondered exactly how old she was. He had assumed her to be at least thirty: now she appeared to be much less than that. Very much less.

His company, the tea which she was sipping, the

muffin which she was eating, the entertainment he had by chance provided, had all combined to make him look more closely at her, and what he saw pleased him. She also seemed more at ease with him than she had been in their previous encounters, so much so that she initiated further conversation by asking him whether he was having any luck with his writing.

'Mrs Britten told me that you were being interviewed by the editor of *The Pall Mall Gazette* this afternoon, with a view to his publishing your work in his magazine. I trust that the interview proved successful.'

'Very,' replied Luke, drinking his second cup of tea but wisely refusing further muffins. 'He has accepted the articles which I wrote when I was staying in Wiltshire recently. I had thought he might find them rather wanting in general interest, perhaps even a little dull.'

Mrs Cowper wiped her hands delicately on her napkin before resuming her sewing. Her eyes on her work, she said, 'Having read your book, Mr Harcourt, I cannot believe that. It seemed very witty to me, but I wonder that you can approve of those whose attitude to life and politics is so immoral.'

'Both of them, in general, being so immoral, seeing that they are concerned with power, which of itself possesses no morality, one cannot be surprised that a philosopher, writing of them, is also immoral,' replied Luke.

He was being deliberately provocative, he knew, but he wished to see her face animated again, and hoped that she would rise to the bait he was offering her.

She stitched very carefully for a few moments before answering him. When she did so, looking straight at him for once, Luke was surprised to see that her eyes were full of tears, her voice trembled, and was so low that he could scarcely hear what she was saying.

'Oh, of course, if power is involved, one must be surprised at nothing which those who hold it do to retain it, or if not, to gain it. Tell me, Mr Harcourt, do you think that it is ever possible for men to use power wisely?'

Luke wondered what he had said to move her so.

'One must hope so. For example, if our laws and constitution were both reformed to give ordinary men more say in ruling the country by allowing them to vote, instead of confining that to the few, then I would hope to see power used more responsibly.'

'And women, Mr Harcourt? You said nothing of women. Are women always to be left powerless—

and exploited? Does your radicalism—for I see that you are a radical—extend to that?'

She said this with great fire. Her dark eyes shone, her cheeks glowed. For the first time she was attacking him, not simply reacting passively to what he had said.

'Well, as to that, Mrs Cowper, seeing how difficult it is being to extend the power to vote to men, then it must be almost impossible for women to be granted more freedom—yet. And, after all, women are fortunate in having men to look after them and shield them from the harsh realities of life.'

He knew, as soon as he had finished speaking, that his answer to her had been superficial and patronising. He was punished for it immediately. Her fine eyebrows rose. Her stitching lay abandoned on her lap. Her mouth twitched ironically.

'Ah, yes,' she murmured. 'The harsh realities of life. You reassure me, Mr Harcourt.'

She paused, and Luke knew that she was mocking him. 'As I am being shielded, and Mrs Britten—and the women who walk the Haymarket at night to earn a pitiful living? And the women whose husbands beat them regularly, and to whom the law offers no redress? Whose husbands may turn them out of their home, penniless, and keep their children from them? I think that you know better than that, Mr Harcourt.'

Her scorn was so fine and fierce that it transformed her. To his astonishment Luke felt helpless before it. There were a thousand arguments which he could have used to try to refute her, to point out that if the Rights of Man were not yet granted then the Rights of Women were hardly likely to gain a fair hearing.

What he actually said was, 'You shame me a little, Mrs Cowper, for I am well aware of the disadvantages which married women suffer—and widows, too,' he added with a placatory smile.

Luke was used to skating on the surface of life when he spoke to women, and mousy Mrs Anne Cowper was the last person whom he would have expected to have mounted such a fierce and logical attack on him. Her usually quiet and apologetic manner had deserted her. But only for the moment, apparently.

For she had taken up the sewing which she had laid down, and was stitching rapidly away, while murmuring, 'Pray forgive me, Mr Harcourt. I should not have spoken so rudely to you. It is not your fault that the law is so unequal, and as a radical you are trying to do something to reform it. Pray let us speak of more pleasant things. I see that there is a *Book of Beauty* at your elbow. We could perhaps admire the plates in it together.'

She was mocking him again! He was sure of it. By assuming the rather vacant tones of a pampered woman, and by referring to the *Book of Beauty*, a publication which was perhaps the greatest example of the superficialities of an idle gentlewoman's life, she was reproaching him by suggesting that such superficiality was all that he expected from a woman.

He countered her with her own tactics. 'By all means,' he replied politely, picking the book up, 'if that is what you really wish.'

Her smile at him was a watery one. 'It is one way of calling truce, Mr Harcourt, and raising a new topic of conversation.'

'So it is,' he said softly. 'So it is.'

He opened the book at a poem of such vapidity, that he almost laughed aloud, and to test her decided to read it aloud. What new situation that might have created was not to be known, for Mary came in with more hot water, and Mrs Britten was on her heels, demanding tea and fresh muffins.

Their contest was over for the day, since Mrs Cowper immediately resumed her role of 'patience on a monument' as Shakespeare once had it, and fell silent again, leaving their landlady to quiz Luke on his afternoon, and to offer him fresh tea, before he returned to his room.

Not to work, but to ponder on the enigma which Mrs Anne Cowper presented to him.

And what do I make of Mr Luke Harcourt? mused Mrs Anne Cowper when Luke had sauntered out after telling them that he was due to attend a great ball at Leominster House—the season having already begun—and would arrive home tolerably late, but would try not to disturb them both when he did.

He was charming and *galant* in the French sense, full of good manners and perfect tact. He was handsome, but not offensively so. His dark good looks, proudly held head and excellent physique showed to full advantage in his careful, but not too careful, fashionable dress.

He had a good and original mind, no doubt of that, either.

Every page of his book bore witness to his intellectual powers. On the other hand, he was plainly a *dilettante*, idling his way through life. The book had been written three years ago when he was still only twenty-four, and he had produced nothing since but light sketches, articles on reform and other political matters of the day which must have been child's play for the young man who had written as he had done of Machiavelli.

The reason for his mode of life was plain. His guardian, Lord Lyndale, of whom he always spoke with gratitude, had settled on him a competence just large enough for him to be pleasantly idle on, to enable him to play at life rather than work at it. She was unaware that he was Lyndale's son, and equally unaware that she was echoing his father's worries about Luke's steel— or lack of it.

Perhaps, she thought, he has not been tested— and perhaps he never will be, which would be a pity. Even as she had been thinking of him, she had stopped sewing and had allowed her work to lie neglected on her lap. A log fell on the fire, and the noise returned her to the present, for thinking of Luke's possible lack of steel had made her remember all too vividly one who might be seen as possessing too much of it.

Mrs Britten, watching her, knew when her protégée's thoughts became painful and took a dark turn. She said lightly, 'Come, my dear Anne, do not repine. For the present you are safe here. Do not think of the past, I beg of you.'

'I was not thinking of the past,' Anne replied, 'or rather, for only a moment. I was wondering why

Mr Harcourt does not make the best use of his un-doubted talents.'

One might think my dear girl to be sixty-two, not twenty-two, to have such grave thoughts, was Mrs Britten's inward and immediate response. But suffering matures one, no doubt of that.

Aloud, she said, as unemotionally as she could, 'My own opinion is that Mr Harcourt is a gifted young man who has not yet found his way in life. It is to be hoped that he will. He has a good heart, as well as a good mind.'

Now which of those two attributes, she privately wondered, has caused my poor Anne to show, for the first time since she sought shelter here, an interest in the outside world?

And what might be the outcome of that?

Luke made his way through the crowds at Leo-minster House, greeting and being greeted. He was looking for James and Cressy, whom he was sure would be there. James was found soon enough, among a crowd of Parliamentary colleagues talk-ing politics—but Cressy, where was she?

At last he saw her. She was over by one of the tall Corinthian pillars, which held up a vast glass dome, chatting to Lady Jersey. His stepmother was looking as delightful as ever in an apricot toilette. She waved at him with her fan, inviting him to join them.

Nothing loth, Luke obeyed her. But as he did so, the oddest thing happened. For nine years, ever since he had first met her, Luke had only to see Cressy to know how much he loved, admired and desired her, and to feel the deepest despair that she could never be his. But…but…tonight the admiration was there, and the love, although that, too, had changed, but desire and despair alike had fled.

Before him was a beautiful and clever woman whom a man loved as he ought to love his father's wife, as he might love a grown-up sister, if he had one. What in the world had come over him? Had he changed? Or had Cressy? It was as though he had been holding a kaleidoscope, which showed him a beautiful and desirable object, and somehow the kaleidoscope had tilted so that he still saw the same equally beautiful object—and yet it was quite changed.

The chains which had bound him to Cressy had fallen off. It was not that she was less to him than she had been—far from it—but that he valued her after a different fashion.

She was smiling at him as she re-introduced him to Lady Jersey, who greeted him in her usual familiar manner. 'You come pat, Master Luke,' she

said. 'We have both been deserted by our husbands, and need someone to escort us to the cold
collation. Lady Leominster's cold collations are
famous. It would not do to miss them. Besides, we
need a man to talk scandal to.'

Sally Jersey was fond of indulging in this sort
of nonsense; her satiric nickname was Silence,
meaning that she was a chatterer. In his new role
of society satirist, Luke was pleased to listen to
her. He offered her his arm, and the three of them
made for the refreshment room.

'You see,' she began, 'we have so much to oc-
cupy us tonight. They say Clairval is invited,
doubtless hoping to discover whether his wife is
here, disguised as a page imitating poor Caro
Lamb chasing Byron, or perhaps hidden behind
the arras—like a character in a play.'

She saw by Luke's expression that he was not
quite following her. 'Ah, I collect that you are not
long back in town and so are unaware of the latest *on dits*. Which of us shall enlighten you? Dear
Lady Lyndale, perhaps. Although, as you know,
she likes to listen to gossip, not spread it.'

Cressy said quickly, 'It is an unhappy story. We
should not joke about such a sad misfortune.'

'Ah, but exactly whose sad misfortune? The
husband's or the wife's? You must know, Mr

Harcourt, that the Marquess of Clairval's wife has run mad, has been confined to her room to spare both her and the neighbourhood—and has disappeared…completely.'

Lady Jersey paused dramatically, aware that she had an interested audience.

'Run mad and disappeared,' repeated Luke slowly. 'Yes, truly a sad story. She ran away, I suppose, with someone—but who?'

'Who knows?' was the lady's somewhat arch answer. 'All that we do know is that Clairval has advertised this very day for knowledge of her whereabouts and is offering a large reward. He has set the Runners after her—she has been gone these six months, they say.

'They also say…' and she leaned forward confidentially '…that she ran so mad that for the last three months of her confinement she was imprisoned in one of the tower rooms at Clairval Castle. Or so the story goes in Yorkshire.'

'If,' Cressy remarked drily and practically, 'the lady has run so very mad, then surely she would be a conspicuous figure in any society in which she chose to settle, and therefore Clairval should have little trouble in finding her! Furthermore, I do not like him,' she continued, putting down her lobster patty in order to speak more plainly.

They were now sitting in an alcove watching the passing show. 'He has neither manners nor small talk.' She picked up her patty again, and said before eating it, 'He has no large talk, either!'

'Who does like him?' asked Sally Jersey spitefully. 'Everyone was sorry for the poor little wretch who married him.'

'Poor?' said Luke being about to seize a buttered roll, seized on this apparent fact instead.

'I speak figuratively, of course. She was actually extremely wealthy. Clairval was the poor one in the marriage. She was the daughter of old "Grecian" Temple. He had been an underpaid Greek scholar at Oxford—hence the nickname—until a distant cousin died and left him a large fortune. He had only this one daughter, who is now Lady Clairval. Her mother died when she was born. She was left quite alone when her father died and her guardians were happy to marry her off to Clairval. She had an odd name, I remember... Anticleia.'

'Not odd at all,' announced Cressy firmly. 'It is the name of Odysseus's mother, the wife of Proteus. Everyone knows *that*.'

Luke's lips twitched as this learned Cressyism was thrown so casually into Sally Jersey's light gossip, but he made no comment, only asked her,

'Clairval is in his forties. How old was Miss Anticleia Temple?'

'Barely eighteen, a poor innocent child to be married to such a brute. They say that her relatives were determined to have a title in the family. Those who witnessed the ceremony said that she looked like a schoolgirl—more suited to be his daughter than his wife.'

'Well, then, there's no wonder that she ran mad,' remarked Cressy irrepressibly. 'I'm sure that I should have done so if I had been married off to Clairval. Yes, I suppose that it was the title which attracted them.'

'And the money him,' put in Sally Jersey, determined to have the last word. 'And look, here he comes, arm in arm with my husband, who I know does not care for him in the least. Only his rank allows him to be tolerated by us at all.'

Luke could not remember having seen Clairval before—other than in the distance. The man looked like the brute gossip had suggested he was. He was massive, not only tall but broad and running to fat. He had conceivably been an athlete in youth but was so no longer.

His face resembled, Luke thought irreverently, a side of tough beef, being streaked reddy-purple and dirty cream. Although his clothes were impeccable, they somehow served not to enhance him, but to demonstrate instead how much his body had gone to seed.

He was reputed to have been handsome in his youth, but little evidence of it remained. His hair was a shop-worn tawny streaked with grey. His manner when he spoke was bullying and intimidatory. One could only pity the poor mad wife. Luke remained quiet whilst Clairval was introduced to Cressy and himself. His own bow was as deep as it ought to be to a nobleman of such consequence and betrayed none of his true thoughts.

Lady Jersey commiserated with him on the loss of his wife. 'And I understand that you have no news of her, none at all. Most worrying for you.' She almost added, Not to know whether she is dead or alive, but thought that under the circumstances it might not be tactful.

Clairval bowed, shook his massive head and put on as melancholy a face as he could before replying in a broken voice, 'Particularly as my poor lady is so lacking in wits that any passing stranger must be considered as able to take advantage of her. I tremble for her—wherever she is.'

He paused, passed a handkerchief over his face, and said sadly through it, 'I blame myself, you must understand. If I had been willing to admit straight away that her mind was unhinged, then I could have called in a mad doctor earlier, and much misery might have been saved us both. As it is...' and he shrugged '... I can only pray that she is still in the land of the living.'

'Poor man,' sighed Lady Jersey after Clairval had walked off, still arm in arm with Lord Jersey who did not look as though he appreciated the honour. 'One really feels for him. He seems quite broken by her loss. Perhaps we have misjudged him.'

No one answered her. Even Cressy made no comment at all—unusual for her, Luke thought. Perhaps, like himself, she believed that Clairval protested too much over his wife's loss, since his remarks on it were a counterpoint to every conversation in which he took part at Leominster House that night.

How sincere Clairval's very public grief was Luke begged leave to doubt.

His doubts were reinforced a couple of days later when James told him that, after leaving the Leominsters, the gossip was that Clairval had made straight for Laura Knight's high-class brothel and had spent the night there with not one, but several of her girls.

A garbled version of this story was also passed on to him by Bayes, who was now urging him to write about Clairval's marriage for his radical weekly newspaper, *The Clarion*. In it, Bayes attacked everyone in high life whom he considered was representative of the corruption of those who ruled England.

'The gossip is,' he whispered confidentially, his finger beside his nose, like a criminal from the parish of St Giles conspiring with one of his fellows, 'that the lady was not mad at all, but that Clairval was saying so to gain the balance of her fortune which was settled on the child they never had. That he was imprisoning her in order to drive her mad, not because she was mad.'

'Oh, come,' protested Luke. 'I can hardly believe that, even of Clairval. I have met him, and he's scarcely likeable...but...'

'There were odd stories about him years ago,' continued Bayes. 'I'll pay you highly if you discover anything new. Imagine how much it would help the cause of reform to expose such a grandee as Clairval.' He was already thinking about writing a poem satirising the wicked Marquess and his unfortunate child bride.

But it was not Luke's notion of what he wanted his life's work to be. He was being asked to dabble in a sewer. It was one thing to write high-minded articles about the noble cause of extending the vote to the common people of England, or comment wittily on the minor *on dits* of society. It was quite another to write salacious pieces about Clairval's private life and dubious sexual habits. He knew that Bayes would find someone else to do it if he refused, but that was not his business.

'You'll end up in prison for criminal libel, like Leigh Hunt did when he attacked the Prince Regent,' he warned.

'But think how many copies of the paper I would sell first,' wheedled Bayes. 'And there's nothing like being a martyr to a cause to advance it!'

As a consequence of this long conference with Bayes, Luke arrived back in Islington late enough for Mrs Britten to offer him supper.

'I have more than enough soup and rolls,' she told him cheerfully, 'to feed the three of us, and besides, my dear Mrs Cowper needs cheering up a little. We should both, I am sure, like to hear of what passed at Leominster House the other night. They say that there was a great crowd there, and that the King himself attended.'

Not for the first time Luke wondered from whence Mrs Britten gained her knowledge of current high life. But soup, and Mrs Cowper's company, sounded pleasant, so he agreed to her request—and the dish of soup turned out to be only a small part of the repast.

'So, Mr Harcourt,' said Mrs Britten, shooting him a conspiratorial glance as Mary removed the soup plates preparatory to bringing in a tureen of stewed pike, 'were you fortunate enough to meet the King the other night?'

'No, indeed,' he replied, joining in the game of cheering Mrs Cowper up. 'I only saw him from a distance, but I did have the honour of meeting the subject of the current most titillating rumour in society.'

'Indeed,' said Mrs Cowper drily, wiping her lips with her napkin. 'And was the subject of your conversation fit for a humble dinner table in Islington?'

Yes, she *was* roasting him, no doubt of that! Luke returned the compliment. 'Oh, our conversation was mild enough for a schoolroom, I assure you, but the rumours about him were something else again.'

Mrs Cowper's fine brows rose. 'A him? And what him was this, pray? Rumours usually have a female subject!'

'Oh, a female subject was also involved,' replied Luke gaily. 'In this case it was the gentleman's or rather nobleman's, wife. It was the Marquess of Clairval to whom I was introduced, and who has most carelessly mislaid his. It appears that not only is the poor lady mad, but also that she has run away, has disappeared quite. Clairval claimed to be most distressed at her loss, was almost in tears as he spoke of it…'

He stopped speaking. What had he said? Mrs Britten was looking daggers at him. Mrs Cowper, on the contrary, had dropped her head and was examining the tablecloth with an earnestness usually reserved for the perusal of a fascinating book. Only the entry of Mary with the pike, potatoes and a dish of anonymous greens lightened the atmosphere.

'Oh, splendid!' cried Mrs Britten gaily. 'I'm sure that they did not serve you anything half so fine the other night. Come, Mr Harcourt, allow me to help you to a succulent piece of pike. It is quite a favourite of mine when well cooked.'

She continued to talk nineteen to the dozen in a feverish and urgent voice, most unlike her usual cheerful one. It seemed, Luke thought drily, that as a topic of conversation the reception at Leominster House had changed in one short minute from being most desirable to something which was not to be persevered with at all.

His belief that this was so was enhanced by Mrs Britten launching into a long and rambling story about a neighbour who was trying to organise a protest against the annual Fair, which was due to take place in Islington the following week.

How he set about it, and his lack of success—
since most of the citizenry of Islington welcomed it—took up the next twenty minutes, but,
as a ploy to cheer Mrs Cowper up, it hardly
seemed to be working, since she remained quiet
and apparently uninterested in anything except
her dinner.

Finally Mrs Britten ran down. Silence reigned.
Luke wondered whether to break it, but was
saved from having to make a decision by Mrs
Cowper raising her head, fixing him with her
fine eyes, and asking him, 'And what, Mr Harcourt, was your impression of the Marquess? I
should be interested to learn it, since I thought
that I detected a touch of criticism in your original remark.'

So much for Mrs Britten trying to dismiss the
subject of Clairval and his wife!

'You are correct in your supposition,' said Luke.
'I must confess that I was not taken by the noble
Marquess, and I thought that his tears over his lost
wife were crocodile ones. Particularly when I was
informed that he had almost certainly married her
for her money and that she was young enough to
be his daughter.'

He did not mention the rumour that Clairval had
driven his wife mad, or had imprisoned her in

order to do so. He saw the gleam in Mrs Cowper's eye and wondered what was coming next. What further question might he expect from her?

Nothing more about Clairval, but before she resumed eating her supper she asked him quietly, 'And what is your opinion of people who peddle gossip, Mr Harcourt?'

Now here was a hard question for him to answer, seeing that Bayes was prepared to pay him good money to do so in *The Clarion*! Luke decided to be honest with her.

'You have me in a cleft stick there, Mrs Cowper, since the editor to whom I sell my articles on politics has promised me even greater fees if I am prepared to write about society scandals instead. He believes that to expose those in high life will eventually bring about a better life for us all.'

'And have you agreed, Mr Harcourt? To make a living out of the miseries of others—such as Clairval's poor wife, whether she be mad or no? Are you ready to do evil so that good may come of it?'

'That is a very harsh statement, Mrs Cowper,' was his uneasy reply.

There was nothing mute or passive about her now. The almost holy calm which she had always maintained before him was quite gone. A becoming flush coloured her usually pale cheeks, her eyes shot fire, her shapely mouth was curled in scorn, not in cool acceptance.

Seen thus she was more than pretty: she was beautiful. Apparently the mistreatment of another woman had brought her to life. And what she had just said to him was no more than the question he had been asking himself.

He was coming to understand that in some ways he was as passive as she was: content to go with the tide, to live his quiet pleasant life, not asking much from it, nor getting much either. He was dodging commitment because to commit himself might disturb the even tenor of his way. Which was what Josette had hinted to him when she had finally turned her back on him in order to marry the man who was prepared to commit himself to her.

He knew what was causing his passivity, but what was causing Mrs Cowper's? The loss of her husband, her consequent collapse into poverty and the necessity to work long hours to gain some kind of a living, so that she must remain quiet in order to endure what must be endured because it could not be cured?

Except—and why was that?—Luke thought that there was more to Mrs Cowper than appeared on the surface: that there was some deeper explanation for her way of life and her presence at Mrs Britten's.

All this flashed through his mind as Mrs Cowper made no answer to him, having decided to concentrate on eating her supper, rather than discuss moral problems over it. The fire and vivacity which had transformed her had died down and she was a humble sempstress again.

Clairval banished from the table, Mrs Britten heaved a great sigh of relief and steered the conversation into quiet backwaters where no monstrous fish, a distant cousin of the pike which they had just eaten, lurked ready to devour anyone who ventured into his territory. Merely to speak of one such as Clairval was enough to grant him power over lives which scarcely touched his. Far better to talk of the coming Fair and wonder what new delights might be on show there.

Perhaps she could persuade Mr Harcourt to escort Anne Cowper and herself to it. Ladies at a fair were always in need of a man's protection.

There seemed no escape from Clairval for Luke. Pat O'Hare told him bluntly during a jolly evening at The Coal Hole that he had accepted a commission from Bayes to write about Clairval's lost wife and his marriage.

'Bayes said that he offered it to you first but that you went all moral on him. Not turning Methodee, are you, Luke?'

'Didn't fancy prying into bedrooms and bou-
doirs,' retorted Luke curtly.

'A man has to live, and Clairval's reputation was
hardly savoury before this,' said Pat lightheart-
edly. 'I've winkled out of a friend in the know that
he's got a former Bow Street Runner trying to
trace her. He thinks that she might have fled to
London, apparently.

'What few relatives the poor bitch has have told
him that if she turns up wanting help from them
they'll hand her over to him. Seems that they think
that she's not shown much gratitude to him for
having made her his Marchioness. A bit rich, that,
when another friend of mine tells me it's common
knowledge in Yorkshire that he treated her worse
than a slave. Locked her up in a cell in a tower.'

Luke thought of Clairval and winced. Shrewd
Pat saw him do so.

'Yes, I know. It's a dirty business. But think of
it this way. If we can expose him as a cur who has
maltreated his wife then we might be able to stop
his little gallop...'

'No chance of that.' Luke was curt again. 'She's
his wife and the law says that he can do as he
pleases with her. You know that as well as I do. It's
a bad business, but that's the way of it.'

So the question of whether or not he ought to

write about Clairval had been settled for him. He went to see Bayes to tell him that he would prefer to continue writing articles on politics or philosophy, and that others could deal with society scandals if they wished.

'Your funeral, not mine.' Bayes was philosophical. 'I suppose you've enough tin to pick and choose, though!'

For some reason this dismissive comment, implying that he was a mere amateur, hurt Luke. He tried to work out why all the way home to Islington in a hansom cab which dropped him off in the High Street. He finally gave up, after deciding that Bayes was wrong. Even poverty, he hoped, would not have seen him scandalmongering to earn a living.

Satisfied by this decision, he settled his top hat at a jauntier angle, and strode for home. If he were lucky, Mrs Britten might invite him to tea and he would have a further opportunity to discuss difficult moral subjects with Mrs Cowper whilst she sewed diligently away.

He had reached a cross path when the noise of an altercation drew his attention. A small crowd had gathered around a low stone wall before a piece of waste ground. In the middle of it a burly man in the leathers of a saddler was shouting at a woman seated on the wall. The watchers were either hallooing him on, or bellowing support for the woman by urging him to 'leave the gal alone!'

Intrigued as ever by the busy parade of low life which filled Islington's streets, Luke stopped to discover what all the fuss was about.

The woman was crouched over something in her lap, her face invisible, but Luke knew immediately who she was. He moved towards her at the same moment that the shouting brute in front of her reached out a hand to seize her roughly by the left wrist, twist it brutally, and pull her to her feet.

Luke thus saw her face for the first time, and yes, as he had somehow strangely known, it was Anne Cowper, and the something which she was holding was a small and shaggy mongrel dog.

'Let go, you bitch. That cur is mine to do as I please with,' the ruffian—for so he appeared to be—howled at her, still clutching her roughly by the wrist. It was plain that he dare not treat her more harshly, or snatch the dog from her because the crowd around him, still growing, was by no means all on his side.

He turned to shout at them. 'Tell her to give it back.'

Anne Cowper spoke at last, her voice low and breathless but quite calm. 'Indeed not. You were thrashing it to death until I picked it up to try to save it.'

The man appealed to the crowd again. 'Aye, and what's that to you? A man may do what he pleases with his own—dog, horse or wife—when they're disobedient. That's what the law says and I'll set the law on yer.'

Luke, fascinated, saw that Anne's pallor was that of fear, but she answered him bravely enough. 'Because a man *may* do what he pleases with his own does not mean that he *should*, if what he does is wicked.'

This brave statement brought answering growls of encouragement as well as jeers from those who supported the notion that right was might where horses, dogs and women were concerned.

Luke thought that he ought to intervene, if only because it was becoming plain that sooner or later the man would use violence to drag the animal from Anne's arms. But the crowd was now so large that it had drawn the attention of a man of law, some sort of beadle, who pushed his way forward demanding to know 'What's a-goin' on, 'ere?'

Even as the dog's owner began to speak, to explain what had happened, to re-state his right to have his dog back and to do as he pleased with it—

to kill it if he so wished—Luke pushed his way to where Anne and her tormentor stood.

He said in as dominant and commanding a voice as he could, 'Allow me to try to settle this unhappy business. I know the lady and will vouch for her good character. More than that, I am prepared to pay enough money to buy the dog from you, sir, and end this whole wretched business.'

The crowd had receded from him as he walked forward, pulling off his hat. He was so very much the gentleman and aristocrat in his splendid coat, buckskin breeches and shining boots that his good looks, as well as his commanding presence, had the women present oohing and aahing and poking one another.

The man said rudely, 'Who the devil are you, that you want to buy a worthless cur from me? You've got more money than sense, like all you young gents, I'll be bound.'

'No more of that,' ordered Luke curtly. He had reached Anne Cowper by now and had put a hand on her trembling arm. The dog gave a frightened bark as he did so.

'Mind that,' cried his owner. 'He's as ill-favoured a brute as a dog can be. Give me a guinea, though, and he's yours.' The beadle, and most of the crowd, nodded agreement at this preposterous proposal, seeing that the dog was worth nothing.

Luke did not attempt to argue with him over the price demanded. He fished a guinea out of his pocket and held it up. 'It's more than you deserve,' he announced severely. 'And more than the cur is worth. But take this, and the dog is the lady's. But you'll get nothing until you release her wrist.'

'A fool and his money are soon parted,' sneered the man, but he threw Anne from him and took the offered coin. She gave a small cry of pain on being released and fell against Luke, her face grey.

'Damn him,' grated Luke, moved both by her suffering and by the determination with which she was still clutching the dog. 'He's hurt you. If I had known that, I'd not have offered him a penny.'

'Too late,' triumphed the man, and made off at the run, grasping his new-found wealth tightly. Luke, pleased to be rid of his presence, contented himself with saying gently, 'Pray allow me to take the animal from you, Mrs Cowper, and then we must try to find you a surgeon so that he may examine your wrist.'

He helped her to sit on the wall again, as the crowd, fun over, began to scatter, but she refused to hand him the dog even when a portly man came forward, saying, 'If the lady is hurt, then allow me to assist her. I am Adam Dobson, a surgeon.'

Mrs Cowper shrank away from both of them, her

eyes shadowed. 'No, please. No. I am not hurt, only a little shocked.'

Both Luke and Mr Dobson, however, could see that her wrist was swollen and bruised. Finally Luke managed to persuade her to allow the surgeon to examine it, and she reluctantly held out her arm. At his first touch, though, gentle as it was, she gave a great shiver, and hid her face.

Whilst Mr Dobson carefully flexed and manipulated her wrist, Luke pulled off his cravat so that by the time the surgeon had finished examining her and had pronounced her wrist to be sprained, he was able to hold out an improvised sling for the surgeon to put on.

'Your wrist has been broken in the past, madam, has it not?' asked Mr Dobson as he finished securing the sling. Anne did not answer him directly, but simply nodded her head. She was still clutching the dog to her with her good hand.

'It was not properly set,' he told her severely, 'which is why it has become damaged again so easily. Some country fool made a botch of it, I suppose. Fortunately, being your left wrist, no great harm has been done. But you must not use it again until I give you permission.'

Still she made him no answer, nor did she look directly at Luke. The surgeon had not done with her, for as she stood up he said, 'Pray allow your friend to hold the dog for you, since you will find walking difficult with both a sling and the animal to manoeuvre.'

Lips quivering, but the colour slowly returning to her wan face, Anne handed Luke the dog, which barked its protest at losing its new friend, but quieted when Luke stroked its shaggy head. He privately agreed with its original owner that it was the most ill-favoured animal which he had ever encountered, but never mind that: it seemed to be pleasing Mrs Anne Cowper simply by existing.

After taking down Anne's address so that he might call to examine her wrist in a few days' time, Mr Dobson bade them good bye, quietly pocketing the guinea which Luke slipped to him. After which Luke, slightly hampered by the dog, helped Mrs Cowper to walk back to their lodgings.

'I haven't thanked you,' Anne said shyly. 'You really were a Good Samaritan, Mr Harcourt. I cannot say how sorry I am that I have teased you so cruelly about your good faith ever since I first met you. I am properly shamed.'

'Oh think nothing of that,' exclaimed Luke, who had suddenly begun to think of Mrs Cowper as Anne from the moment when he had seen her crouched on the wall, braving a bully twice her size and weight. 'But you were risking yourself, you know, to defy such a brute.'

'I know,' she admitted 'But I cannot bear to see anything beaten. And such a little creature. He would have killed it, I am sure.'

Luke could not but agree. 'All the same,' he told her, a trifle severely, 'I want you to promise me that you will never do such a reckless thing again. I might not be there to help you the next time.'

'No, indeed. The problem was that I could not afford to buy the poor little creature from him, you understand. You will allow me to pay you back a little at a time, will you not?'

'Certainly not!' replied Luke warmly. 'Think of it as a reward for your courage. Particularly when you bore the surgeon's manipulations so bravely. I could see that he was hurting you.'

Anne's smile was wan, but a smile. 'A trifle, a mere trifle,' she told him. 'And now I have only one worry. What in the world will Mrs Britten say when I arrive home with my poor little charge?'

'Oh, no need to trouble yourself on that score.' Luke's reply was as confident as he could make it. 'I know that there is an empty kennel in the back yard. Her dog died of old age about six months ago and I cannot think that she will turn this poor scrap away.'

Nor did she. Exclaiming alternately over Anne's poorly wrist, the dog, and Mr Harcourt's fortunate arrival on the scene, Mrs Britten also made sure that all four of them, including the dog, had an even better supper than usual, and Anne was sent to bed with a glass of hot toddy to ease the pain of her damaged wrist.

What troubled Luke a little, although he said nothing to anyone about it, was not only the knowledge that Anne Cowper's wrist had been broken before, but the fact that as a result of tiredness and strain, her slight limp was a little more prominent than usual as she bade him goodnight. He was sure from everything he saw of her that her married life had not been happy. The other thing which he was sure of was her uncomplaining courage.

What she needed was someone to look after her, he concluded, since it was plain to him that no one had ever looked after her before.

The dog, christened Odysseus—Dizzy for common use—spent a happy night in his new home.

Chapter Three

Pat O'Hare was sitting quietly in his rooms in Stanhope Street, near to Regent's Park, when he heard a banging on the house door. Next the door itself was flung open, and a man's voice began to shout imperiously at his landlady. In the commotion he heard his own name shouted.

He walked to the head of the stairs—his rooms were on the first floor—and called down, 'What is it, Mrs Rouncewell? What's the trouble?'

'No trouble,' said the imperious masculine voice, 'and now I know that you are at home, O'Hare, I shall come upstairs to see you at once. Fernando, Jem, follow me.'

Fernando and Jem were two burly men who followed their master upstairs. Pat knew at once who his visitor was. He had seen him about town, in Laura Knight's exclusive brothel, and driving a curricle in Hyde Park. It was the Marquess of Clairval, all fifteen stone of him—he was even larger than his two footmen who resembled pugilists more than house-trained servants.

One of them was a boxer whom Pat had seen in Jackson's gym. On Clairval's orders they stood, one on each side of the door into Pat's study, like a pair of Praetorian guards, armed with muscles not swords.

Clairval threw his hat and whip on to Pat's desk, remarking conversationally, 'That stupid bitch downstairs said that she wouldn't let me up until she had first announced me. Who the devil does she think you are? Fat King George himself incognito, instead of a jumped-up cur of a journalist who spends his time slandering his betters?'

He was so plainly bent on mischief that, even before his last words, Pat had retreated behind his desk, which stood in the bow window.

'Aye, you may well run away from me,' sneered Clairval, hurling some galley sheets from the printer towards Pat, half of them landing on the floor, the other half on his desk. 'I've just been interviewing the toad who owns *The Clarion*. He confirmed, oh so politely, what an informant of mine had already passed on to me: that his scandal sheet was ready to publish filth about my mar-

riage. Filth which you had written. Shall I give you
the taste of the whip which I gave him?'

Pat said from behind the shelter of his desk,
'I'll set the law on you if you do, Marquess or
no Marquess.' He wasn't feeling half so brave as
he sounded.

Clairval said in a bored voice, 'I thought that you
might threaten me with that. So did Bayes, but I
persuaded him that, if he did, I knew some scandal about him which might land him in Newgate.
I can't say that he took his medicine like a man.'

He gave a great exaggerated yawn. 'Now, I
couldn't find anything to blackmail you with—not
that you're as pure as the driven snow, mind—so
instead I've brought Jem and Fernando along with
me. I hear you consider yourself a student of the
Fancy so you may face the pair of them at once
and take your medicine like a man.

'Any complaint from you and they will swear
that what was done to you was done by accident
in sparring practice. That little lesson should cure
you, once and for all, of peddling inaccurate scandal about me and mine.'

'Here?' queried Pat desperately, his voice rising.
'They're going to thrash me here? Mrs Rouncewell might tell a different tale from theirs.'

'It's my experience,' said Clairval, bored again,

'that the Mrs Rouncewells of this world will say anything if the money offered them is right.'

He looked at Pat, began to crook a finger at his bully boys, and then dropped it. 'On the other hand, you can save yourself a beating, which might leave you with a broken wrist, which would prevent you from writing anything at all—let alone about me—if you will only do as I wish. Not only that, if you agree to my proposal, I shall see that you will receive a reasonable reward.'

Pat looked at the two bruisers, who were plainly eager to set about him immediately, and decided on surrender. He knew that it was useless to plead with the monster before him.

'What is it that you want of me?' he asked. He could only hope that what was required of him didn't compromise his already-stained honour overmuch.

'A small enough favour.' Clairval's tone was almost indifferent. 'As you well know, my poor mad wife escaped from her home where I was making sure that she received every attention her sufferings and her rank deserved. I have reason to believe that she fled to London, the more easily to hide herself away. I dare not think what ill fortune might befall the poor little thing in this corrupt city.' He heaved a great sigh.

'Now I know you go out and about in society. You hear all the gossip and the rumours—' and he pointed at the scattered galley sheets '—so, I wish you to try to discover where she may have hidden herself. Someone must know, for I am convinced that she is not alone. I have an ex-Runner on the job, but he only has access to criminal haunts and the like, not those in society like you. And you are shrewd, as your writing proves.

'Bring me anything you find as soon as you find it—and don't try to trick me. Jem and Fernando are disappointed, I know, that they may not use you for sparring practice. Don't give them the opportunity to do so.

'You will also oblige me by writing a pamphlet setting out the true history of my poor mad wife—that should silence the lies of the gossips and the Radical writers when I publish it.' His grin at Pat was feral.

All Pat knew was that he had been reprieved, but only at the expense of tracking down the *poor mad wife*, whom rumour said had been brutalised by the man before him, and by doing his dirty work for him into the bargain. Yet what alternative had he? Like many young gentlemen with little money, Pat desperately needed what he earned from his journalism to stay afloat and not end up in a spunging house. He had been counting on this money from Bayes, and now he had lost it.

Besides, it was always possible that Clairval was telling the truth about his wife: that she was mad and needed the protection which he could give her...

He nodded agreement, and as a reward Clairval tossed him a purse of guineas: it was far more than Bayes would have paid him.

Pat took it and felt like Judas.

'I must say,' remarked Luke, 'that Dizzy improves with knowing—and with all the good food he has been scoffing.'

He was in Mrs Britten's small back yard, watching Anne put out a large bowl of scraps for the happy cur, who barked his pleasure whenever he happened to see either of them.

'I don't think that he had ever been fed properly before,' replied Anne, 'or looked after, either.'

'No, indeed. Care and attention works wonders for us all.'

Luke forbore to add that the remarks which they had made about Dizzy could have been made about Anne. In the few weeks since he had first met her, everything about her—her looks, her skin and her general appearance—had improved wonderfully. The gaunt and haggard scarecrow was slowly changing into an attractive young woman.

Every week he revised her age downwards. From first judging her to be in her early thirties and then in her late twenties, Luke now thought it possible that she was in her early twenties. And this despite the fact that her conversation and her general demeanour were those of a woman much older than that.

For her part Mrs Cowper—who was not to know that Mr Luke Harcourt now always thought of her as Anne, however punctilious he was in addressing her as Mrs Cowper in conversation—thought that Mr Harcourt also improved the more one knew him.

He was so kind! She had not thought that a man could be kind, let alone as kind as Luke Harcourt was. Such had not been her experience of life. The fear which she had thought that she would always feel for all men deserted her when she was with him. She could almost bear for him to touch her. When he had helped her home after they had rescued Dizzy she had found, to her astonishment, that the strong arm on which she leaned was welcome to her.

Last night, when they had been talking after supper, which Luke now invariably ate with her and Mrs Britten instead of having it brought to his suite of rooms, he had told her that he had refused to write about Clairval's marriage.

'Not, you must understand,' he had said, 'that that means that no one will do so. He has already commissioned a friend of mine to undertake what I refused to do.'

'I am sorry to hear that,' she had said.

'Let me be honest,' Luke had told her earnestly. 'Had I needed the money, as my friend does, I doubt whether I should have allowed my scruples to overcome my need to earn a living. But I do have private means, and Pat does not, so you must not think too harshly of him. A man needs to eat. Bayes twitted me by saying that my small fortune enabled me to be nice in my conduct.'

He had paused— Why was he telling her this?— but something drove him on. 'I am not a very noble fellow after all, you see.'

Anne had done something which had surprised him. She had put out a hand to cover his where it had rested on the tablecloth. 'Necessity drives us all on to do things of which we are not proud, and none of us may judge another lest we ourselves are ready to be judged. At least you resisted temptation, for I think that you were tempted to accept Mr Bayes's commission, were you not? As at times we are all tempted.'

Luke had given a little laugh. 'All of us, Mrs Cowper? No, I cannot believe that you are to be included in the all of which you speak.'

Her smile for him had been a sad one. 'We none of us know the secrets of another's heart, Mr Harcourt. In that respect we are less fortunate than poor Dizzy, who has no secrets at all, and does not know whether any others of his kind have secrets, and is therefore, in that respect, always happy!'

How is it, Luke had thought afterwards, that Mrs Cowper and I so often end up speaking of such serious and moral matters? Not that I mind doing so, of course. Now Josette and I, until our last meeting, never really spoke of any serious matters at all. Cressy and I did, though. As do Cressy and James.

Mrs Britten had ended their conversation, deliberately Luke had thought, by talking nonsense about the odd-job boy who claimed to be frightened by small harmless Dizzy, and shot past his kennel as though a fire-breathing dragon dwelt there.

Anne had finished feeding Dizzy. Luke offered her his arm back into the house, and said, to show that he could make light conversation, 'You will accompany Mrs Britten and myself to the Fair next week, will you not? She seemed to think that you might refuse.'

She did not tell him that she had an aversion to going into large gatherings or being in a public place where she might be seen—and recognised—even though only recently she would have done. On the contrary, for some reason the thought of being escorted to a fair by Mr Luke Harcourt was a strangely exciting one.

'Oh, no,' and the bright blue eyes which looked up at him were sparkling. 'I shall be delighted to accompany you. I have never been to a fair. My father disapproved of them, and my late husband considered them beneath his notice. I have never been to Astley's Circus, either, and I suppose it is the notion that they were both forbidden to me which makes them seem so attractive.'

'Never been to a fair or to Astley's!' echoed Luke in a teasing and disbelieving voice. 'What a gap in your education, madam. I see that we must fill it. But I must warn you, you are not to put on your best bonnet, nor wear your most elaborate toilette, for if you do you are likely to become a target for pickpockets.'

She gave him a smile as teasing as his own. 'Then I pity the poor thieves, Mr Harcourt, for they will find nothing in my pocket to pick! They will have to rely on yours.'

'Oh, I am not so well breeched these days,' he retorted truthfully; the reason being that he was trying to live on his own earnings and not on the money which his father had settled on him. 'Fear not, though, I shall have enough to enable the three of us to join in all the fun of the fair.'

He bowed to Mrs Britten, who was watching them both from her chair by the window, an odd smile on her face.

Later, as he was leaving to join Pat O'Hare for a night on the town, Mrs Britten approached him as he was shrugging his greatcoat on.

'A word with you, Mr Harcourt, if you please.'

She was so grave that Luke wondered for a moment if she had suffered some bereavement and needed assistance. Not so, for taking his silence for consent, she continued. 'I know very well that you are as good-hearted a young gentleman as ever I let rooms to, and that is why I am daring to speak to you on this matter.

'I hope that you will take no offence at what you might see as meddling, but I must beg of you not to take any advantage of Mrs Cowper. I have seen the pleasure which you take in each other's company—which is very fine—but I would not wish your acquaintance with her to go any further than it has done. Mrs Cowper has had a hard life, with a great deal of suffering in it, and I would not like her to suffer any further pain.'

Luke said, as coolly as he could, although he was stung by the notion that his landlady thought that he was trifling with her friend, 'Would it reassure you, Mrs Britten, if I tell you that my intentions towards Mrs Cowper are strictly honourable?'

'Indeed, Mr Harcourt, I never thought that they were otherwise. It is simply that I trust you not to...' and she searched for the right phrase to use that would not offend him 'raise her expectations, as it were.'

'Oh, you may trust me not to do that,' he replied drily, so drily that Mrs Britten, her face troubled, caught at his arm.

'Oh, Mr Harcourt, do not take what I have just said so amiss that you cease to speak to Mrs Cowper at all. Since you returned from Wiltshire, she is a changed woman, and it is mostly your doing. Put down what I have said to you as the fears of an older woman for her protégée who deserves more than the unhappy life which has been hers so far.'

So, he had been right in his suppositions. Mrs Cowper's married life had not been a happy one. He said impulsively, for he knew his landlady well enough to be aware that she was no mere busybody, 'No offence taken, madam, I assure you. I have noted what you say and you may trust that my behaviour to her, as to all women, will be as proper as a gentleman's should.'

This seemed to reassure her, for she bowed her head, saying simply, 'Thank you, Mr Harcourt. I knew that you possessed a good heart.'

Luke smiled at her little compliment, and added a rider to his reassurance. 'You will allow me, I trust, to escort you both to the fair. I know that Mrs Cowper is looking forward to her visit very much.'

'Of course, Mr Harcourt. And I am greatly looking forward to going with you as well.'

He bowed and she curtsied. The strange little interview was over, leaving Luke with the distinct impression that, yes, there was some mystery about Anne Cowper which was making Mrs Britten so determined a protectress of her. He absolved himself of any wrong thoughts about her, since he had never viewed her as prey.

But it was also apparent that something must have changed in the manner in which he and Mrs Cowper spoke to one another and which had caused Mrs Britten to be troubled enough to speak to him.

Well, at least they had parted friends, although what she had said caused Luke to lie awake that night after an unsatisfactory evening's pleasure, and ask himself exactly what his intentions were concerning Anne Cowper.

To which he found no satisfactory answer.

Islington Fair was not so big as Bartholomew Fair—nor Greenwich Fair, for that matter—but it was big enough. Half of the citizenry welcomed it, the other—respectable—half most emphatically did not, since fairs not only attracted a small army of pickpockets and cutpurses, but also a band of gypsies. These were even more suspect than the thieves, but with less reason.

The smaller, uncovered booths were arranged down the High Street in front of the shops; another source of annoyance to the local townspeople, since they provided a fierce source of competition for them.

The larger covered booths, and the main attractions such as the menageries, and the small theatres under canvas called penny gaffs, were sited in the market place and on a piece of waste ground near by. The fair was officially opened by the Town Crier, a ceremony which Anne witnessed by accident when she delivered her latest batch of work to the shop in the High Street which had commissioned it.

She had never seen anything like it in her short, unhappy life, as she dawdled, wide-eyed, back to Mrs Britten's down the row of booths which were selling everything from gingerbread, sweets, oysters, wicker baskets and pegs to books and pamphlets.

The strangely dressed people who were tending the booths, the noise, and the sight of a troop of gypsies arriving on horseback, all held her entranced. It was as though the little joys of childhood that she had never been allowed to experience were being gifted to her now that she was a grown woman. More than one man gave her bright and sparkling eyes a second glance as she wandered along, and said to himself, 'Why, there's a pretty gal!'

'My dear, I thought that you were lost,' exclaimed Mrs Britten breathlessly when Anne finally arrived home with a pair of gingerbread men wrapped in a screw of paper which she handed to her friend.

'Oh, I see that you have been enjoying yourself at the Fair. Mind, the best of it will not be ready until later today when Mr Harcourt will be our escort. But was it wise of you to be alone for so long in such a public place among so many?'

Anne's smile was apologetic. 'I must confess that I never thought of that, but I can't believe that anyone would come to look for me in Islington.'

'Hmm,' snorted her friend. 'From what you have told me, I think that *he* might follow you to Hell, let alone Islington, in order to find you.' She was always careful never to name Anne's pursuer, even in the safety of her own home.

'But you will let me accompany you and Mr Harcourt this afternoon, won't you?' wheedled Anne.

'I'm not sure that I am wise to encourage you, and I admit I did agree that we should all three go, but dear Anne, do take care. Even with Mr Harcourt, take care.'

Anne dared not admit to herself what Mrs Britten might be hinting, and said, 'I cannot believe that Mr Harcourt has any sinister motives where I am concerned.'

'He is a young and handsome man, and that is enough,' declared Mrs Britten robustly. 'I know that he is a good-hearted one, but even good-hearted young men have their limitations and temptations.'

She would never have agreed to Mr Harcourt taking the pair of them to the fair if she had realised how far matters had gone between him and Anne—never mind that they were largely unspoken. She considered that the most dangerous thing of all was that neither Luke nor Anne fully understood what was happening to them. A foolish thought, perhaps, given Luke's undoubted experience of life

and love, but meeting Mrs Anne Cowper had taken
the pair of them into unknown territory.

Mrs Britten was concerned that they did not become lost there.

She was even more concerned when she saw
the easy pleasure with which they greeted one another when the time came for them to visit the fair.

Luke had followed his own advice to Anne and
had dressed down rather than up in a pair of grey
woollen breeches which had seen better days,
leather gaiters, heavy half-boots and an old brown
coat. They were clothes which he wore when he
visited Haven's End and engaged in country pur-
suits; they had never seen any better days at all,
only worse ones.

'Why, Mr Harcourt,' Anne told him merrily, 'I
don't think that I would have recognised you were
it not that you are in Mrs Britten's hall waiting for
us to come down.'

She put her head on one side, and rallied him by
saying, her mouth curling with amusement as she
finished, 'I do believe that I admire your hat most
of all!' It was the kind of hat a haymaker might
wear—or perhaps a coachman—brownish in colour, with a wide round brim and a low crown. But
he had swept it off to greet them with all the flourish of a dandy of the *ton*.

'Now, Anne,' reprimanded Mrs Britten with a smile which robbed her tone of offence, 'you must admit that whatever he wears, Mr Harcourt always looks the gentleman.'

'Oh, dear, then I have quite failed in my objective,' mourned Luke. 'I did not wish to appear gentlemanly at all. Up from the country, rather. An honest yeoman, hardly worth robbing.'

He held out his arms for them to walk one on each side of him. 'Come, ladies, yeoman that I am, I shall be the envy of all at the Fair this afternoon.'

Luke thought that Anne had never looked better. Her gown was a pale mauve one, as befitted a widow, and was certainly not cut in the latest mode, or, indeed, in any known mode at all. The only thing which relieved its plainness was the cream-coloured collar which she had crocheted herself. Her bonnet was a tiny straw with a black velvet band and a couple of mauve silk pansies— also made by Anne—decorating it.

But it was not her clothing which was giving her a new glow; it was the slight blush in her cheeks which enhanced the ivory pallor of her face. Her face had lost its hollows, and her tender mouth was curving up, not down, as it had done when he first met her.

Humour informed it, and that humour had

spread to her eyes, which sparkled and shone at him beneath her finely arched eyebrows. However was it that he had once thought her plain?

Islington Fair was roaring when they reached it. The noise was so great that before the day was over most of the small shopkeepers would be petitioning for it to be restrained. Children, eating gingerbread men or sucking sweets, ran about shouting. Men and women stood before the gaudily decorated booths, proclaiming their many attractions at the top of their voices.

All the small entertainments were in full swing. A gypsy fiddler was playing for an impromptu dance being performed by soldiers and their young women alongside a man who had three inverted thimbles before him on a small table.

Fascinated, Anne asked Luke what the man was doing. He smiled and told her, 'He lifts the thimbles to show you that there is a pea under one of them. He then covers them, moves them round and asks you to bet under which thimble the pea is to be found. If you guess correctly, you will win the bet, and he will pay you.'

'I know—' and Anne's voice was guarded '—that I am an innocent, but I would have thought that the man with the thimbles would make only a poor living, since it would be easy for anyone who watched him carefully to know exactly where the thimble with the pea is.'

'You think so?' Luke smiled at her. 'Come, let me pay for you to try to find the thimble with the pea.' He laughed gently at her hesitation. 'It will not be a costly lesson, I assure you, but a useful one.'

He threw a florin on to the table, saying to the man, 'The lady wishes to play the game.'

'And so she shall, young sir.' The man, thickset and wearing a battered top hat, crooned his patter at them. 'Look, pretty lady,' and he lifted the thimbles to show that the pea was under the middle one.

'Mark well what I do.' He began to move the thimbles rapidly around whilst Anne stared hard at the one under which she knew the pea was hidden, until he stopped suddenly, lifting his hands and leering at her.

'Now, pretty lady, where is the pea?'

'There!' And Anne confidently pointed at the right-hand thimble.

'Lift it, then, my pretty dear—and see whether you have won your bet.'

Anne lifted the thimble, to find beneath it— nothing!

'No, that can't be,' she wailed at Luke. 'I watched his hands so carefully that I was sure that it must be there.'

Luke and Mrs Britten were both laughing at her surprise. Grinning, the man said, 'Let me show the pretty lady where the pea is. Watch, dearie,' and he lifted the other two thimbles to reveal that the pea was under the middle one.

'I could have sworn that it was in the thimble on the right,' lamented Anne as they walked away. 'And I lost your florin for you, Mr Harcourt. I'm so sorry.'

'Oh, think nothing of that,' Luke said tenderly, pressing her hand which had somehow found its way into his. 'For it was I who was tricking you, as well as the thimble-rigger—which is what the man who runs that game is called. You see I knew that you couldn't win, because whichever thimble you had lifted you would have found nothing. The man palms the pea—that is, removes it and hides it in his hand—when he turns the thimble over at the beginning.'

'Oh, but, Mr Harcourt,' cried Anne, 'how can that be? There *was* a pea under the middle thimble, and look, someone has just won!'

She pointed at the thimble-rigging man who was handing money over to an ill-favoured rogue in a blue and white spotted neckerchief, who had been among those around the stall while Anne had been playing there.

'He simply palmed the pea again,' Luke in-

formed her, 'and put it under the thimble even as
he seemed to uncover it. The man who appeared
to win was the thimble-rigger's assistant, there to
make you think that *you* can win.

'There is a similar trick involving three playing
cards, one of which is the Queen of Hearts, called
Find the Lady. The fair people call those who bet
on such games, marks—which means innocents.
You see, there is an old saying, "The quickness of
the hand deceives the eye."'

Anne was secretly amused. A game called Find
the Lady, indeed! Despite herself, she began to
laugh. 'I was a mark, was I not? Were you educat-
ing me, Mr Harcourt, so that I should not bet my
non-existent fortune, and lose it all?'

'I was teasing you, because I wanted to see your
face when the man lifted the thimble and the pea
wasn't there. It was, indeed, a picture I shall always treasure.'

Forgetting everything—Mrs Britten, the deport-
ment which had ruled her life and which had
seemed to bring her nothing but misery—Anne
did something which she had never thought she
could or would. Her face alight with mischief, she
slapped lightly at Mr Luke Harcourt's hand. 'Oh,
you wicked creature, to tease me so. You are as big
a rogue as he is.'

Also forgetting himself and everything which he had promised to Mrs Britten so recently, Luke caught the slapping hand, bowed over it and kissed it before he could stop himself. 'So pleased to have amused you,' he murmured. 'Now, what shall I follow that with?'

'Nothing,' said Mrs Britten smartly. She had been watching her lodgers and was displeased with them both. They seemed to have lost the sense they had been born with. Particularly Anne, who also appeared to have forgotten how precarious her position was. 'You must allow the showmen to entertain us now.'

And so they did. Luke, who knew all about fairs and had visited many before, found his enjoyment in watching Anne's. Eyes wide, lips parted, her face rosy with pleasure, she found entertainment in everything she saw.

She hid her face in Luke's chest when the sword swallower began his act. 'Oh, no. I can't endure the sight of that,' but surprisingly was enchanted when Luke paid for them to enter the booth where Madame Giradelli, The Fireproof Lady, performed her magic tricks, holding her hands in the flames of a brazier and apparently swallowing fire without any ill effect.

She wore the oddest costume which Anne had

ever seen: an elaborately frilled gown which ended just below the knee to reveal a pair of heavily frilled pantaloons. Her feet were bare, and she had a ring with a giant winking stone on one of her toes.

After that, Luke bought them all oysters from one of the large booths, which boasted gaily striped coloured awnings, and where a pretty girl danced up and down before it, trying to persuade the passers by to sample the goods. She winked at Luke, calling him 'a fine upstanding young feller,' when he handed his money over.

Anne had never eaten oysters in the public street before, nor had she ever visited a menagerie, so her pleasure was guaranteed, as well as his, when they entered the big tent where Mr Wombwell had assembled in tiny cages some of the most ferocious animals on earth. Or so his posters, and the barker outside, informed them.

Next Luke took them into Mr Richardson's penny gaff which gave Mrs Anne Cowper more pleasure than the one visit to the theatre which she had been allowed as a young girl before she had been married.

She joined in hissing the villain, cheering the handsome hero, and in clapping the happy ending when the hero and his pretty girl were reunited after he had killed the villain in a duel. Never mind that both hero and heroine were rather long in the tooth, their remarkable and garish costumes more than made up for that.

'Oh,' sighed Anne blissfully when they were in the open again. 'I did enjoy that.'

Luke, about to offer her his arm, was struck, as though by summer lightning, with a most blinding revelation. She was standing by him so that he was seeing her in profile, and the expression of pure delight on her delicate face had an extraordinary effect on him. As thunder follows lightning, so Luke was overwhelmed by the realisation that this, this, was nothing other than love.

He also knew that he had never truly experienced it before. What he had felt for Cressy had been something quite different. Most of all he wished to protect the innocent creature beside him. He had never felt the need to protect Cressy, for she had never been vulnerable, had always been self-sufficient. But Anne—oh, that was a different matter.

And yet, at the same time, he wanted her. He wanted to be as near to her, as close to her, as a man might be to a woman. He wanted her in his arms, not only to tell her that he wished to love and care for her, but so that they could join together in experiencing all that men and women were made for: the age-old ceremony where they would become not two, but one.

All this in a moment of time. He was saved, either fortunately or otherwise, from saying or doing anything by a familiar voice hailing him.

It was Pat O'Hare.

Chapter Four

'Good day to you, Harcourt, and to you, mes-
dames,' cried Pat, all Irish charm as he swept off
his hat. 'I believe you know my friends, Jackson
and Thomas. What the devil are you doing in that
get-up? Rehearsing for a part as a yokel in Drury
Lane's next pantomime?'

His keen eyes swept over Luke and the two mod-
estly dressed women with him. The younger one
looked rather like a slow-burning charmer, one of
those who improved as you got to know her. Trust
Luke Harcourt to know where to find them!

'Come, O'Hare,' retorted Luke. 'You know how
many pickpockets and cutpurses haunt these fairs.
I'm less likely to be a target than you are, togged
out fit for a reception at Devonshire House.'

'Pooh, nonsense,' was Pat's reply. 'Aren't you

going to introduce us to the ladies?' His smile at Anne was a winning one.

He didn't win Anne. Inwardly she shrank away from him. She had been so happy alone with Luke and Mrs Britten. She still feared all men except Luke, so she stood mumchance, head bent, until Pat decided that he had been mistaken about her. She was simply a dowdy-goody with an attendant friend to whom Harcourt was being stupidly kind by taking them to the Fair.

All in all, the next quarter of an hour was not a happy one for Anne until Jackson proposed that they visit the penny gaff. It enabled Luke to say that they had already visited it and that he had promised Mrs Cowper that she should see The Learned Pig, who had so recently impressed a crowd of assorted scholars and savants, so they begged to be excused.

Excused they were, and Luke could not resist a quiet smile when, as he left them, Pat went to pull his watch out of his pocket—and found that it, and his handkerchief, had disappeared quite.

The grin which he gave Luke's party was a rueful one. 'You are not to crow over me, Harcourt,' he offered sadly. 'I doubt whether I could bring myself to wear that get-up, even to save my watch.'

This sally set Luke's party, as well as his own, laughing.

Anne, her arm tucked in Mrs Britten's, whispered to her kind friend, 'Mr O'Hare seemed a pleasant enough gentleman, but I am not sorry to see him and his party leave us. It is so much cosier when there are only the three of us.'

Mrs Britten silently agreed with her. She was only happy when Anne Cowper was not in too much company. Even to be at the fair at all was perhaps a mistake. On the other hand, this friend of Mr Harcourt's could scarcely be seen as endangering her…

Anne enjoyed seeing the animals most of all, from the monkeys on sticks to The Learned Pig who turned out to be just as learned as promised, proudly displaying his knowledge of French and German. She also admired the farm animals, from sheep to cattle, whose owners all boastfully proclaimed that they were the largest of their kind in the world.

It was when they were inspecting a ewe so large that it appeared almost deformed that a man whom Anne had already seen watching them, and who had a most fearsome appearance, walked up to Luke. He said in the strangest accent she had ever heard, 'All you *gorgios* look alike to me, but I knew at once that you were the only one who ever ate a *hotchiwitchi jogray* with us and claimed that you enjoyed it. Welcome, brother Luke,' and he held out his large hand.

Seen near to, he was no less fearsome, but beneath the long hair on his head and face he possessed a kind of hawklike handsomeness. He was wearing a jacket like Luke's, only the buttons on it were half crowns—and as if that were not enough, those on his flashy waistcoat were spaded half guineas.

His breeches were similar to a gamekeeper's, except that they, and his jacket, were made of velveteen, and his leggings, unlike Luke's, were not leather, but of a buff cloth, furred at the bottom.

But it was his hat which was the strangest thing of all. It had a high peak like a Spaniard's. The whip he carried was ornamented with a huge silver knob. His holland shirt was finely made and was a brilliant white. All told, he made Luke look shabbier than ever.

A couple of other men, as strange and fine in dress and appearance as he was, stood a little way behind him, like the courtiers in the playlet which they had recently seen in the penny gaff.

'Jasper!' cried Luke. 'You're a long way from home.'

'Oh, brother Luke,' smiled Jasper. 'All places are home to us. You should know that. And this is your pretty wife?'

Anne blushed and looked away. Luke said

briefly, 'This is my friend, Mrs Anne Cowper, and our landlady, Mrs Britten. They are doubtless wondering what a *hotchiwitchi jogray* is.' He turned to them, explaining, 'You have Jasper Petulengro, the king of the gypsies, no less, to tell you what it is.'

'A hedgehog stew,' translated Jasper. 'And you know, brother Luke, that we Romanies have no king. True it is, though, that I am their Pharaoh. I am sad, Luke, that you have not yet found your mate—but you will bring your pretty *rackley* and her friend to drink tea with us, will you not? We are camped yonder on the nearest thing to a heath that we could find. Come.'

'You may not call yourself a king, Jasper,' Luke riposted, 'but you behave like one—and that is all that matters in this world!'

Mrs Britten, fearful of the gypsies, as so many townspeople were, whispered to Anne, 'If we were not with Mr Harcourt, I should be afraid to go to their camp, but I don't think that he will allow any harm to come to us.'

Even as she spoke, a group of gypsies on horseback galloped up, led by one of the most handsome men Anne had ever seen. He said something in a strange language to Jasper and to Luke, whom he greeted with a flourish of the hand and a bent head. There was nothing humble about his manner, and he nodded condescendingly when Luke replied, haltingly, in the same strange language.

When Jasper saw that Anne was listening, fascinated, to them both, he said, 'They are speaking Romany, pretty lady, the language of the gypsies. Brother Luke is one of the few *gorgios*—that is, people who are not Romanies—who has taken the trouble to learn it. We honour him for doing so.'

Led by the horsemen, they reached the encampment, which was made up of small tents, with wagons drawn up behind them. Before the tents were tripods from which iron cooking pots hung.

A small woman, who greeted them, turned out to be Jasper Petulengro's wife. She was finely and strangely dressed. Her dark hair hung in long braids, and she had huge gold hoops in each ear. Anne wondered if the pearls around her long, proud neck were real. If so, they were worth a small fortune, as were the gilt ornaments on her dress.

She kissed Luke on his cheek, before taking his hand and bidding them all to sit so that they might drink tea and break bread with them. The handsome horseman had dismounted, and was staring boldly at Anne, so boldly that, a little afraid, she turned her head away.

Luke saw that the man's attention worried her.

Quietly he said, 'Do not be afraid. His name is Tawno Chikno which means The Small One, although he is so tall—just as we call Lady Jersey, who chatters so much, Silence. He has an ugly middle-aged wife who adores him, and he her. Jasper has told me that many *gorgio* women have begged him to marry them, but he has always refused! So, you see, there is nothing to be afraid of.'

Jasper overheard Luke, and also tried to reassure Anne. 'Brother Luke tells you true. But then he always does. He should have been one of us.'

He handed Anne tea in a fine china cup and saucer. 'Eat and drink with us, my pretty.'

Anne thanked him shyly. Luke thought that he had never seen her look so well. There was a slight flush on her face as she drank her tea and ate the coarse bread which Mrs Petulengro gave her. The woman had been watching her carefully, and spoke at length to Luke and Jasper in Romany.

Luke listened to her, then told Anne, 'Mrs Petulengro thinks that you have an interesting face, and that she would like to read the leaves in your cup after you have drunk your tea. She is a *chovihani* or a fortune teller. They call fortune telling *dukkerin* in their own language.'

He did not tell her that Mrs Petulengro had also said, 'Yon *rackley* will be your doom, brother

Luke,' meaning that Anne was his fate, or his future. When he had shaken his head at her, she had lifted her shoulders and said, 'You may not alter the future, brother Luke, howsoever you might try to. But it is no great matter since you have no wish to do so. I see your heart and her name is written there.'

She leaned forward when Luke had spoken, holding out her hand to take Anne's cup. Hesitantly, Anne gave it to her. She did not believe that the woman could tell her fortune, and she hoped that she could not tell her past. She watched Mrs Petulengro stare at the pattern of the leaves at the bottom of her cup as intently as she had previously stared at Anne and Luke.

'Your hand,' she said at last, putting the cup down. 'Give me your hand, my pretty dear, that I may read it, for the tea leaves are not as plain as they ought to be.'

She spoke as though she were intoning some strange ritual, and her eyes were as fixed as though she were looking, not at Anne, but at some distant horizon. Anne found herself falling into something resembling a trance as Mrs Petulengro took her hand and fixed her strange yellow eyes on her.

At last she spoke in a lilting, singsong fashion, not at all like that of her normal voice. 'I see you imprisoned on high in a strange place far from here. You have come to us after a long and dangerous journey. You look small and frail but you have a courage as strong as that of a Romany's. Two treasures are yours, and the second is not gold. A faithful loving heart is better than riches, and that, too, you possess.

'All before you, and all that is past is dark and mysterious, but at the end is light, and you shall have your heart's desire, but not before much suffering. Suffering, they say, purifies, and suffering has already purified you and will purify you more. I will give you the power, not only to endure, but to see the truths of life and love.'

She dropped Anne's hand and looked into her eyes for a long minute, as though she were searching her very soul. She spoke again, her voice so faint that only Anne could hear her.

'Most strange it is, dearest *chal*. Through the darkness around you I can see that your destiny and ours are entwined, though how and why, I do not know. You are in great danger, but fear not, all shall be well.'

She paused, spoke only to repeat what she had said earlier,

'At the end is light…and that is all I can see…that, and the gift that I bestow on you.'

Silence followed, until, 'Did I speak?' she asked
Anne. 'Did I prophesy?'

'You spoke darkly of the past—and of the future,'
replied Anne. 'But I think that I understood you.'

Oh, yes, the woman before her had somehow
seen something of her past life. Anne had said
nothing to her beforehand which might have
hinted of imprisonment, suffering and flight—but
she had seen them. She had also spoken of a future where Anne would achieve her heart's desire—but only after more suffering. Her heart's
desire! What would that be?

Anne looked up, and saw Luke's eyes on her. In
that moment she knew, not only that she loved
him, but that he loved her. She looked at the handsome young gypsy, and knew that what Luke had
told her was true. He loved his plain and middle-
aged wife dearly. It was as though many things
which had been hidden from her, so that she had
walked the world as though she were asleep, were
made plain.

And Mrs Britten, what of her? For the first time
Anne could see quite clearly the goodness of her: a
goodness which few possessed. She twisted her
hands together. Could she live with this new power?

Mrs Petulengro was still watching her even
though she had sunk exhausted to the ground. She

said, again for Anne's ears only, 'Oh, *chal, chal*, do not repine. Accept, and although everything has changed it will be as though nothing has. But the power will not leave you.'

Anne looked at Luke again, and the revelation was still there, but did not blind her. Accept, yes, she would accept.

'*Chal*?' she asked him. 'And *rackley*? What do they mean?'

'*Chal* means child,' Luke said. '*Rackley* is woman.'

He could see immediately that Anne had changed again as she had been changing since he first met her. But this change had been rapid, not slow, and he could not put a finger on what it was. Always he had been aware of her brave spirit behind the submissive face that she showed the world, but now that spirit was suddenly visible.

In some way she had been blessed. He had not heard what Mrs Petulengro had said to her. No one had for, although Anne had heard her voice as loud and compelling, the others had heard only a low muttering. He knew, though, that the change was connected with the *chovihani* and her divination.

Jasper Petulengro, who had been intently watching all that had passed, said gently, 'Eat, my children, eat. The breaking of bread together seals friendship. My wife has made your lady one of us, as you are one of us, brother Luke, so is she our sister. There is always a home here for you.'

Mrs Petulengro suddenly spoke in her prophetic voice again.

'Aye, and it may yet be needed. Give me your remaining bread, *chal*. I feel faint and you have had some of my strength.'

Anne handed the bread over, and Mrs Petulengro tore at it as though she had not eaten for days. She rose and walked towards the tents, saying, 'I must sleep.'

Her husband, his face troubled, watched her go. He said to Luke, 'It is not often that the strength leaves her after the spirit has spoken, yet it has done so today. But remember this, she always speaks true.'

In a lighter tone, he added, 'Come, pretty lady, brother Luke and the lady's protectress, come and see Chikno school the horses. It is a sight to please mortal men and women more than a little.'

So they did, and a fair sight it was, and after that one of the gypsies came with his fiddle and escorted them back to the Fair, bowing low before he left them, blessing them in Romany.

Anne's long and happy day was over, and exalted, she walked back to Mrs Britten's, her hand in Luke's, knowing that not only did she love, but that she was loved.

Before they had parted Jasper had bid her farewell, adding, 'Remember, pretty lady, that though the *chovihani* spoke so surely of the past and the future, all that we mortals ever have is the present. Enjoy that, for the past is gone, and may not be relived, and the truth of the future is unknown, even though we may have had a glimpse of it, since sometimes that glimpse may be deceitful. Meet your doom as it comes to you. Seize the day.'

That night, for the first time since she had arrived at Mrs Britten's, Anne's sleep was peaceful, her dreams were happy ones, and Luke walked through them all.

'Pray, Mr Harcourt, did you enjoy the hedgehog stew of which Mr Petulengro spoke?'

It was the following afternoon. Luke had come down to the drawing-room where Anne was working. Her face had lit up when he entered, for her visit to the gypsies had liberated her, and she no longer feared to let him know how much she enjoyed his company.

'Not very much,' he answered her, 'but it would not do to say so. I was only a boy when I first met the gypsies, and Tawno and his men cured me of

my fear of horses. My gratitude to them is so great
that I would do nothing to hurt them. Letting me
eat with them and share their life a little is an honour not given to many *gorgios* and I am very sensible of that.'

'Afraid of horses,' echoed Mrs Britten incredu-
lously. 'You do surprise me, Mr Harcourt, you
ride so beautifully.'

By her expression Luke saw that Anne, too, was
surprised by his confession.

'Oh, yes,' he went on. 'I had a bad fall when I
was very young, and although my guardian
thought that I had recovered from it, my recovery
was only a physical one. I had to exercise my will
every time I went riding. I dare not confess my
cowardice until one day, when I was at the gypsy
encampment on the heath near my home at
Haven's End, Tawno Chikno dared me to ride one
of their half-broken horses. I think that he sensed
my fear and wanted me to confront it.'

He paused, and continued as though the memory
still pained him. 'I will not bore you with the details of how he cured me. Suffice it that he did, and
that the lesson was long and hard. Afterwards I
found riding a joy, and not a penance, and he taught
me some of the simpler equestrian tricks he knew.

'They do not share the whole of their knowledge

with us, only a little. They are fearful that, if too much is shared, the spirit of the Romanies will die, and they will become like *gorgios*—than which there is no worse fate.'

Anne bent her head over her work. She did not want to discuss the Romany's powers. She had thought that the ability to read men and women would pass from her as soon as she left the gypsy camp, but it was still with her. She found that she even knew what Dizzy was feeling—she could not call the blur which surrounded him thinking! But his happiness when he saw her was more tangible than ever.

What touched Anne was discovering how careful of her Mrs Britten was, and that she was determined to protect her from Luke in case he began to think wrong thoughts about her. She had also found that she had another talent. If she wished, she could blank out her awareness of others' feelings.

I wonder what she is thinking, mused Luke, watching the slight play of emotion on Anne's face. He sighed. He really ought to be paying attention to his own problems, not troubling about Anne's. Ever since he had turned down Bayes's commission to write scandal about Clairval, he had been finding it difficult to write at all.

Anne heard the sigh. It told her that Luke was

worried, but not what was worrying him. She looked at him under her lashes. His brow was furrowed, and there were signs of strain on his handsome face. Even her new powers of intuition were not powerful enough for her to divine exactly what was wrong with him: that having decided he would no longer live on his father's bounty, he was finding it impossible to make a living at all.

And then she knew! She said, as off-handedly as she could, 'Pray, what new articles are you writing for Mr Bayes? Or have you accepted a commission for another editor? Do not answer me if you think that I am prying into your affairs.'

Luke decided to tell her the truth. He might feel better if he shared his feelings of despair with someone. 'You are not prying, Mrs Cowper. Indeed, it is kind of you to ask. No, I have not begun any new articles for Mr Bayes, or for anyone else. Nor am I like to. The nub of the matter is that I seem to have lost all my powers of invention and I am beginning to wonder whether I ought to have settled in the safe haven of Oxford's cloisters after all.'

'You are not writing of society's scandals, then?'

Luke stirred restlessly in his chair. 'That is part of my problem. It is not the kind of work which I wish to engage in, but refusing it seems to have dried up my muse. I wish… I don't know what I wish…'

Anne put down her sewing, and said earnestly, 'I think I understand you, Mr Harcourt. It occurs to me that, since writing scandal about high life is not your true *métier*, you might be happier engaged in writing the truth about low life.'

His head, which had drooped a little, jerked up. Luke said, struck by her suggestion, 'What exactly did you have in mind?'

'Why, seeing how much we enjoyed ourselves at the fair yesterday, and the rapport that you so obviously had, not only with the gypsies, but all the showmen and women present, you might use that rapport to write about them.

'Truthfully, of course, for it seems to me that I have never come across any really good prose which told of the lives of those who, after all, make up the greater number of the citizens of Britain. Do not the humble deserve to be celebrated as well as the great? And because you sympathise with them, who better than you to do it?'

Oh, how beautiful she looked, as well as clever and kind! What a splendid notion she had offered him. Luke's busy brain had already begun to see the possibilities of what she was saying.

Thinking by his silence that he was perhaps not impressed by her suggestion, Anne added in an encouraging tone, 'I believe you said that Mr Bayes was ready to hire someone like Mr Cruikshank to illustrate your work for you when you were writing scandal. If so, then could he not draw The Learned Pig, or the thimble-rigger in action instead?'

Luke could not contain himself. Mrs Britten or no Mrs Britten, duenna or no duenna, he was out of his chair at one bound, and was pulling Anne to her feet in order to kiss her vigorously on each cheek.

'Oh, my dear. What a splendid girl you are! There was my destiny staring me in the face, and I could not see it for looking, but you could. I can write about the gypsies and Mr Petulengro and try to make people understand their true nature, instead of believing myths about them! I do believe that if Bayes does not want me, then there are others who will.'

He whirled her around as though they were dancing together—a vigorous kind of waltz, perhaps—before he tenderly settled her back in her chair again.

'Really, Mr Harcourt,' exclaimed Mrs Britten, scandalised. 'I would never have thought it of you, such a perfect young gentleman as you used to be. Mrs Cowper deserves more consideration from you.'

'And so she does.' Luke was jubilant. 'Let me do this in proper form!' He went down on one knee before the blushing Anne. 'Dear Mrs Cow-

per, allow me to thank you for your splendid suggestion. When I have made my fortune, I will offer
you a suitable reward. There! Will that do?' He
kissed her again: on the hand this time.

Anne was laughing. 'Oh, Luke,' she said, forgetting all decorum, all proper forms of address between a single young man and a young widow.
'Thank me when you have sold your first paper
describing scenes from low life.'

'And that, too, is it,' declaimed Luke. 'My title.
"Scenes from Low Life". Why, I do believe that
there may be a book in it!'

Mrs Britten had never seen him behave so before.
He had always been quietly courteous, so gentlemanly, so decorous. Whatever had got into him?

Anne Cowper had got into him. That, and his
sudden understanding that she had just pointed
out to him the way he ought to go. His first paper
could be written almost from her point of view:
that of someone who was seeing the fair for the
first time.

He was on fire to begin at once. 'My dear Anne,
you will forgive me, and Mrs Britten, you too. I
must go upstairs immediately and begin to write
before the muse deserts me. Tomorrow I shall visit
Bayes, and if he doesn't want me, why, I know
several other editors who I am sure will.'

The door closed behind him. Mrs Britten opened her mouth to remind Anne that she ought to go with care where Luke Harcourt was concerned, but the expression on her friend's face stopped her.

My dear Anne, he called me. And then he kissed me. That was all Anne Cowper knew, and all she needed to know.

Chapter Five

When had he fallen in love with her? Luke was in no doubt that what he felt for Anne was more than a mere passing fancy. It was both deep and true and had only been fully revealed to him when he had seen her innocent pleasure at Islington Fair—which did not mean that he had been struck down by his passion for her at that exact moment.

No, looking back, he could remember a hundred small things which should have told him that she was slowly turning into the one woman in the world whom Luke Harcourt wanted for a wife.

He remembered the night when he had seen Cressy at Lady Leominster's and had realised that he still loved her, but was no longer in love with her. Could Anne have been the reason for his change of heart? Surely not, for then he had scarcely known her. Was it conceivable that from the very first time that he met her she had begun to wind her way around his heart?

Luke was sure she was good: he also knew that she was both clever and kind. She was hardworking as well: stitching conscientiously away at gossamy baby clothes in order to earn a meagre living, and yet at the same time quietly and unobtrusively helping Mrs Britten about the house.

She was not at all the sort of young woman with whom he might have thought that he would fall in love. That woman would have been outgoing, perhaps a little racy in manner—in short, a woman like his stepmother Cressy.

But if Anne was quiet and retiring where Cressy was voluble and forthright, she possessed an integrity of character wholly admirable in one so frail and defenceless. Without either wealth or position she yet gave off an effortless aura of moral authority. Like Cressy, she was brave, but her bravery took a different form from that of his stepmother's, who had always lived in a protected world.

No, Anne was living at the margin where pennies were scarce and both men and women were exploited, but the influence which she was beginning to exert on him was a profound one. For the first time, Luke had begun to question his own life and to find it wanting.

Whose example but Anne's had made him determine to live as little as possible on his father's money, and instead try to carve out his own career? He had been a dilettante, idling his life away whilst pretending to be a writer; a typical younger son surviving on the edges of the great world of society, frittering away his talents.

If he had any, that was! Well he would soon find out. He had followed Anne's advice to write about the Fair and its people. He had worked far into the night, the words tumbling from his pen, his newly roused mind driving him on. Why had he never thought of writing about the life around him before?

He had been stuck in a rut where he poured out high-minded, moralising copy about the political world, or stale and perfumed gossip about the people he met in high society. And all the time he had possessed a talent for something quite different— and without Anne Cowper's prompting he would never have found it out!

By morning he was handing the newly written, unblotted sheets to Bayes, saying, 'I couldn't write scandal for you, sir, but here is something I *can* write, and which you might like to print. You could perhaps persuade Cruikshank—or someone like him—to illustrate them. If you approve of the idea, I would like to write a series about low life in

London and the country and the gypsies who frequent the fairs.'

Bayes had begun to read Luke's work with a patronising smile on his face. He had always considered Harcourt promising as a writer, but held back by his being fundamentally unserious as a result of his class and his small, but dependable, income.

His smile faded. 'Good stuff, Harcourt!' he exclaimed. 'Damned lively. Didn't know you had it in you. There's a public for this, you know. The people with money walk by this world and never see it. And you're right about an illustration. Yes, I'll take it, on the condition that you write me something like this for every number.'

The strength of his enthusiasm surprised Luke. Bayes was basically a cynical manipulator, but he had a keen eye for what people would pay to read. Here was an immediate source of income for him—and it was all owing to Anne Cowper's suggestion. Bayes picked up the first page again and began to read it more carefully.

'With this,' he enthused, 'we'll get our readers coming and going in every number. O'Hare can do the society stuff and you the low life.' He thought a moment, said, 'That's it, that's the title: "Scenes from Low Life"!'

Luke forbore to tell him that Anne Cowper had

been there before him. Let Bayes think that he was the originator. If the series was a success, he would doubtless soon be claiming the idea as his own. Well, let him, so long as he paid Luke Harcourt a good fee.

'You think that you can keep this up?' Bayes asked him anxiously.

Could he keep it up? Luke, who had resolved to go back to Islington and start writing immediately, now that inspiration had begun to flow, assured him that he could.

'My next will be about the tricksters at the fair, and then I'll probably write two about the gypsies—with your approval, of course.'

'Splendid, old feller. If Egan can have the public enthusing about boxers, then why not gypsies and tricksters from Harcourt, eh? Your name's a bit fancy, though, for someone writing about low life, ain't it? How about Solomon Grundy instead?'

The idea of being Solomon Grundy took Luke's fancy, if only because the name seemed to belong to someone vastly different from his own carefully dressed and well-mannered person.

'What a splendid notion,' he exclaimed approvingly. 'Solomon Grundy it shall be—so long as you don't address me as "Solly boy". I don't think that I could stomach that.'

'You'll stomach the money you're going to earn by using his name,' remarked Bayes shrewdly. 'Come to the ordinary with me and have a steak and kidney pie, and we'll agree terms while we eat. "Scenes from Low Life",' he repeated thoughtfully. 'I like it.'

On the way home, having decided that he must keep his expenses down, Luke stopped at the livery stables to order the proprietor to sell the horse he kept there, even though it hurt him to part with Tiger. Another problem was that he had agreed to have a night on the town with Pat O'Hare after he had dined with James and Cressy. It was too late for him to cancel it, but such self-indulgent treats must be a thing of the past until he had a steady income.

In the morning he would visit Jack Hatfield, who published a lighter magazine than Bayes, called *The Talk of the Town*, and offer him a little piece which was already running through his mind on fashionable slang and thieves' cant. It was just the kind of piece Hatfield was willing to pay for. He had a copy of Captain Robert Grose's elderly Dictionary of the Vulgar Tongue, and he could easily bring it up to date.

It was quite extraordinary how fertile his imagination had become since Anne Cowper had

seeded it with her original suggestion. His gratitude would take the form of inviting her to visit
Cremorne Gardens with him—Mrs Britten could
act as their duenna. Alas, neither of them was at
home so Luke left for dinner at Lyndale House
without thanking her.

James and Cressy thought that he was rather
less forthcoming at table than he usually was.
Later that evening, after their last guest had left,
dinner having been taken at the fashionable hour
of four-thirty, Cressy chose to raise the subject of
Luke with her husband.

'James, do you not consider it a trifle odd that
Luke has scarcely been seen in society this season,
has dined with us most infrequently, and tonight
was very unlike his usual self? He can't be ill,
surely? He didn't look ill,' she added doubtfully.
'What's more, he told Frank Belsize that he had
sold Tiger when Frank asked him to ride with him
in the Park on Saturday.'

'Sold Tiger!' exclaimed James, more struck by
his son doing such an unlikely thing than by the
fact that Almacks, Devonshire House and other
haunts of high life were being neglected by him.
'What an odd thing to do! I trust that he's not been
extravagant lately and run into debt. I know his allowance isn't huge, but he's never done such a

thing before. I would never have thought that he'd sell Tiger.'

'Well, that had occurred to me, too,' confessed Cressy, 'that he had run into debt—but when I asked him if he were strapped for cash, because if he were then I might be able to help him out, he was quite short with me. Short for Luke, that is,' she amended. 'You know how astonishingly polite he always is.

'He told me in no uncertain terms that, on the contrary, he was living well within his earnings, and intended to continue doing so. He did remember to thank me for my offer, though. As prettily as usual. Perhaps I'm being fanciful.'

James said slowly, 'I shan't reproach you for offering to bail him out if he were in trouble. And I don't think that you were being fanciful. He struck me as having changed in some way...'

'Perhaps he's fallen in love,' Cressy offered hopefully. 'But who can he have met to do so? Frank told me later that he has hardly seen him this year, either. If he's not going into society, he won't be meeting anyone suitable.'

She saw James's face change and, as usual, read it correctly, and said faintly, 'Oh, no, never say that he's fallen in love with someone *un*suitable!'

'It's possible. I know that he's always been

steady, but very often it's the steady ones who kick over the traces when they do at last fall in love with someone.'

They stood silent for a moment before James took Cressy into his arms 'Do not fret, my love. He's a grown man, and in some ways he's been too chained to the pair of us for too long. He's going his own way now, and we mustn't stop him. Trust in his basic goodness, Cress, as I do.'

He rarely called her Cress, and she knew that, for all his brave words, James was worried about his son—who had never before given them the slightest occasion to think that he might kick over the traces.

'Very well, James. So long as he knows that there's always a haven for him with us.'

'Our home has an appropriate name. Haven's End, my love. It's his refuge as well as ours if ever he needs one—which I pray that he never will.'

Having a night on the town in company with Pat O'Hare and a crowd of other young bucks was not half so much fun as taking Anne to the fair, Luke was discovering.

They had begun by visiting a silver hell off the Haymarket, so called because it was not so expensive as some of the gaming halls where the top-notch swells went. Luke had never been a great gambler; that night he didn't want to gamble at all.

'Oh, come on, Harcourt,' grumbled Pat. 'You're a regular wet blanket these days. Risk a penny if you can't risk anything else.'

'Don't want to risk anything,' returned Luke equably while watching Pat in some surprise. Pat had already gambled a considerable sum, and for the moment luck appeared to be with him, since he had managed to double it. Idly, Luke wondered where Pat was getting his money from. He was usually short of the ready, but tonight he was flush with it. He certainly wasn't selling enough of his writing to Bayes, or anyone else, to have so much cash at his disposal.

'You're not as jolly as you used to be, Harcourt.' Pat was already half-cut. 'And you ain't drinking, either. The drink's free, you know.'

Cynically, Luke thought that the free drink was there to fuddle the few wits of the committed gamesters who always believed that a really big win was waiting for them just around the corner.

Another thing just around the corner was Laura Knight's, which Pat wished to visit, although the rest of the party wanted to patronise The Coal Hole.

They ended by wrangling at the entrance to a dirty alley off the Haymarket, Luke wishing him-

self anywhere but where he was. He was wondering at the enthusiasm with which he had, in the
past, joined in this type of excursion. Some wanted
to go one way, some another, Luke was just about
to perform his own judgment of Solomon by suggesting that the party cut itself in two when he
heard a woman's wailing cry coming from halfway down the alley.

'Help me, oh, help, please.' The last word was
cut off in mid-shout.

'What's that?' Luke turned towards the direction
of the cry.

'That? Oh, some doxy complaining that her
client is being a little too enthusiastic. Come on,
Harcourt. Where do you want to go? Oh, the devil,
he's gone to rescue the ladybird!'

There had been something so desperate in the
woman's cry that Luke felt that he could not ig-
nore it. He ran down the alley towards a pair of
open gates before a large courtyard.

A small group of men were gathered there, watching another man, a large one, who had a woman
pinned against the wall, his fell purpose quite plain.
His watchers were so lost in their concentration on
him, cheering the woman's attacker on, that Luke
was through them, his companions streaming after
him, before they realised that he was there.

He took the man by the shoulder in order to pull him away, which allowed his victim to scream at Luke, 'Oh, Gawd, mister, save me! Oh, I wants me Ma!' Except that it was not a woman who was the subject of public rape, but a girl who was little more than a child, her clothes torn, her face streaked with tears, her thin arms held up to protect herself.

It was fortunate for Luke that his friends had followed him. The girl's attacker was large, but no larger than his companions, who looked like a group of bruisers on holiday: they would have made short work of Luke had he been alone.

Instead, Luke's party got between them and the man he had swung towards him. Pat O'Hare took the child by the hand to pull her away from where Luke and the girl's attacker were struggling. Another of Luke's friends shouted, 'I'll fetch the Watch,' and ran back up the alley.

By now the man Luke held twisted almost free, sufficiently so to turn to confront him so that for a moment they were eye to eye. Luke almost let go of him in shocked surprise at discovering that the man whom he was holding on to so grimly was none other than the Marquess of Clairval. Clairval was equally shocked on recognising Luke.

'Damn you!' he gritted between his teeth.

'Loose your hold on me, Harcourt. I'll let no man's bastard interfere with my pleasure, even if Lyndale is his father.'

'And damn you, too,' retorted Luke, all his usual mild and courteous charm missing at the sight of a man publicly violating a child for the amusement of himself and his companions. 'I'll hand you over to the Watch to deal with when they come. You'll face the magistrates in the morning, I'll make sure of that.'

Clairval was almost spitting with thwarted rage. He tried to strike Luke in the face, but failed. His men were fighting and struggling with Luke's party until one of them saw that in the excitement of the fracas the child had disappeared after wrenching herself free from Pat.

He grasped Clairval by the arm and shouted, 'Stop, m'lord, stop. The doxy has scarpered. Neither the Watch nor the magistrates can do anything to you without anyone to snitch on you!'

His voice was loud enough to end the struggle. Clairval stood back, laughing at Luke, just as the Watch arrived, a gross fat man, self-importance personified.

'What's this, then? A girl child attacked and like to be ravished? Let me see her—and the man accused.'

Still laughing and now the picture of aristocratic arrogance, Clairval strolled languidly forward, pulling a guinea from his breeches pocket, he pressed it into the watchman's hand.

'A misunderstanding, look you. Take this for your wasted errand. I am Clairval, as my companions will testify. Those who have drunk too deep, like our friend here—' and he waved a contemptuous hand at Luke '—often see what isn't there. Look around you, there is no child, there never was a child, as again my men will testify.'

Which they did, surrounding the Watch and loudly informing him that their master was the Marquess of Clairval, a friend of the King, who would not stoop to attack anyone or anything publicly—least of all a woman.

'You lie, damn you,' cried Luke, seething with rage. He looked reproachfully at Pat, who had carelessly allowed the girl to run off. 'We all saw her—and you, as *my* friends will testify.'

'I don't know, nor do I wish to, what bees are buzzing in your bonnet, Harcourt. I am supposing that you are usually light in the attic, but I would advise you and your friends not to make reckless charges which you cannot substantiate,' drawled Clairval, now quite at his ease. He saw that, the excitement of the moment over, none of Luke's companions, who had not seen the worst of the attack on her, was willing to accuse him without the girl child being present.

They were only too well aware that the Marquess of Clairval was a great and powerful man whom a bench of magistrates might find it difficult to accuse without an overwhelming reason. Worse, they might also fear his revenge if they persisted in their accusation and it proved to be groundless.

Luke looked around him to see that Clairval had judged the matter correctly, and that his friends were hanging their heads and looking away from him.

He controlled with difficulty the red rage which was rapidly overcoming him, and said as coolly as he could, 'Both you and I know exactly what you were doing, Clairval. You may fool the Watch by your lies and intimidate my friends with your rank so that they will not testify against you, but it doesn't alter the fact that you were violating a girl child in public.'

Pat O'Hare pulled at Luke, before Clairval could reply. 'Leave it, Harcourt. Why make an unnecessary enemy? You've no hope of proving anything against such as Clairval without a cast-iron case.'

It seemed that Clairval had won, as Luke suspected that he always did and always would. Armoured by his rank and the deference paid to it by those below him, he might do as he pleased— short of murder. He must accept that it was his turn to be thwarted and that to betray his anger at Clairval's escape would only serve to add to Clairval's pleasure at having done so.

Clairval, indeed, was openly laughing at him, only waiting to throw a final triumphant sentence at Luke as soon as the Watch had walked away, apologising profusely and humbly to m'lord for taking the liberty of troubling him.

Once he had disappeared, Clairval thrust his ugly face in Luke's. 'I'll not forget this, Harcourt. I always make sure that any man who seeks to injure me subsequently pays a heavy price. Walk carefully, keep out of my way as much as you will, you will not escape me.'

'Perhaps not,' replied Luke hardily. 'But "the pitcher may go too often to the well" is a saying you might remember next time you attack a child.'

'Not if the man's name is Clairval,' replied the Marquess arrogantly.

Pat was pulling at Luke's arm again, 'Come away, Harcourt. You do no good bandying words with him.'

Clairval gave Pat a knowing nod. 'Well said, sir. It's a pity that your friend is not as wise as you are. I bid you both goodnight,' and he strolled off laughing, his lackeys behind him, guffawing their amusement.

Luke turned angrily on Pat. 'No need for you to say anything to placate him, O'Hare. If you had kept tight hold of the child, he would be singing a different song by now. Whatever possessed you to let her go?'

'Come now, Harcourt, no need to rail at me. She did you a good turn by disappearing. Nothing but trouble could have come of it, if you had succeeded in getting us all involved in a public fracas in court with Clairval. He would have demanded to be tried in the House of Lords by his peers, if it was decided that there was a case against him. As it is, you've made a bad enemy of him for life.'

'Well, I don't want him as a friend, that's for sure: an enemy's better,' retorted Luke, who was finding depths of anger and determination in himself which he had never known existed. He was still annoyed with Pat, whose carelessness had allowed Clairval to escape punishment for his brutality.

Luke now believed that all the whispered stories about Clairval's mistreatment of his young wife were true, and he pitied any woman who found

herself in his power. All desire to make a night of
it, never very strong, had completely vanished.
He felt only a desperate weariness of spirit.

Clapping him on the back, Pat said cheerfully,
'Leave it that you did the right thing, Harcourt.
Let's forget Laura Knight's and go to The Coal
Hole instead, and drown our sorrows, eh?'

Luke shook his head at him and his fellows, who
obviously agreed with Pat that visiting a brothel
after what had passed was not quite the thing.
'Sorry, O'Hare, I can't forget that child's face so
easily. I'm for home.'

Home? Where was that? he thought, as he hailed
a Hackney cab to take him back to Islington. Mrs
Britten's, like Haven's End, was simply a tempo-
rary place where he might lay his head. The truth
was that he had no home. For the first time in his
carefree life he thought longingly of a different
kind of haven where a woman waited for him, and
children, perhaps.

As for Pat, he didn't feel very proud of himself
for having saved Clairval's bacon by allowing the
child to run away. Not to have done so, however,
would have brought immediate vengeance down
on his head from Clairval who, notoriously, never
forgave a slight, an insult or an enemy. He had successfully diverted Clairval's anger from himself to

Luke, but afterwards he drank himself senseless at The Coal Hole, in an effort to forget his treachery towards a good friend.

Chapter Six

'Let me take your bag from you, mam. It looks a little heavy.' Mary put out a willing hand to help Anne by carrying the bag full of linen and fine cotton that she had just collected from the drapers as part of her next commission. It was the material for a layette for a baby who was expected in the autumn, and making it would be a welcome addition to Anne's small income.

Smiling, she shook her head. 'Thank you, Mary, but no, I can easily manage to carry it up to my room these days.'

'Not surprising,' said Mary boldly, 'seeing as how you look so much better now.'

Privately she put this improvement down to Mr Luke Harcourt's influence. Why, she remembered how ill and weak Mrs Cowper had been when she had first arrived in Islington; so pale and listless that she didn't seem likely to be long for this world. And now, look at her! Cheeks rosy, eyes shining, her step lively, and looking as sleek and rounded as a well-fed kitten!

All this since Mr Harcourt had arrived back in the spring. Well, who could be surprised at that? A nicer, kinder gentleman never existed. Hard-working, too, these days.

Mary was not to know that if Mr Harcourt had improved Mrs Cowper, Mrs Cowper had done the same for Luke. Even Anne did not know how potent her influence had been. It was true that, on the morning after Luke had sold 'Scenes from Low Life' to Mr Bayes, he had come down to breakfast just as Anne and Mrs Britten had been finishing theirs and told them the good news and had also thanked Anne most heartily for her suggestion.

'And,' he had added, tucking into Mrs Britten's good porridge with a will, 'I shall take you both to Cremorne Gardens, if you will so allow. You, my dear Mrs Cowper, for providing me with inspiration, and you, Mrs Britten, for having taken Mrs Cowper in as a lodger. Now, ladies, thank me, as I have thanked you.'

Of course, she and Mrs Britten had thanked him vigorously, and agreed to accept his kind invitation. As with Islington Fair, Anne had never been allowed to visit anywhere as cheerfully doubtful as Cremorne was reputed to be, and for that very reason was all agog to go there.

For all his easiness of manner, Anne had thought that there was something troubling him. He had a bruise on his cheek and his left hand appeared to pain him a little. On neither of these small injuries had she seen fit to remark, although Mrs Britten had asked anxiously, 'I trust, Mr Harcourt, that nothing went amiss with you last night. You are carrying a nasty bruise on the face and I see that you favour your wrist. Perhaps a visit to an apothecary is called for.'

'By no means.' Luke was firm. 'A trifle, nothing else.' He seemed to think a moment before he had added, 'I met a most unpleasant fellow last night, and the fact that he was a Marquess, the Marquess of Clairval, in fact, did not exactly endear him to me. A man of his station should know better than to act like a common bully.'

He had been a little surprised, Anne had not been able to help noticing, at her and Mrs Britten's strong reaction to this statement which had been as far as he had been prepared to go in explanation. What Clairval had been interrupted in doing was no fit subject for ladies' ears.

Anne had turned pale and looked down at her

empty plate. Mrs Britten had put a protective hand
on her arm, and at the same time had tried to di-
vert Luke's attention from her sudden malaise,
and the possibility that it might have been caused
by his remark.

'I have heard nothing but ill of the Marquess,'
she had said. 'I am not all surprised if you witnessed him behaving badly. Anne, my dear, I
thought you looked rather pale this morning.
Would you care to lie down for a little in order to
recover? I am sure that Mr Harcourt would not object if you were to leave the table.'

If Luke had thought that up to the moment when
he had mentioned Clairval's name Mrs Anne Cowper had looked in singularly glowing health, he
had not said so. Anne, herself, had thought that it
was the most feeble excuse for her sudden faint-
ness and pallor which she could ever hope to hear.
What had surprised her the most was the fact that
even to have Clairval's name spoken in her presence should have caused her such distress. To
learn that he was in London and troublemaking
had been even more shocking.

'Thank you, no,' she had said. 'It is a passing fit
only, Mr Harcourt. It would be a poor reward for
your kindness if I fled your company at the first
opportunity. Yes, I will go with you to Cremorne.'

And so it had been arranged.

'Do you think it wise to visit such a public place, Anne?' Mrs Britten had asked her when Luke had gone up to his room to write.

Wise? What was wise? Having had her life ruined by the arrangements of all those who had thought that they were being wise on her behalf, Anne had not been sure what being wise consisted of. Besides, she could not live her whole life paralysed by fear. Her youth and her regrown strength were all drawing her towards Luke, and she had the feeling that he was, equally, being drawn towards her.

Now, all things being as they were, this was perhaps the most unwise situation in which she could find herself. But the notion of living her life in a kind of purdah, like the poor ladies in the Sultan's *harem*, who were forbidden to go out of doors, had filled Anne with horror.

'No, it is not wise to go to Cremorne Gardens with Luke,' she had said with a firmness which Mrs Britten had never seen her exhibit before. 'But I cannot live on my knees, and oh, my dear friend, I have never in my life enjoyed those pleasures which most young women of my age have always taken for granted. Do not deny me this one!'

Neither had Mrs Britten ever heard her call Mr Harcourt Luke before, but he had been Luke in

Anne's thoughts for some weeks now. If she had betrayed herself, and she had known that she had, then Mrs Britten had been tactful enough to say nothing—although she obviously had thought a great deal!

She had put her arms around Anne and drew her to her ample bosom. 'Oh, my poor girl. Of course you shall go to the Gardens. And you are right not to wish to hide yourself away in constant fear. But you heard what he said about Clairval…'

'No,' Anne had drawn away, her eyes aflame. 'Do not mention his name to me. I shall go to Cremorne, and I shall be friendly with Luke, and if this is wilful and dangerous of me, then in the past I have always lived an exemplary life—and you well know what that has earned me!'

After such a brave declaration, Mrs Britten could have denied her nothing, although it had been a great relief when they had gone to Cremorne Gardens and the only person who had accosted them had been Luke's friend, Pat O'Hare, who had had a lady of dubious virtue on his arm in the waltz, and who had waved to them from afar. So her own and Mrs Britten's fears had been all in vain…

Which had only served to add to Anne's pleasure when Luke had asked her to waltz with him. This had been so delightfully daring that Anne had almost turned him down as he had stood before her, his handsome head bent low, though not so low that she had not been able to see the light of admiration in his strange amber eyes.

After that, refusal of him had been impossible, and spinning around the dance floor, in the gathering dusk of a warm summer's evening, had been paradise enough for anyone, and Anne had been able to ask for nothing more of life.

She came back to the present. Mary was saying, a little timidly, 'I am sure, Mrs Cowper, that the missis would wish me to bring the tea board in for you, once you have put your work away.'

'I can't gainsay you, Mary. I must admit that a cup of tea would be most welcome.'

'And muffins,' offered Mary, as Anne made for the stairs. And Mr Luke Harcourt to eat and drink with, she added to herself, matchmaking. I'll go and knock on his door at once.

So it was that when Anne entered the drawing-room, she found Luke already there, the sofa table before him already laid for two, only awaiting the tray carrying the tea pot, hot water jug and Mrs Britten's silver muffin basket.

He rose to his feet immediately and bowed. His punctiliousness, his whole charming person, enchanted Anne even more than it usually did. She noticed that he was more casually dressed than she had recently seen him—several stages up, perhaps, from the yeoman's clothing he had worn to Islington Fair, but a stage or two down from his young gentleman-about-town's outfit. He was sporting a sober black coat and trousers, light boots and an unassuming cravat.

It didn't really matter what he wore, Anne concluded happily. He would be attractive in the clothes of a labourer or a London clerk.

'Mary tells me that she doesn't expect Mrs Britten back for some time, and has orders to see that we were looked after when you came in. She was so firm that I hardly dared to deny her. She also told me that Ben, the odd-job boy, has already fed Dizzy for you, so that you are not to put yourself out by going out to look after him. Ah, here come the tea and muffins. Allow me.'

He had walked over to take the big silver tea tray from Mary, who was staggering under its weight. 'Oh, you shouldn't, Mr Harcourt,' she told him reproachfully. 'It's no task for a gentleman.'

'Oh, but I'm not a gentleman any more, Mary,' he informed her. 'I'm that new-fangled thing, a journalist—or so Mr Bayes tells me.' He looked at Anne as he set the tray down in front of her.

'He's sending me to the House of Commons to-morrow to report on one of the debates there.'

So that was the reason for his quiet attire—and his ink-stained fingers—he was taking his writing more seriously. It occurred to Anne that when he had first arrived in London he had spent most of his time enjoying himself, going 'up West' as the saying had it. Not so, recently. Perhaps he had lost money? No matter.

'We seem to spend much of our time together eating muffins,' Anne ventured, only to reproach herself inwardly for offering an observation which might be taken in two ways.

'I can think of worse ways of passing the time,' said Luke, before biting carefully into his warm and well-buttered muffin. 'And few better. There! I have manoeuvred my muffin successfully today—a feat I do not always accomplish.'

This mild attempt at a joke set Anne laughing. Jokes had rarely come her way, Luke concluded, since she found so much pleasure in even the weakest of them. He could offer to take her to the theatre and enjoy himself watching her reactions to the farce, which always preceded the tragedy.

He suggested such an excursion immediately. Anne's reaction surprised him.

Almost before he had managed to get the words

out, she was shaking her head vigorously. Go to the theatre! No, that was far too public a place, and plenty of the quality were sure to be there—and she might be seen.

'Oh, it's very kind of you, Mr Harcourt, and I thank you for the invitation, but no.' She sought for a reasonable explanation of her refusal. 'I find being in a crowd such as the one at a theatre very trying. It's weak of me, I know…'

How charming she looked! Every time Luke saw her he found her more enchanting. Her modesty pleased him the most of all. He was not used to such gratitude from the young ladies he met in society. Privately, he considered that even if Mrs Anne Cowper had been one of the well-dowered young women who took him for granted her manner to him would have been the same as it was in Mrs Britten's humble drawing-room.

Enchantment had him leaning forward to offer her another muffin, and saying, 'Not weak at all. It is something over which you can have little control. Would it be too great a hardship, or a breach of manners, for you to address me as Luke?'

Anne considered him with her great grave eyes after she had refused the muffin. 'I think that perhaps we ought not to be so familiar—' for she rightly judged that he dearly wished to call her

Anne '—but we must consider Mrs Britten's feelings concerning propriety, as well as our own. After all, I am so recently widowed…'

She let the sentence hang in the air, and saw with what grace and tact he accepted her refusal.

'You are right, of course. We may not always please ourselves. When we have known one another a little longer, perhaps?'

'Perhaps.' And if she had admired his tact, it was now his turn to admire hers. She put up a finger. 'I think that I hear Mrs Britten arriving. We must not give her cause for worry.'

'Indeed, not. Especially since she has no cause to.' And that, Luke privately thought, was a matter for regret. How he had refrained from taking her in his arms once they were alone together, he would never know.

But it was not Mrs Britten at the door, it was Mary, bringing more hot water and more muffins. She looked at them, bright-eyed, hoping that they would take full advantage of being left alone together, but something which she rather doubted. The gentry were queer folk and, for all her poverty and working as a sempstress, Mrs Cowper was plainly a gentlewoman—and one who needed a husband, poor love. What on earth was Mr Harcourt holding back for?

A question which Mr Harcourt was asking him-self. He appreciated the opportunity which Mary had offered him, but instinct, rather than reason, told him that he must go carefully with Anne, or risk losing her altogether.

And then something occurred which drove rea-son and prudence out of his head. Her tea and muffins consumed, Anne remembered that work awaited her, rose, excused herself and walked to the door. Ever the courteous gentleman, Luke leapt to his feet to reach the door before she did and open it for her. By ill luck—or was it good luck?—after he had done so he turned too quickly and his hand brushed hers.

Such a small contact, to have such a sudden and remarkable result. As though they were a pair of Signor Galvani's frogs subjected to an electric current, a powerful impulse passed between them.

Anne looked at Luke; her eyes were luminous with love for him, and Luke could not resist lean-ing down to kiss her. As he did so her eyes closed, and he kissed her on the lids as gently as a butter-fly alighting. To his surprise, he found that this delicate caress gave him a sensation more erotic than the most passionate kiss on the lips.

He shuddered.

She shuddered.

Anne opened her eyes and looked at him again as he released her and that look told him everything. But what she said also told him that she was not quite ready to accept what was happening to her.

'No,' she said, 'no, we mustn't… I mustn't. Oh, Luke…'

'Why not?' he could not help asking. 'You must know how I feel about you.'

'So sudden,' she said, 'so sudden,' and he could sense her withdrawal from him. She was a shy bird, caught in a thicket, and perhaps he had gone a little fast for her. But he could not, must not lose her, and if she required him to be patient, so be it. At least he now knew that his love for her was reciprocated; for the moment, that must be enough.

The Marquess of Clairval paced around his study: a tiger confined. He had the unpleasant feeling that those who disliked or feared him were laughing behind his back. What more foolish and silly fellow, he imagined them saying, was there than a husband who could not control his wife? A man, moreover, whose wife had disappeared so successfully that, despite all his wealth and power, he had not been able to find her.

There were times when he hoped that she was lying dead beneath some hedge or in a ditch—

except that, if that were so, her wealth would be lost to him.

No, dead or alive he needed her body. So far, not even the small fortune which he had promised to give to anyone who brought word of her where-abouts to him had succeeded in flushing her from her bolt hole. In the meantime he was also paying a noted thief taker to look for her—another waste of money, no doubt.

There was a timid knock on the door. 'Come in,' he roared, his roar being all the louder for the fact that he was feeling so much at odds with the world.

His secretary, a harried-looking man—all Clairval's servants except the bruisers who did his dirty work for him looked harried—entered.

'Jenkinson to see you, m'lord.'

'Then send him in, man. Why are you delaying? There are times when I believe that no one was ever served by such a pack of fools as I am.'

The man waiting outside could hear Clairval's upraised, railing voice even through the massive oak double doors which the secretary had carefully fastened behind him. He grinned to himself, and was not surprised when the secretary emerged from m'lord's study looking more harried than ever.

'His lordship will see you now,' Browne said distastefully to the foxy-faced fellow who sat on the edge of his chair, visibly pricing everything in the vast ante-room, from the painting of Jove on the ceiling to the Aubusson carpet which graced the floor.

M'lord's study was equally grand. It could have served as a chamber of state instead of a room where a brutal nobleman bandied words with an ex–Bow Street Runner who had been dismissed on suspicion of bribery and corruption.

'Well, d'you have any news for me?'

'Not yet, m'lord, but soon. I am on a hot trail. I can tell you that you were right about one thing—it *was* your steward who helped your wife to escape.'

'As I thought. I hope he's rotting in the hell to which I have consigned him. And that's all? Something I'd already guessed and have seen to myself!'

'Not quite, m'lord. Did your wife ever speak to you of a Miss Latimer, who married a parson, Eli Britten? She was m'lady's governess before her marriage to you. I found that he had a living at Moorcroft in Surrey. I visited the parsonage there, only to discover that he had died prematurely some years ago.

'Their neighbours told me that he had left his wife but a small competence so she had decided to move to London and open a lodging house for the gentry—to make ends meet, they said. They also told me something else. Apparently she had received regular letters from one of her old charges and the local postmaster said that the letters came from Yorkshire.'

Clairval uttered an oath. 'What, in the devil's name, has all this to do with my wife? She never prated about governesses to me. She hardly ever spoke at all, damn her!'

'Only that, so far as I can discover, she had no other person to whom she might go for help. Her relatives have taken your part in this matter—so she would not go to them.

'I made further enquiries. She and this Mrs Britten were very close. Her father refused to allow her friends of her own age—he was a recluse himself, and intended that she should be one. He approved of her friendship with the governess, though. I should like to follow this up, but the thing is that I've run out of blunt. If I'm to trace the governess, I need some more of the ready.'

Clairval stared at him. 'And that's it? Some whim-wham about a governess, and maunderings about letters from Yorkshire? Half England lives in Yorkshire! Dammit, man, you came highly recommended, and this is all you can offer me? And you have the gall to demand more money from me! Be damned to that for a tale. I've a good mind to tell you to take your Friday-face away!'

Jenkinson surveyed the unsavoury swine before him. What a bastard! No wonder his missis had run away from him. He pitied any poor bitch in his power—wife or what-have-you. It was almost enough to make him give up the job—but he needed the money.

'I told you, m'lord. It's the only lead I can find: a last resort, you might say. If it's a dead end, then I'll give up—and someone else may have a go. The neighbours said her rooms would be highly respectable—she hoped to take in the gentry. The name's uncommon and I can enquire among all the fly young fellows wanting lodgings who might have heard of her. I ain't hopeful—m'lady might be lying in a ditch somewhere, dead soon after she scarpered.'

Clairval sighed. A last resort. Yes, it was very much a last resort. And this fellow was supposed to be one of the best in his unsavoury profession. What, in God's name, could the worst be like? Incompetent idiots, all of them, no doubt.

'Tell my secretary to give you five guineas. But that's the last you'll get from me, mark you. If you do turn up trumps, then I'll see you well rewarded. Be off with you. I seem to have done nothing but throw guineas at you and get nothing back.'

'Short of the ready, is he?' Jenkinson asked the secretary as he was handed his guineas. 'Never met a fellow so bound and determined to get his money's worth. The fly word is that that's why he wants his missis back. She's the one with the blunt and without her he can't get at any more of it.'

If the secretary agreed with him, he did not say so. M'lord's temper was so uncertain these days that a still tongue in one's head was the best attribute any of his servants had—and even that might not save them from trouble.

Jenkinson took the money. As he reached the door he turned to say casually to Browne, 'm'lord had a steward, did he not? Name of Leethwaite or so I was told. If he helped m'lady escape, he might have something useful to tell me. Except that I can't find him. Left m'lord's employ and disappeared—just like m'lady. Not the same day, but soon after. Know where he might have gone?'

'No, I do not.' The secretary was brief.

'No, nor wouldn't tell me if you did. Frightened of him, I dare say. Oh well. Never mind. He might turn up—like m'lady.'

'He didn't run off with her, if that's what you mean,' said the secretary shortly. 'He was fifty, had a doxy in Wakefield about as unlike m'lady as a woman could be. He's probably taken himself as far from m'lord as he could go. M'lord put the blame on him, but I have no notion of the truth of the matter.'

'Aye, happen so,' agreed Jenkinson, 'as they say in Yorkshire. Odd, though. But then, the whole business is odd.'

'You will excuse me, but I have work to do. I can't stay gossiping with you.'

Jenkinson forbore to say that gossip was the life's blood of a man on the trail of those missing. He had once thought that the secretary might have helped m'lady to run off but, looking at him, knew that was another dead end. A right desiccated cold fish, concerned only with himself.

So it was with considerable surprise that he heard the secretary, looking away from him, murmur in a distant voice as he finally walked through the door, 'The steward may have taken himself off, but all I can tell you is this: that no one saw him again after m'lord found that m'lady had gone.'

Chapter Seven

All that golden summer Luke did two things: he worked diligently at his writing and patiently, oh, so patiently, courted Anne Cowper.

After his first two papers had appeared in *The Pall Mall Gazette* which Bayes had transformed into a weekly on the strength of the work with which Luke and Pat and some other young men were providing him, the publishers, Chapman and Hall, approached Luke to suggest that he write either a book about gypsy life, or a novel based on his knowledge of it. Mr Chapman had been impressed by the paper which Luke had written about the gypsies at Islington Fair.

'But I've never even tried to write a novel,' Luke protested faintly. 'I'm sure that I shouldn't know how to.'

'Nothing to it, young man,' Chapman told him

severely. 'My partner and I consider that your work shows great promise in that line. Your account of your conversations with the gypsy king told us all that we needed to know.'

Luke wanted to say that Jasper wasn't a gypsy king, but held his tongue. The terms that Chapman was offering him if he liked the novel were attractive ones. Chapman saw him hesitate.

'Come, young fellow,' he said, 'at least try. What can you lose?'

'Nothing,' exclaimed Luke, almost laughing aloud and, without meaning to, giving the publisher the benefit of all his famous charm. 'Nothing at all. Yes, I'll rough out a few chapters for you, and you can tell me if they're what you want.'

'Famous,' said Chapman warmly. 'I can see we shall deal well together. Let's shake hands on it.'

So they did, and Luke rushed straight back to Islington to tell Anne the good news. After all, she had started him on this road and who knew where it would end? He said nothing about his new career to his father or Cressy. Best to keep quiet until he had achieved something substantial. But Anne, oh, Anne was different—she was his muse, his inspiration, his *alter ego*—so he informed her, pouring out his hopes and aspirations about the novel which Chapman had suggested to him.

'Oh, Luke, I'm so pleased for you!' Anne's face was aglow.

They were alone in the drawing-room, for Mrs Britten had not expected him to be back so early. Had she known, she would have made a third and acted as duenna, but she did not, and had gone for a walk, leaving Anne to get on with her sewing.

Luke determined to take full advantage of the situation.

'How shall I reward you?' he asked her, his amber eyes glowing. He had never looked so handsome, never looked more like his unacknowledged father.

'Oh, it's not necessary to reward me,' Anne said. 'You have done this yourself.'

'Not so,' replied Luke energetically. 'Surely you know that you are my inspiration. Oh, Anne, ever since I first met you my whole life has changed. I was so aimless, so careless, but your example, your encouragement have served to transform me. I feel that I could move mountains, never mind write a novel for Mr Chapman. You have given me a purpose in life.'

Anne had never been so moved, so touched. Looking at him, she knew that he was speaking the truth. Almost without meaning to, she had reached out and influenced another human being, and that human being was someone she had come to love.

Luke's essential goodness shone out of him. To some extent it had held him back, since the hint of steel, of resolute determination, which all men and women need if they are to succeed in this life, was missing because of it. But loving Anne, wanting to feel that he was worthy of her, and would be able to ask her to marry him once he had succeeded in the career on which he had embarked as a result of her encouragement, had roused in him the desire to excel.

'If that is so,' Anne said at last, 'then you have made me very happy. And I am as sure as Mr Chapman that you will succeed in your new venture. Having met the gypsies, I can't wait to read your novel about them.'

She dare not say more. Oh, if only her circumstances were different, she could have made the answer that would have had her in his arms. She sighed at the thought, which frightened as well as attracted her.

Luke mistook her slight hesitation. He thought that it sprang wholly from fear of him; that he was going too quickly. 'My dear,' he said gently, 'I did not mean to be so enthusiastic that I overwhelmed you. But I felt compelled to tell you how much you have come to mean to me. I haven't been overbold, I trust.'

'Oh, no, not at all,' exclaimed Anne, who was torn by two contrary desires. For while she did not wish to encourage Luke, for their case was hopeless, she also didn't want to lose his love; the sweetest thing which she had ever experienced was to hear him tell her how much he loved her. After all, that must have been what he meant by his recent declaration to her.

If only she could reciprocate by telling him how much she loved him! Tears sprang into her eyes. She bent over her work so that he should not see them. He mistook her again.

'I have overset you, and I will leave you. What's more I must justify both your and Mr Chapman's faith in me, and start work as soon as possible.'

No, no! He must not think her so weak a creature. 'Indeed, not, Mr Harcourt. Far from being overset, I am delighted by your success, and honoured that you think that I have a share in it.'

Impulsively, not thinking what she was doing, and forgetting what had occurred on the last occasion on which they had touched, Anne put out her hand to lay it on his in a spontaneous gesture of encouragement.

Again! It had happened again! As they touched, that strong electric current passed through them both. It was of such magnitude that, before he knew what he was doing, Luke had cupped her face in his hands and was giving Anne the kiss which he had been longing to bestow on her all afternoon.

And she was responding to it. Like a flower bud responding to the touch of rain, her mouth gently opened to receive and give back his offering. Of the two of them, Anne was the more surprised. First, because the shock which her whole body had received at his touch was something which she had never experienced before. Second, because before Luke kissed her on the lips she had always thought that she would reject any form of love-making, however slight, because not only would her reason forbid it, but her body would reject it vigorously too, as a consequence of her husband's brutal mistreatment of her.

Far from it! Far from rejecting him, Anne's arms, of their own volition, wound themselves around Luke's neck, and she was stroking his face as he was stroking hers: the kiss went on and on, growing ever more powerful and passionate. What brought the whole unexpected and delightful business to an end was the sound of footsteps—Mrs Britten's this time—advancing down the corridor towards the drawing-room door.

Neither of them was so far gone that they did not instantly spring apart. Anne's face was flushed, her mouth had softened and her whole body glowed as a result of her first experience of true love.

Luke's face had also changed. It was that of a man who had been given a most unexpected present. Knowing Anne's delicacy, her shrinking from any form of physical contact with anyone or anything except poor Dizzy, her timid response the last time he had kissed her, he had been half-expecting her to fight him off. Instead, he had met delighted co-operation. Regrettably, from his point of view, Mrs Britten's coming through the door to discover them now decently apart, and Anne on the point of leaving, meant that he had no opportunity to extend her co-operation further.

No matter. The ice having been broken, as it were, the winter would end and spring must surely follow. The only thing which remained was for him to assure her that his intentions were purely honourable, and this he would do as soon as decently possible.

He had no desire to hurry matters overmuch. Anne's kiss had told him more than she could know. Married she might have been, but her response had been that of an unawakened woman. Which begged a question which had been puzzling him for some time. What kind of marriage had Mrs Anne Cowper experienced? Again, no matter. This—and other problems—could wait until their better acquaintance had made it easy for them to talk of such intimate affairs.

Mrs Britten surveyed him suspiciously after she had poured out her tea. Mr Luke Harcourt looked like the cat which had just swallowed the canary. She was not to know that he was contemplating wooing Mrs Anne Cowper with just the kind of innocent courtship which his fly friends who visited Laura Knight, and others like her, would have laughed at him for proposing.

He might have laughed at himself, too, before he had met Anne. Instead, all that he could think of was that Anne loved him, and knowing that he went at once to his room and to win her he began to write... Exactly as Chapman had prophesied, the words flowed easily from his pen as he told of Jasper, his followers and the open road which was their home.

Later, Anne sat on her bed, her work unregarded, her hands held to her hot cheeks, her whole body vibrating after its first experience of passion. Whatever had she been thinking of? Instead of pushing Luke away as she ought to have done, she had encouraged him. But, oh, how sweet it had been to be held in a man's arms and kissed so gently and lovingly on the lips. Nothing in her marriage had led her to believe that love-making could be other than a torment for the woman, however much it seemed to please the man.

Whatever might have happened if Mrs Britten had not arrived to disturb them? No words had been exchanged between them afterwards, so Anne had no means of knowing whether Luke was toying with her; whether the kiss meant anything—or nothing.

This was all so new to her. She had never had a friend of her own age to talk and giggle with about young men and what they meant by sly glances and stolen kisses. One minute she had been barely out of childhood and the next she had been chained to a ruthless, cruel and selfish man who saw her as merely the means to get him an heir.

The worst thing of all was that she knew that she was falling in love with Luke.

No! Amend that. She *had* fallen in love with Luke and had some reason to believe that he might be in love with her. Which was hopeless, quite hopeless. There could be no future for them which embraced marriage, and so she must not encourage him, not tempt him to…to…

For the first time something which had always been abhorrent to Anne—the bodily union of a man and a woman—no longer seemed so.

* * *

It was to Anne that Luke brought home in triumph each copy of *The Pall Mall Gazette* that contained his articles and each part of the novel that he was writing as it came out every month. Chapman had been so pleased with the first chapters of *Lords of the Road*—the title Luke had given his novel—that he had taken the risk of issuing it in parts. If this put pressure on Luke, it was welcome, and he rapidly found that he was running ahead of publication.

More, the sales of the first part were so good that Chapman had raised the amount he was paying him for it. He had taken the pseudonym of James Linley for the work he was doing for Chapman and for Jack Hatfield. Solomon Grundy was reserved for his work for Bayes.

Hatfield had enthusiastically taken up his suggestion for a series of light articles on fashionable and thieves' slang and cant, thus providing him with another source of income. If this continued, he would be able to offer marriage to Anne with a good conscience. This happy thought made him work the harder.

The one thing which he found difficult to understand was Mrs Britten's lacklustre reaction to the growing rapport between himself and Anne. He would have thought that she would welcome any chance of a marriage for her young protégée that would rescue her from grinding poverty. Luke knew that Anne sewed and embroidered into the night watches to make enough to keep herself from starving.

Mrs Britten stopped him one day after he had left the drawing-room where Anne was working in the good light of the large bow window. He had just given her the latest copy of 'Scenes from Low Life'. She said to him, without preamble, 'I hope you are remembering what I said to you earlier. About Mrs Cowper, I mean.'

'Oh, indeed.' Luke was a trifle stiff. 'You may rest assured that my intentions towards her are strictly honourable.'

'I have no doubt of that, Mr Harcourt. What worries me is Mrs Cowper's position. After all, you are the son of a member of the *haut ton* and Anne is but a sempstress.'

'I am a working writer, a journalist. I no longer wish to live on my father's bounty.' Luke was uncharacteristically blunt. 'I see little to choose between us.'

Mrs Britten stared at him helplessly. She could not, dare not, say more. To do so might put Anne in jeopardy. On the other hand, if Luke knew the truth about Anne, he would at once realise how hopeless his dreams were. Which was a sad pity, because he was just the sort of young man who would have made Anne a good husband...

She could not tell him that earlier that day, when she had been escorting Anne to the shop that commissioned her work, Anne had pulled her arm free and said in a distressed voice, 'Someone is staring after me. I am sure of it. Someone who means me ill, I fear.'

Her face had turned quite white, and she had been shivering. Mrs Britten had said, 'Where? I see no one.'

'Nor I, either.' Anne's agitation had been extreme. 'I cannot see him, but I know that he is somewhere hereabouts. A foxy-faced man with red hair. He has been watching and following me.'

'Not seen him?' had queried her protectress dubiously. 'How then do you know that he is following you?'

Anne had hung her head a little and had looked away. 'I have not chosen to tell you—or Luke— but ever since I visited the gypsy fortune teller I seem to have developed an odd sense, something which I can't explain. I can tell people's true thoughts, their true characters, and I know when they are thinking about me, even when they are not present. Oh, not everybody, not everything all the time, but in odd flashes, which come and go. It is a most inconvenient gift—for gift it was—from the fortune teller. She told me so.'

She had looked up at her friend. 'You see, I know for sure that you and Luke are both good people, and that neither of you would ever harm me. This man who has been watching me is not evil, but his watching me is dangerous and can only do me harm.'

'My poor girl. Do you know what you are saying?'

Anne's smile had been melancholy. 'I dare say that you think me mad. Stricken mad with suffering, I suppose. But it is not so. I should not have spoken of it.'

She had shivered again. 'He is nearer to me now than he was. Not very far away.'

Even as she had spoken a man had walked out of the shop next to the one for which they had been making. He had been dressed in reasonably good clothing, similar to that of a superior clerk. He had worn a broad-crowned beaver hat, beneath which his reddish hair could be seen escaping in tight curls. His face had been undeniably foxy. He had walked by them without looking at them.

Mrs Britten had looked helplessly at Anne. She had thought a moment before exclaiming, 'Now,

I know what caused *that*! You must have seen him out of the corner of your eye and he was sufficiently odd-looking for you to be frightened of him. And no wonder. In your case I should be running mad with worry.'

'But I am not mad,' Anne had answered with the gentle firmness which was her trademark. 'Please, we will talk of it no more. I wish you will say nothing to Mr Harcourt of this. I would not for the world have him think that I am turning simple-minded!'

Mr Harcourt! Mr Harcourt! He was all that Anne could think of when she ought to be thinking of her safety. No doubt of it at all, was Mrs Britten's sad reflection, she had forgotten all prudence from the moment she had met him. If only she could be frank with Mr Harcourt, but she dare not. She sighed helplessly as she watched him bound upstairs to his room—to start work again, she supposed. She would warn Anne not to encourage him, but that, too, would probably be useless.

Even more useless than Mrs Britten might have imagined. As Anne stitched happily away, foremost in her mind was Luke's face when he had given her the latest copy of *The Pall Mall Gazette*. Mrs Britten's gentle admonitions went unheeded. Except that later that night Anne started up from sleep, crying out, the tears running down her face.

Her dream had begun as a happy one. She had been walking along Islington High Street, Dizzy trotting along in front of her, her hand on Luke's arm. She had looked up at him and he had been smiling down at her, his face so loving that in her dream her heart had given a little skip of delight. And then...and then...the foxy-faced man had come out of the shop, just as he had done that morning and walked towards her.

But instead of passing by, as he had done that morning, he had put out a hand, caught her by the wrist and pulled her towards him...and as he had done so, Luke, Dizzy, and Islington High Street had all disappeared. The foxy man disappeared, too, and all that was left in the world was—HIM. She was in a wood with HIM, and she could not tell whether it was night or day, only that she was alone with her doom.

Helplessly she awaited it, and as HE advanced towards her she found herself screaming...and she was back in her bed in Islington, and Mrs Britten was seated on it beside her, holding her to her broad bosom and trying to stop the hiccuping sobs which had succeeded the screams. Luke stood in the doorway, a candle in his hand. He was wearing a brocaded dressing-gown, just like a Chinese mandarin's. His hair was awry and the look on his face was so agonised at the sight of her distress that Anne felt for him, not for herself.

'There, there, my pet,' soothed Mrs Britten. 'A bad dream, was it?'

'Yes,' whispered Anne, recovering herself. 'Oh, I'm so sorry. I did not mean to wake the house, but the dream was so real...'

'Never mind, my darling, never mind.' Mrs Britten began to rock her so that Anne closed her eyes, leaned against her friend, and surrendered herself to the maternal love which surrounded her. She had never known anything like it before, just as she had never known what it was to be truly loved by a man. She turned her head into Mrs Britten's bosom, her eyelids fluttered and after a little time, exhausted, she slept.

Mrs Britten laid her gently back on the pillows, and Anne stirred a little, smiling in her sleep. Neither Mrs Britten, nor Luke, knew that in her dreams Luke was with her again, and another presence was also there, the *chovihani* who, unseen and unheard by Luke, whispered in her ear, 'Never fear, I shall be with you both, even in the darkest hour of the night.'

Then the dream disappeared, and Anne slept, but the smile remained.

Luke walked to her bedside, disregarding his

landlady's disapproving stare. He looked down at
Anne and his heart was filled with such protective
love that he thought that it would burst. Mrs Britten took him by the hand, whispered, 'Come, let
her sleep,' and led him to the landing so that he
might return to his rooms.

But he resisted her, saying with the look of
agony still on his face at the memory of Anne's terror, 'Tell me, Mrs Britten, does this happen often?'

'I will not lie to you, Mr Harcourt. When she
first came here these fits occurred every night, but
of late, no, she has not suffered from them.' She
did not think that it was wise to tell him that
Anne's terrible nightmares had ceased when he
had returned to Islington.

'And the cause,' Luke said urgently. 'What is the
cause? Do you know why she should suffer so?'

'Again I will not lie to you. Yes, I know the
cause, but I cannot tell you of it. I cannot break
Anne's confidence.' She hesitated. 'But I fear that
this episode may have been caused by Anne's believing this morning that she was being followed
by someone who wishes her ill.'

It was as much as she dare say to him, and perhaps it was too much, but Mr Harcourt was a good
young man. If he thought that Anne was in danger, then he might be prepared to protect her.

'And was she being followed?'

'That I do not know. I saw nothing which might lead me to believe that she was, but Anne is not normally fanciful, you understand. Now I think that we ought to return to our beds.'

Luke wanted to ask her more questions, for he was beginning to think that there was something strange about Mrs Anne Cowper, more than met the eye. He could see, however, that Mrs Britten looked nearly as exhausted as Anne had done, so that, although he thought that she was being evasive, he said no more.

If Mrs Anne Cowper needed protection, then making her Mrs Luke Harcourt was the best protection he could offer her, and soon.

'I think, m'lord, that I may have tracked down your missis—beg pardon, her ladyship.' Jenkinson paused, smiling.

Clairval sprang to his feet. Jenkinson had arrived some time ago and had been made to wait to see him as a punishment for his failure so far. He knew at once that Jenkinson was playing cat and mouse with him to pay him back.

'Go on, man.' His voice dangerous. 'You cannot afford to palter with me.'

'No paltering, m'lord. I am not yet completely

certain, you understand. Another day's work will doubtless do it. I have found the governess, Mrs Britten. She lives in Islington and keeps a respectable lodging house in Duke Street. Some months ago, according to local gossip, a poor young woman, alone and penniless, arrived at her address, seeking shelter. She was granted it and is living there, earning her keep as a sempstress. The young woman is uncommon like the miniature you showed me when you hired me some months ago—though badly dressed.'

'In that case,' Clairval bit back at him savagely, 'why are we waiting? Why cannot we go there immediately?'

Jenkinson managed to look more foxy-faced than ever. 'Because, begging your pardon, m'lord, I do not think that you ought to go off half-cock like, if she proves to be the wrong young woman, seeing the scandal as would follow, Mrs Britten being a most respectable party.'

Clairval turned his eyes to heaven. 'What next?' he declaimed nastily. 'Am I to be taught etiquette by a dirty hireling who does not know his place?'

Forelock touching from Jenkinson managed to convey neither suitable penance nor respect for his betters. 'Tomorrow,' he promised. 'I am taking out the other young woman who lives in the house,

Mary by name, a servant, and will winkle out of her the exact date when our young woman arrived. If it matches the date you gave me for m'lady's flight, why, then you may storm Duke Street and claim your lady back.'

'And about time, too. However, if you have found m'lady and I recover her person, I shall pay you the reward I promised you.'

Aye, you will that, thought Jenkinson nastily, as he tugged his forelock again, especially since I have found something out about you, milord Marquess, which you would not want the world to know. Bilk me, and the whole world will know of it, this I promise you.

All this whilst he appeared to be listening to Clairval make arrangements for him to accompany the party that would visit Duke Street, if the young woman proved likely to be his missing wife.

Clairval could hardly wait to get his hands on her. He would teach her a lesson that would keep her from straying from home again. The thing which touched him most on the raw was to learn that m'lady Clairval was earning her living as a sempstress.

Chapter Eight

'Keep this up and you're a made man,' Chapman had told Luke after the roaring success of the second part of his novel, and after he had passed on to him the fourth part. He had read the third and was convinced that the praise—and consequent sales—which had accompanied the first two parts would be redoubled. Luke had discovered his true profession at last. The cleverness which was so essential a part of him had never before found an outlet: now it had.

He could hardly wait to rush home to Islington. He was compelled to accompany Chapman to a chop house—as with Bayes, a sure sign that he was valued—but he was chafing inside all the time, and refused the porter which Chapman tried to press on him. He would not propose to Anne with drink on his breath, that was for sure.

All the way home in the cab he prayed that she would be in her usual place on the sofa in the bow window, and lo, to his delight, there she was, head bent and stitching away. Well, once she was Mrs Harcourt she would no longer need to spend all her days working. He was already visualising a little cottage Chelsea way, where he might have a room overlooking the river to work in, and Anne somewhere in it, his love and his helpmeet.

Washed, his shirt changed, his hair brushed, his fingers and nails free of ink, he took himself to the drawing-room with a further prayer that, it being Wednesday, Mrs Britten might be out shopping at the market, Mary in attendance on her. She had been a little short with Mary lately.

It seemed that Mary had found an admirer and had become less diligent in her duties. Her mind was on her lover, no doubt. The foxy-faced man had been careful never to meet her at her place of work in case he was seen or recognised, preferring instead a rendezvous in a small park nearby.

Luck was with Luke again. Fortune favours the brave, as the saying went, and it certainly appeared to be favouring him. Anne looked up from her work when he entered the drawing-room, and if he thought that she had never looked so pretty and desirable, she thought that he had never looked so handsome.

'I had hoped to find you alone.' He had decided that he had better not be too roundabout in his approach to her, for he wished to make his proposal before Mrs Britten returned. 'May I inform you that you look more lovely than ever.' So saying, he dropped on to one knee before her and took her small hand in his large one.

Anne did not repel him. She allowed the hand to rest there, but said in a voice which neither encouraged nor discouraged him, 'You did not ask me if you might do that.'

Positioned as they were, his face was on a level with hers so that he could look straight at her. Amber eyes and dark blue eyes met and meshed. 'And would you have refused permission if I had asked?'

'I should not have done,' was her reply, 'but I ought to have done.'

'Then,' said Luke gaily, 'what a good thing I did not ask,' and he bent his head in first to kiss her hand before he lifted it to kiss her cheek.

'You should not have done that, either,' said Anne slowly, lifting her own hand to touch her cheek exactly where his lips had brushed it.

Luke decided to be naughty, since he was greatly enjoying the game he was playing with her. 'Ah, I see that rather than being too bold I was not bold enough. Does this please you more?' This was a kiss directly on her lips, which she resisted a little at first before she surrendered to the delight that it induced, responding to him as freely and frankly as he could have wished.

The kiss went on and on. It changed in character, became wildly passionate, so that all the pent-up longing for her which Luke had kept inside him during the long weeks in which he had first known, and then loved Anne, found at last its true expression.

Dropping his head, he kissed her neck and then the tiny shadow which showed above the neck of her dress. Oh, such delight! So much so that he delved further as he pulled the dress down, using his hands as well as his mouth to stroke and caress her.

And she was with him all the way! She made no resistance. Her fear of him, and of all men, had vanished under the tenderness of his caresses, for he was careful not to distress her by allowing his passion to overcome him to the point where he no longer considered her feelings, but only his own. He willed himself to go slowly as she quivered and gasped her response to each delicate caress. Even when he pulled her dress further down still, gently, gently, until his mouth enclosed her right breast, she still shuddered with joy against him, her own hand rising to stroke his neck and head.

He must not frighten her! Whatever her dead husband had done to her had, Luke was sure, destroyed her ability to respond easily to an openly passionate assault on her senses, however much she might love the man who made it. If he could persuade her that she might join him in joy, and not in terror, then his battle was won. He could make his offer secure in the knowledge that she would not shrink away from him.

Far from shrinking away, she had begun to caress him, murmuring his name as he murmured hers, so that when his hands moved again to stroke her everywhere she still made no resistance. He lifted himself on to the sofa to lie beside her, to make their love-making the more easy, and still she did not resist him. Eyes blind, Anne was lost to the passion that was beginning to consume her and that she had never felt before.

Suddenly, how Anne never knew, she was on her back and Luke was above her. He was now lost to everything but the need to consummate fully the passion which they were sharing, and he began to fumble with the buttons on his breeches flap, desire making his hands clumsy.

He was never to know exactly what particular caress, what murmured endearment, or perhaps the direct evidence of his arousal, caused his love's sudden change of heart. One moment she was panting and sighing beneath him, the next she was pushing him away, pulling her bodice up and her skirts down, exclaiming wildly, 'No, no. I can't. I shouldn't. I mustn't. This is wrong of me. I shouldn't allow you...'

'No, not wrong,' cried Luke, 'never wrong,' and he tried to pull her down into the circle of his arms again. 'I love you. I want to marry you. I never meant to go so far so soon, but once I began to make love to you I was lost. Oh, Anne, marry me as soon as possible. Be my wife and make me the happiest man in England.'

This declaration, which was so patently, so vividly truthful, had quite the opposite effect from the one which Luke had expected. Anne sprang to her feet, retreated across the room to lean against the wall facing him, both hands in front of her mouth. Great tears began to rain down her face. Sobs shook her body.

'No, no! Do not ask me! It's impossible,' and now she held both her hands out in front of her as though warding off an enemy, not a man whose one desire was to make her his wife, and whose passion for her was as great as hers had so plainly been for him.

Luke, his hair awry, his dignity gone, unable

even to stand until he had pulled up and fastened his wretched breeches, gasped at her, 'Oh, my darling, don't reject me now. Not now, when you have proved that our love is mutual.'

'Oh, Luke. I love you so—' and this declaration came out through a hail of sobs '—but I cannot marry you. You must not ask me why, for both our sakes. Oh, I cannot be your wife and I should never have fallen in love with you, but I have... I have... God help me... God help us both. Oh, I cannot stay here now. I cannot. We can't...we can't...'

Her pain and distress were so strong that Luke was quite unmanned at the sight. All the pleasant equability and charming self-control with which he had previously faced life had gone. He was across the room and by her side, trying to take her into his arms.

'Why cannot you marry me? Why? You are a widow. Why should we not marry...?'

Anne did not, could not, allow him to finish, saying again, through her agony, 'Do not ask me. Please, I beg you.'

The very power of her passion, of her newly awakened senses, added to and compounded her distress. To see his beloved face before her, to want him and his love so desperately, and at the same time to know that she could not have him, must not have him, was like the torture of the damned. She threw herself face down in the nearest armchair to wail into the cushions. Luke knelt down beside her, alarmed by the strength of her misery.

'Oh, my love, my dearest love, only tell me what is wrong. You know how much I love you. I can't bear to see you in such despair, it is almost worse than suffering myself.'

Even as he spoke, Luke suddenly knew that the years of love which he had felt for Cressy were as nothing to the depth of the passion which he felt for Anne. So strong was it that her pain was his. Never before had he experienced the sensations which were overwhelming him now. That other love had been a mirage, something which, because of its hopelessness, had allowed him to distance himself from true feeling and true commitment to anyone else.

'Only tell me what is wrong,' was wrenched from him at last, 'and we can meet and overcome it together.'

But all that that produced, despite the tenderness with which he held her, was a shake of the head, before she buried it in the cushions again, until she raised herself once more to show him a face now tearless.

'I must be brave,' she said, her composure as

great as it had always previously been. 'I must not behave like a hysterical fool, however deep and desperate my feelings are. Believe me, Luke, I love you to distraction, and because of that I cannot tell you of the burden which I carry round with me. I cannot, must not, share it with you— ever. You must let me go and try to forget me. I should never have allowed myself to fall in love with you, never have accepted your love-making.

'Once we began I should have stopped you, for I was being unfair to you to allow you to continue. But oh, my dearest love, you, and all the love which you have offered me, have overwhelmed me quite, have made me forget what I am, and what I must do. I will leave Mrs Britten's and you must try to forget me, as I must try to forget you.'

She turned her head away from him so that she might not see his suffering face.

'Forget you!' Luke's voice was a mixture of agony and disbelief. 'Look at me, Anne. How can you ask such a thing of me?'

But she only murmured, her head hung low, her voice calm—except that he could feel the pain beneath her outward composure— 'No, no, Luke. You must do as I ask you, please.'

It was hopeless. She was adamant. The strength of her will impressed Luke even as it distressed him, because it left him no hope. He rose slowly to his feet, his whole body still throbbing with the misery of passion rejected, and the equal misery of the knowledge that his suit was doomed to failure. Anne had become his guiding star. She had given him the spur to change his life so that he had begun to achieve what he ought to achieve, but at the very moment when success was in his grasp, he was about to lose her.

'You mean this, Anne, knowing that you have been my saviour, that you have given my life the point and purpose which it lacked until your encouragement? Can you not trust me with the reason why you are rejecting me?'

She shook her head. 'Believe me, Luke, it is for your benefit even more than mine, that I must remain silent. And yes, oh, yes, I must not be tempted to give way to your persuasions. Oh, if only I could speak, but I cannot. Please go, Luke. My heart is broken—as I can see that yours is. Be brave for me, Luke, if you truly love me. Think only that I have helped you.'

Be brave! How right she was. To rail at the fate which was keeping them apart—whatever that was—was to play a coward's part. If she could face him, her face white with pain, and endure what she must, then he would be less than a man if he gave way to the misery which was consuming him. If at one bound he had passed from heaven to hell, then so be it, he must live with it on his feet like a man and not on his knees, wailing.

Luke walked to the door.

His hand on the knob, he turned for one last look at her. She had not moved. Her face had resumed its usual stoic passivity. She was silent, her longing eyes fixed on him, only him. He must be silent, too.

But he could not stay at Mrs Britten's, for to do so would be to drive her away from what had plainly become her haven. More, to face her daily would be, as Anne had already seen, simply to compound their misery, so he must play the man and leave as soon as could be arranged.

'Goodbye, my love,' he whispered to himself as he left her, and accepted the gift of courage which she had conferred on him.

He had lost her. Except that he had never possessed her. He knew now that, as he had sometimes suspected, there was a mystery attached to her presence, here as a humble sempstress in Mrs Britten's home. What could it be that held her in such terrible thrall, that made her reject him and his honourable proposal so decisively? He would ask Mrs Britten when she returned, but he knew, even as he made this decision, that she would tell him nothing.

All the warnings which she had uttered, her evident unhappiness at the sight of him and Anne falling in love with one another, made a terrible kind of sense if she knew that there were some strange circumstances which must keep them forever apart.

Nevertheless, when he heard Mrs Britten return, he ran down the stairs to confront her, to tell her that he had made an offer to Anne and that she had refused it in terror and distress. If she knew that, for some unexplained reason, his case was hopeless, she could at least assure him of that, if nothing else, and that it was not mere shrinking nervousness which held Anne back.

He caught her before she had a chance to speak with Anne, who had fled to her room as he had fled to his. He told her an edited version of what had just occurred and she heard him out in silence, although the face she turned on him was a compassionate one.

'Oh, Mr Harcourt, I did try to warn you not to become too involved with Anne, or she with you, but I could see by the behaviour of you both that it was not answering. I cannot tell you why she has refused you, and is right to do so, for I am bound to secrecy. If, as you say, she has told you to forget her, then you must try to do so. That is all I can say, and it is little enough.'

'But I cannot forget her,' Luke cried passionately, and then a suspicion, which the nature of her refusal had created in him, had him saying, 'She calls herself a widow, but is she truly one?'

He thought a shadow passed across Mrs Britten's face, but her answer was firm. 'I cannot tell you more than she has told you herself, Mr Harcourt. You must understand that.'

'Which is nothing,' Luke murmured sorrowfully. He could not badger the good woman before him any more. 'She says she will leave here,' were his last words, 'but it is I who must leave, for I can see that this is the only refuge which she has, whereas I can afford to leave—and must—even though it will break my heart to do so.'

The pity on Mrs Britten's face almost unmanned him, but if Anne were brave, then he must be, too. 'I will look for new rooms tomorrow, although I cannot hope to find a kinder landlady or a happier place to live.'

Mrs Britten did not say him nay, but sorrowfully watched him mount the stairs. He was bereft of hope, who had recently been so hopeful.

Once in his room, Luke thought that he might not be able to write, but to his surprise the words poured from his overful heart as he described the miseries of his gypsy hero, who had seen the girl he loved married to another. It was himself of whom he wrote. Later in the year when the part he was writing was published, his audience grieved and suffered with him, so powerful were the emotions which his own sorrow had enabled him to put on paper.

He did as he had promised Mrs Britten and began to look for another home, far from Islington so that he might not accidentally see Anne. He knew only too well that he could not bear the pain of knowing her near and being unable to approach her. As for Anne, on Mrs Britten telling her that he was about to leave, she almost lost her stoic poise.

'I am driving him from the home he has come to love,' she wailed. 'It is I who ought to leave.'

'Nonsense, child,' returned Mrs Britten briskly, 'for he has money—even if he has renounced the income from his father—and he has homes to go to, apart from his rooms, whereas you, you have only me, and I am sure that he knows that is the case. He is a good young man, and more's the pity that it is not possible for you to marry him.'

I will not cry, Anne thought, and held her head proudly high while she waited each day for Luke to leave the house before she came downstairs, and retreated to her room before he returned in the evening.

'The day after tomorrow,' Luke told Mrs Britten one morning, 'I shall leave. I have found a snug little cottage in Chelsea, near the river, and I shall say goodbye to you with a heavy heart.'

'You have the consolation of doing the right thing, Mr Harcourt.'

'But it isn't enough,' Luke said sadly, 'as you well know. You will tell Mrs Cowper from me how sorry I am to go, and that I wish her well. I think that it would harrow us both too much if I were to try to bid her a formal farewell.'

He walked painfully upstairs to his room. His writing had become a consolation for him, and a means of escape. He was not aware of how ill he looked, or of the pity with which Mrs Britten looked after him.

Later, she said to Anne who sat in her usual place on the drawing-room sofa, sewing, 'Mr Harcourt leaves us tomorrow. He asked me to say goodbye to you, and that he is sorry to go. He thought it wise not to try to see you before he leaves.'

Anne did not immediately reply, but kept her head bent over her work before saying in a stifled voice, 'It is better so.'

The two women sat in silence. Mrs Britten did not wish to leave Anne on her own. Despite Anne's bent head, she could see the slow tears falling down Anne's face, and sighed a deep sigh over the wicked vagaries of an unkind fate which had brought Anne and Luke together, knowing that the love which would follow could never come to fruition.

The morning dragged on. Mrs Britten had, most unusually for her, taken up a novel—she never normally read before noon, that was for the afternoon's leisure—and her book did not capture her whole attention. Consequently, the sound of a coach, a grand affair, drawing up outside, and the bustle which accompanied it, had her rising and walking to the window.

To turn, her face pale with shock, to hiss at Anne, 'Up with you, my dear. It is he, your husband. He has tracked you here, but he must not find you.'

'Never say that it is Clairval!' Anne sprang to her feet, her sewing dropping unheeded on to the carpet as she ran to join Mrs Britten at the window, just as the Marquess of Clairval helped by a footman and followed by the foxy-faced, red-haired man whom she had seen and feared a fortnight earlier, stepped down from his coach.

'Oh, I am lost just when I thought that I was safe.'

Mrs Britten seized her by the hand. 'No! He

shall not have you, but we must be quick. He will be in the house in a few moments, for Mary will undoubtedly let him in, such a grand personage as he is to come a-visiting here. Up the backstairs with you, at once.'

She ran to the door, dragging Anne with her, and the two women dashed along the corridor to the kitchen, fortunately missing Mary, who was already on her way to the front door to answer the peremptory ringing of the bell as well as the banging of m'lord Marquess's gold-topped cane on the front door!

Through the kitchen they ran like the wind, and up the narrow uncarpeted stairs, which were the back way to the first floor and then to the servants' quarters at the top of the house.

'Where are we going?' gasped Anne, as Mrs Britten's route took them across the first-floor landing to knock on Luke's door.

'Oh, no,' she cried, trying to drag her hand free. 'We cannot involve Luke. Think what Clairval would do to him if he found out that he had helped me, that he loved me.'

'Think rather of what Clairval will do you if he captures you here,' retorted Mrs Britten practically before knocking on Luke's door, and pushing Anne into his room. Luke started up from his work to stare at them, so wild and sudden was their arrival.

'There is no time to explain now,' gasped Mrs Britten at him, too distressed to straighten her widow's cap which had fallen awry in the violence of her dash upstairs.

'You must take Anne away from here as quickly as possible, lest a further great wrong be done to her. Go down the backstairs, out through the kitchen door, to a place as far away from here, and as secret as you can find. She can explain to you later. Now, you must go at once,' she almost roared at him, 'for I must leave you. I shall say that Anne is not here, has gone a-marketing, and is not his wife. Anything to prevent Lord Clairval from taking her away.'

'Clairval!' Luke stared at Anne as Mrs Britten shot out of the door. All was suddenly plain to him, but there was no time to think of that. 'Of course, I shall help you, Anne.' Like Mrs Britten he, too, took her by the hand and began to urge her out of the door. 'Quick now, before he demands to search the house.'

'This is not my wish,' began Anne, 'Believe me, I never meant to involve you in my troubles, Luke…'

'No time for that, now,' replied Luke briskly. 'Explanations later.' He had not stayed to put on his coat, and together, he in his shirt sleeves rolled up to the elbow, Anne in her shabby morning gown, ran through Mrs Britten's garden towards safety—wherever that was to be found.

Mary smiled confusedly at her recent suitor, the foxy-faced man, who had followed m'lord Clairval into the house and ushered them both into Mrs Britten's drawing-room. Her mistress, her cap restored to its proper dignity, rose from the armchair in which she had apparently been reading. She placed her book on a side-table and curtsied profoundly to the great man before her.

'I believe that you wish to speak to me, m'lord. How may I be of service to you?'

So this was Anne's husband. He was staring around her room, a look of utter and complete contempt on his face. Mrs Britten could plainly see through its ruin the good looks that he had once possessed. She could also see his cruel mouth, and even crueller eyes.

He fixed them on her and said without preamble, as though he were speaking to the veriest serf, 'You may fetch my faithless and disobedient wife to me, woman, so that I may take her home—to the punishment which rightly awaits her.'

Inwardly quaking, Mrs Britten yet decided to be

bold. 'Your wife, sir? I think that you must be mistaken. I have no Lady Clairval lodging with me here.'

For a moment she thought that he was going to strike her with the gold-topped cane which he was carrying. Instead, he banged it on the floor, and ground out, 'Do not lie to me, woman. I know that you were her governess. I also know that you have been harbouring her here under the name of—' and he snapped his fingers at the man standing behind him '—which is, Jenkinson?'

'Cowper, m'lord. Mrs Anne Cowper, who has been lodging here these many months,' his minion dutifully supplied.

'You heard him, woman! Summon her here immediately from whichever room she is hiding in before I send Jenkinson to fetch the authorities to remove her for me. I do not want a scandal, nor should you. Do you hear me? Or do you add deafness to your other incapacities?'

His voice had risen to a bellow on his last words.

Mrs Britten, fearful of him though she was, yet held her ground. 'She is not here, m'lord. She has gone to the shop where she collects her work as a sempstress. I cannot believe that Mrs Cowper is your wife.'

'So, woman. You are a double liar. You know quite well that she is my wife, and Jenkinson's man, who has been watching your house this morning, informed us that no one has left it.' Clairval's expression was baleful, mixed with grotesque triumph as he came out with this.

'Nevertheless, m'lord, I fear that you are mistaken. Mrs Cowper is not here.'

His face uglier still, Clairval swung round to address his henchman, who stood there silent, considering the brave defiance of the valiant woman before them. 'Search the house, Jenkinson. Spare no pains, and do not consider the feelings or possessions of the lying bitch before you. She is aiding and abetting a felony by keeping my wife from me.'

Not quite a felony, thought Jenkinson but he sped to do m'lord's bidding, Mrs Britten crying after him as he left the room, 'She is not here. You run a wasted errand.'

'Be quiet,' thundered Clairval. He flung himself into the armchair which Mrs Britten had earlier vacated, mannerlessly leaving her to stand, the better to inform her how little she—or any woman—mattered in the Marquess of Clairval's scheme of things.

Silence followed.

Mary could be heard crying in the distance. Was Jenkinson bullying her? Mrs Britten comforted herself with the knowledge that Mary knew nothing, and so could betray nothing. She hugged that thought to her when Jenkinson at last entered, his face glum.

'M'lady is not here, m'lord. I have searched the house. The maid says that to her knowledge she has not left it—but I cannot find her.'

'Then where the devil is she? She could not have escaped by the chimney.' He rose and roared at Mrs Britten with such ferocity that she retreated before him. 'Where has she gone?'

Jenkinson did not like to admit that he might have been careless, but honesty compelled him to say, 'Through the kitchen, perhaps, while the maid answered the door. There is a back way through the garden by which m'lady may have fled.'

'Oh, a back way, you say? Remind me of that when the time for settlement comes. The bird has flown and all is to do again. As for you, woman, your house will be watched, back and front, night and day, and if my wife so much as shows her face here, I'll have the pair of you before the magistrates.'

It was over. Mrs Britten, her legs failing her, sank into the armchair so lately occupied by m'lord. For the time being Anne was safe. She had no idea where Luke might have taken her, which was as well, for Clairval might yet return to try to drag the truth from her. But so far he had failed to find the lady!

She could hear him thundering his thwarted wrath at Jenkinson. Whatever he was saying was not pleasant, she was sure. Presently the front door opened and closed. They were gone.

She ran to the window. The coach was being driven at breakneck speed along the road towards London, but Jenkinson was not in it. He was standing on the pavement, gazing after it with a most malignant stare. M'lord had just turned him away without a penny, shouting that he had been light in the attic to trust such a fool to do his work for him.

'Not a penny,' he had bellowed at Jenkinson. 'Not a penny. You have spent my time and my money and all for nothing! The woman's loose again, leaving me like a gaby haring after her. You may find your own way back to town. Do not show me your curst face again.'

Oh, but I *shall* show you my curst face again, m'lord, and a sorry day it will be for you when I do, was Jenkinson's inward litany as the coach and Clairval disappeared round the corner.

Once he was well away from Mrs Britten's, Luke slowed down and tried to think where he might safely take Anne, whose hand lay so trustingly in his. He was struck by a sudden inspiration.

Josette! he thought, as they finally reached the

road which led towards London. Josette will help me, I am sure. She is a good girl, and if she is not still in her rooms, then her friends will. Clairval will not be able to find us there, for Mrs Britten does not even know that Josette exists, let alone what her address is.

They walked briskly along the road, regardless of the stares which their inadequate dress attracted. Luke had just enough money in his breeches pocket to pay a hackney cab to take them to Josette's. He bundled Anne into it after he had paid the cab driver, who had demanded to see the colour of Luke's money before he consented to take them to the lodgings in a back street behind the Haymarket to which Josette had returned after she had broken with Luke.

Luck was with them. Josette's landlady was out, and it was she who answered the door.

'Luke Harcourt!' she exclaimed, looking from him to Anne. 'What are you doing here?'

'I shall explain in a minute,' Luke said gravely. 'I am well aware that I have no right to do so, but I have come to ask of you one last favour. This is my friend, Mrs Anne…Gordon, who is in need of a safe place to live. She is being pursued by her husband from whom she has fled, and who has treated her abominably.

'He can have no idea that she is here, but we shall both understand if you feel that you cannot help us—at least for one night, until I find somewhere safe to hide her.'

Josette looked doubtfully at them both. Something in the quiet desperation written on Anne's face touched her heart. That, and the tender way in which Luke was looking at her. Josette bore Luke no malice; he had been a kind and considerate lover, and very soon she would be back in the village where she had been born and Luke and his doings would have no part in his life.

'Of course, your friend may stay with me overnight Luke and longer, if it proves necessary. Pray sit down, Mrs Gordon,' she added kindly. 'You look as though you are about to faint.'

'It is most good of you to help me,' Anne replied. 'Particularly as I have been unable to bring anything with me. No money and no clothes.'

'You may forget them both,' returned Josette. 'I am sure that I can find Mrs Gordon some night rail and something to eat. You may safely leave her with me, Luke, and if it is so necessary for her to disappear, then you must be off to find help for her as soon as possible.'

Anne did not wish Luke to leave. He was her sole remaining link with Islington and Mrs Britten, where for a short space she had been happy. Josette saw that she was distressed and, when Luke had gone, came over to sit by her.

'You are not just a friend, are you?' she asked. 'That is a tale he told to protect you. Luke loves you, does he not? Truly loves you.' Her voice was wistful.

From some depth of knowledge, never before fished in, Anne found words to answer her. 'He cares for you, too. A different form of love. He would not have brought me here, otherwise.'

Josette nodded. 'You were fortunate to find me here. I am going home this weekend, into the country, to marry my true love. I will be honest with you. I once thought that...someone else... was my true love. I was wrong.'

Anne had known from the moment that she had first seen Josette that she and Luke had been lovers... But what he did before he met me is past and gone—as is what happened to me before I met him at Mrs Britten's.

She trembled a little again as she thought of Clairval and what she must say of him when she next met Luke, and also at the thought of what might be happening to her good friend in Islington once Clairval found that his prey had eluded him again...

* * *

Once he had left Josette's Luke tried to assemble his muddled thoughts and decide on a sensible plan of action. He could not leave Anne with Josette for very long. It would not be fair to Josette since, if Clairval found that she was sheltering his runaway wife, Luke had no doubt that he would wreak vengeance on her.

That might sound as though they were all living in a Drury Lane melodrama, but Clairval's reputation was so suspect that nothing must be left to chance. But where could he take her where she might not be found? He was so distracted that he did not hear his name being called until a hand touched his shoulder.

He looked up. Of all people, it was Tawno Chikno, as raffishly handsome as ever, and leading a prime horse.

'Luke, my brother, what's amiss?' He seemed to have acquired a little of the *chovihani*'s second sight, for he added, 'I sense that something is wrong with you. May an old friend help?'

May an old friend help? Luke gaped at him. Had providence sent Tawno on his journey especially to help him? Now, that was demanding too much of life, but a thought, daring in its simplicity, struck him like a thunderbolt from Jove's hand reaching earth.

'Tawno, my beauty! Where are you all en-camped?'

'Nigh to Greenwich. We shall be at the Fair.'

'And then, Tawno? Where do you go, then?'

'Why do you ask, friend Luke? You know as well as I do that after Greenwich we wend west, towards Bristol. Was it not near Haven's End that you and I learned to trust the horse so that it might, in return, trust us?'

Salvation! Salvation was before them—for now Luke knew that his destiny and Anne's were inex-tricably intertwined.

'A week, then? You leave in a week?'

'Indeed, friend.' Tawno stared at him. Like Pat, he had never seen Luke Harcourt so frantic, so un-like his usual controlled self.

Luke collected himself. 'If I asked a favour of Jas-per, friend Tawno, would he be likely to grant it?'

'You know he would, Luke. You are almost one of us.'

'Then take me to him, Tawno. For I must ask it of him immediately.'

Chapter Nine

'Luke!' Josette had been waiting for his return, not in her room, but in the drawing-room of her land-lady—a concession grudgingly granted to her. 'I have something to say to you. I have decided to return to Kent on the night coach today instead of waiting until the end of the week. Anne can rent my room until you find somewhere safer for her to hide—the landlady has already agreed that she may take it over.'

He had, after all, done the right thing in asking Josette to help him. Luke's new, and less selfish, attitude to life told him that he hardly deserved her generosity, and so he informed her in no un-certain terms.

'Pooh!' Josette waved his thanks away. 'We are still friends, I hope. It is the least that I can do for you both. I have given her a nightgown and a change of clothes—they are not those which I shall be taking back to Kent. They belong to my...different...life here and are unsuitable for country wear.'

How could he thank her? He bent down and kissed her cheek. A brotherly kiss. The look which she gave him in return told him that she had no regrets but was looking forward to her new life. They could wish each other well in perfect amity.

He let himself into what was now Anne's room—to find her asleep in her armchair. He did not disturb her but stood looking down at the picture which she presented. In sleep, as when awake, she possessed a lovely calm, a composure which he found astonishing when he tried to imagine what her life with Clairval must have been.

He didn't deserve Anne, as he hadn't deserved Josette, but he would try to make himself worthy of her. So thinking, he bent down and stroked her cheek. She awoke, to smile at him.

'You are back. I hadn't expected you until tomorrow. You know that Josette is leaving?'

'Yes, and I have said my farewells to her.' Luke sat down beside her and took her hand in his. 'I have good news for you. I have found a way for us to leave London secretly. First, though, let me assure you that Mrs Britten has not suffered as the result of your husband's visit although her house is being watched in case you try to return.'

'Mrs Britten! How ungrateful of me to fall asleep so easily, forgetting that she might be in danger. She has been so kind, and has now saved me, not once, but twice. First when she took me in, and today when she helped me to escape.'

'Hush,' said Luke. 'You must not reproach yourself. She sends you her love and the hope that you may escape from Clairval again.'

'And you?' asked Anne anxiously. 'He does not know that you helped me to get away from him?'

'No, indeed. And that is our greatest strength. I may not stay with you tonight, but tomorrow I shall come to you, and put my plan into action. I shall tell Mrs Britten that I am going into town to see my publisher, which will not be a total lie, seeing that I have the last part of my novel to deliver to him before I come to you. And then we shall leave London, but I shall not tell her where we are going.'

'Yes. Best that she knows nothing. Clairval is a pitiless man, as I well know,' and she shivered.

'Oh, Luke, I feel that it is only fair that I tell you my story before you commit yourself to trying to rescue me. It is not only that I wish to explain myself, I must inform you of the danger in which you stand if you help me.'

Luke was keenly aware that, as usual, Anne pitied everyone but herself—who needed it the most.

'Think nothing of that. Think only, that with my help, you may escape him again. And, if it pains you to tell me your story, then you need not do so. I have only to know Clairval to understand what your life with him must have been.'

It was Anne's turn to put out her hand to take Luke's. 'No, in a strange way I believe that it may help me. The plain truth is that Mrs Britten and I have been deceiving you all these months—for the best of reasons, it is true. But I have always been painfully conscious that I was not being honest with you. Now I must be, as I hope always to be in the future.'

'But I fully understand why you could not be,' protested Luke.

'True, and that is all the more reason why I should be open with you now. I was not always a rich heiress. Until I was sixteen years old I was simple Miss Anticleia Temple, although I was always known as Anne. My father was a poor scholar, a parson with a living near Oxford. My mother died when I was born, and my father did not remarry.

'We were very happy together until a distant cousin died and left my father a large fortune and a gloomy neglected house in Yorkshire. He felt it his duty to give up his living and look after his new estate, but I think that the move may have killed him. In six months he was dead and I was his heiress, left to the guardianship of relatives I hardly knew and who were determined to use my wealth to marry the family into the aristocracy.'

Anne stopped and shivered. 'This was how I came to meet Lord Clairval. I was not yet eighteen, and he came to visit my cousins at their express invitation. They saw only his title, his old and honoured name, not the man he really was. You must remember that this was nearly five years ago and he was still handsome...'

In telling Luke her sad story, Anne found herself back in the past again. She could remember quite plainly the first time she had met Clairval. He had been charm itself, and had spoken to her of the things which interested her, of books and music. He was always dressed in black—her cousins had told her that after his first wife had died suddenly he had gone into perpetual mourning, so stricken was he by her death.

He had made no secret of his relative poverty, so that he might not be accused of being a fortune hunter because he had concealed it. He had even laughed over it a little sadly, and she had felt sorry for him. Tears were in his eyes when he spoke to her of his late wife, even though she had died two years earlier. She had honoured him for his devotion to her, and told him so, not in words, but in the kind sympathy which she showed to him.

Even so, she had at first been a little shocked when he had, through her cousin and guardian, John Temple Masters, proposed to her. After all, he was over twenty-five years older than she was.

'But you like him,' John Masters had protested when she had demurred a little. 'And think what you are gaining. A man, not a boy, and one of England's oldest titles. His estates are a little encumbered, true, but your settlement will take care of that. We can arrange things so that your fortune is not swallowed up by his debts. Sufficient of an income can be assured to him so that a steady recovery will see Clairval's lands solvent again.'

That Clairval might not see matters in exactly the same light did not occur to her guardian, nor to Anne herself. She had lived a life far removed from the world which Clairval inhabited, and could not be aware of the deep and passionate tides which lay beneath the easy carelessness with which Clairval faced her relatives and her.

The true carelessness in the matter lay with her guardian, who should have heeded gossip more.

The gossip which told of Clairval's darker side; the gossip about his conduct to his first wife. But the man and his name bedazzled him. Nor did he pause to think that if he made Anticleia's money really safe from Clairval's depredations, then the person who might suffer the most from this might be Anticleia herself.

As for Clairval, he told himself that however tightly her guardian might tie up Miss Temple's estates before her marriage, what might happen to them afterwards would be a very different thing!

The girl seemed young and biddable, and a little awed by him and his title, so he concentrated on pouring his charm over her, and her bedazzled connections. Consequently, the marriage, which took place at York Minster under the aegis of the Archbishop himself was arranged as a glorious pageant, ushering in a golden age for Clairval and his estates.

At this point in her story Anne stopped, and looked at Luke, her great eyes filling with tears.

'I was stupid enough to think that he truly was my fairy prince or, better still, the older man who was going to take the place in my life which my father had always filled. And he, he had not the common sense to go slowly with me at first. I suppose that he thought that I was an obedient fool to whom he might do as he pleased.

'He made the mistake of drinking too much on our wedding night, and it was a disaster. Oh, I cannot speak of it. One moment we were in the Minster, looking like figures in a fairy story, and the next…

'The next I was finding that I had married a man who could only gain pleasure from another's pain. That first night I told myself that it was the drink which had done the damage, except that I soon discovered that, sober, he was more vile than when drunk. There was a coldness about him then. He told me once that the sooner I was with child the more I should please him, for then he could be off to find better entertainment elsewhere, and I might sleep alone.'

She looked away from Luke when she told him her carefully edited tale, for it was beyond her to reveal the true story of the brutality with which Clairval had treated her from the very first. She felt Luke stir, heard the oaths he muttered below his breath, and knew that he guessed much of what she was not telling him, what she could not tell him—for very shame—for Clairval's cruelty seemed to demean her as well as he who had inflicted it.

'My dear,' Luke said, 'if it pains you too much, you must stop.' He was remembering her broken wrist, her slight limp and the manner in which she had flinched away from him when she had first known him, before she had discovered that she could trust him.

She shook her head. 'No, for you do not yet understand the total of his brutality, what he might do to you, or cause to be done to you if he discovered not only that you had helped me, but that we love one another. After a time, some months in all, when no child came, he began to find trying to create one…difficult.

'It was then that his brutality became worse, made the more so because only the birth of a child to me would bring him the extra money which he claimed to need for his estates but which, I think, he meant to spend on debauchery. He became so careless in his treatment of me that he had to excuse my appearance by my clumsiness, making fun in company of what he called "my wife's inability to walk downstairs without falling over".

'And still a child eluded him, so one day he brought me a paper to sign which would give him control of my money without the birth of an heir. When I refused to sign it, for by now I was finding the strength to defy him, he threatened me with worse than I had already endured.

'He had, it seems, begun a whispering campaign about my sanity, and was telling the world that I had run mad and needed to be confined to my room. A man as powerful as Clairval can always find tools to do his bidding, and two of his hirelings solemnly examined me and pronounced me out of my wits. Only, what the world did not know, was that my room was a cell in one of Clairval Castle's towers, with the promise of imprisonment in a madhouse if I did not do his bidding.

'He vowed that he would beat me into submission, and the more I defied him, the crueller he grew. He could not believe that one poor woman would defy him so constantly. Where I gained the strength to oppose him, I shall never know. Oh, I prayed to God to help me or, failing that, to release me through death from a life which had become hateful, but all seemed in vain.

'Shortly before he had had me certified mad, I had written to my late guardian, John Masters, begging him to rescue me from the hell in which I was living. Alas, Clairval convinced him of my madness, and he, and others to whom I appealed, wrote to me, telling me to listen to my husband, take the medicine his doctors prescribed and behave myself. It seemed hopeless to try to escape him.

'Until one day, the steward who had been my gaoler came to me and said that he could see me mistreated no longer. He feared that what had happened to Clairval's first wife would happen to me, and his conscience would not let him bear the double dose of guilt which my death would bring him.

'He said that he would release me, find me sanctuary, delay the news of my flight and would then fly himself and take me to wherever I wished to go. The only person I could think of was my dear Mrs Britten, and so it was arranged.

'Except that, although he released me, he never joined me afterwards. I was hidden away in a poor cottage on the Nottinghamshire border where his brother and mother lived. One day his brother went to Clairval Castle to discover why he had not left Clairval's employment as he had promised.

'When he returned, he gave me just enough money to pay my coach fare to London. He told me that the steward had disappeared, and that the rumour in the servants' hall was that Clairval had likely killed him for freeing me. I was to leave as soon as possible, lest Clairval discover my whereabouts and punish them for harbouring me. The sooner I was gone, the safer they would be.

'So now you see the danger which you run by trying to save me. I already have one man's death on my conscience, and, oh, Luke, I would not have yours. If you love me, leave me.'

This plea was so wild, so impassioned, that it almost unmanned Luke.

He took his beloved girl in his arms, and whispered in her ear, 'No, never, my darling. What sort of cur should I be to compel you to bear this dreadful load on your own? I would have suggested that we go to your relatives and ask for help, but everything which you have told me, and the *on dits* about Clairval which are already circulating in society, have served only to convince me that that would be a hopeless cause.

'Years ago, only the fact that Lady Strathmore's relatives were rich and powerful, and were on her side, was able to save her from the similar wickedness of Stony Bowes. But your relatives have already refused to help you, and my father is a member of the government and a magistrate sworn to uphold the wicked law which condemns you to be treated as a chattel. You have no one but me to protect you, and what a poor insignificant prop I am, my darling heart, even if I love you truly.'

Without further touching, stroking or lovemaking they lay in one another's arms. It was not so much that their passion was spent, but that in the light of Anne's dreadful story it seemed inappropriate.

Presently Luke whispered, 'After what you just have told me, my dearest, it is all the more imperative that we leave London in secret as soon as possible. Today I visited Jasper Petulengro and the gypsies who are at present camped at Greenwich Fair, and they have promised us sanctuary. To rescue you, I must propose something which I at first thought a trifle melodramatic, but since hearing your story I am convinced is a necessity.

'Jasper and the Romanies are on their way west to Bristol—slowly—for they stop at country fairs and horse shows in order to earn their living. Once we reach Bristol, we can take a ship for the Americas under false names. Jasper will marry us according to the custom of the Romanies—he says that by their laws a marriage such as yours to Clairval cannot stand. Even Clairval would find it difficult to find us if we cross the broad Atlantic.

'It means leaving behind everything that we know, and making a new life overseas, but a man may use his ability to write in order to earn a living wherever he settles, and our life could hardly be harder than the one which you have endured since your marriage.'

Anne did not immediately answer him. She wriggled away from his arms to look him full in the eye, her own eyes glowing. 'Oh, Luke, I will go with you anywhere, and although once I would have thought it a sin to live with you as your wife when I am married to another, I no longer do so. If Ruth in the Bible could follow Naomi into a new country, then so can I follow you! But it is not I who should make this decision, for it is you who are the greater loser if we do as you propose.'

'Oh, brave,' said Luke softly, taking her ardent face between his two hands and kissing it gently. 'You shame me when I think of what you have suffered and endured whilst I was leading my idle, careless life. And even now, you think of me before you think of yourself.'

'Dear Luke.' Anne had responded to his caresses by taking one of his hands, turning it towards her mouth and kissing it on the palm. 'When I see what thinking only of one's self has done to Clairval, how can I put my own wishes and desires first? That would be to be as poor and shameful a thing as he is.'

What could Luke say to that, except to kiss her again? He might have wished to love the afternoon away, only there was much to be done if they were to join the gypsies on the morrow. There was Clairval to deceive.

And if he had once thought to involve his father and Cressy in Anne's troubles, he no longer wished to do so—for he dare not risk Clairval using the law to claim Anne back. And once he had done so, possession being nine points of the law, then even James, Lord Lyndale's name and power might not be sufficient to free her again.

For the law saw the wife's obedience to her husband as absolute. If he loved Anne, and were to save her—or try to—he must be prepared to give up everything, and make a new life where Marquesses had little power, and where a man was respected for what he was, not for the bedroom in which he had been born.

'You will be safe here tonight,' he said. 'And I shall come for you tomorrow afternoon, without fail. Mrs Britten shall not know that I am disappearing, nor anyone else—safer so. Tomorrow we shall be Mr and Mrs Gordon, on their way to set sail for a new life.'

'You are sure, Luke,' Anne asked him anxiously 'that this is what you want?'

He gave her one last kiss before he left her. 'It is what we must both want, Anne. For you cannot return to a monster who, at best, would consign you permanently to a madhouse, and at worse would kill you.'

'Welcome, friend Luke, and your woman, too. But if you are to ride and live with us, then you must look like us. You are both far too sleek to be Romanies as you are.'

Everything had gone according to plan. Luke had even spent part of the previous evening at the last great reception which James and Cressy were giving before they left London for Haven's End. Clairval had been there, giving Luke one of his most ferocious stares. Luke had no notion whether or not Clairval knew that he had been living in the same house as his wife, but he thought not. He was sure that Clairval would have accosted him otherwise.

He overheard him telling one of his friends that he hoped to recover his missing wife soon. 'The sooner the better,' he declared piously. 'The poor creature must be in dire need of medical help and careful nursing by now. Those who had charge of her are of the opinion that the longer she is out of their care, the worse she will grow.'

Luke did not know how he contained himself. The memory of Anne's story, and of her suffering face as she told it, was still strong in him. His father, who also overheard Clairval, growled something short about 'not believing people who protested too much,' but added, 'It is to be hoped that she continues to elude him, because once discovered, there is nothing that could be done for her, other than to hand her back to him.'

'A cruel law, that,' exclaimed Luke indignantly, 'which treats a man's wife as less than a serf, no more than a horse or a senseless thing like a chair or a table, for him to dispose of as he pleases.'

His father looked at him curiously, so strong was his son's indignation. There was some emotion in Luke's voice which he had never heard before. 'Most men treat their wives decently,' he said, a trifle defensively.

'Not all men are like you,' Luke proclaimed, and then changed the subject. It was imperative that no one, absolutely no one, should be aware that Luke Harcourt and the missing wife of the Marquess of Clairval had anything to do with one another.

Without revealing his plans to Mrs Britten, he had left her a farewell letter and enough money to pay for his rooms until the quarter ended so that she should not be out of pocket. He had no need to tell her why he was disappearing—she knew that Anne's safety was paramount with him.

As for Anne, she had so little in the way of possessions that a large shawl, its ends knotted together, contained the few items of clothing which Josette had given her. She had fled from Clairval Castle with nothing, and now had fled from Islington after the same fashion.

Luke collected her from her rooms, gave the

landlady a tip for her kindness, and then hired the cab which would take them to Greenwich Fair—and the gypsies.

For the first time in his life he was being careful with his money. He had been to Coutts Bank, had withdrawn most of his holdings there, and had hidden his guineas about his person. He thought that he would give Anne part of his small horde of wealth so that if, by chance, anything happened to him, she would have something of her own.

It was a strange feeling for him to be quite alone in the world without the cushion of his father's name and wealth to support him. He was not even Luke Harcourt—which was a made-up name in any case—but once they took ship for the Americas he would become a fictitious Mr Gordon, travelling with his wife to God knew where. For she was his wife, in the eyes of God, if not in the eyes of man, and he would cherish and protect her and bring her at last out of the shadows and into the sunlight.

Perhaps it was as well that Anne had so little with her, for the *chovihani* came to welcome her, to take her by the hand and say, 'We meet again, as I thought that we would, and you will be my companion for a little while—but first, if we are to hide you, we must arrange it so that you appear to be one of us. Come.'

Luke watched Anne walk away with the *chovi-hani*. She turned at the tent's flap to give him a smile, and he found himself smiling back. Long afterwards he was to remember everything about that golden late August afternoon; the friendship of the gypsies, Tawno Chikno riding by with a troop of horses, and raising a hand in greeting.

He would never forget the warmth of the welcome which they all gave him, and Jasper's praise for the story which he had written of their life and work.

'For you have not betrayed us, friend Luke,' Jasper told him, 'as so many have done before, but you have told the truth about us as far as in you lies, since as you well know, no man is ever completely truthful about anything!'

This was Jasper all over. Inside his tent Luke pulled on the clothes which were to make him one of the Rom: worn blue velveteen breeches, a heavy linen shirt, and a leather jacket decorated with arcane patterns burned on it with a hot poker. His fine boots were packed away with the rest of his gentleman's clothing. Instead he was given a pair of soft half-boots such as Tawno and his riders wore. The elegant gentleman which he had once been had disappeared quite.

'And you must allow your hair to grow,' Jasper commanded, 'for you will be part of Tawno's troop. He knows that you can haggle over horses, but the wretch has a passion to see you try to learn some of the more difficult tricks with which we entertain the mob.'

'Not the one where he rides at full gallop, then twists and turns to lie beneath the horse's belly, I hope,' riposted Luke with a grin.

'Even that,' smiled Jasper, 'if he so commands. You wish to be one with us, you and your woman, so you shall be one with us, and defy the devil and all his works. The *chovihani* says that the omens are good. Look where she comes, and your woman with her.'

He would scarcely have known that it was Anne who held the *chovihani*'s hand. She was wearing a dress which only reached to her mid-calf, deep blue in colour, matching her eyes, and trimmed with saffron-coloured lace. Her feet were bare and her lustrous dark hair had been loosened and fell about her shoulders. Around her neck was a chain of some base metal, and from it depended a star whose centre was a cluster of small pearls.

'Stella,' pronounced the *chovihani* solemnly as she presented Anne to Luke. 'That will be her name among us. Star because her vision will guide not only you, but us.'

Anne smiled and hung her head a little shyly, but

the *chovihani* would have none of that. She seized her by the chin and lifted it up so that Anne faced the world full on, eyes high. 'Nay, child, be not abashed. Courage is yours, and courage is never shamed.'

'Truer words were never spoken,' Luke told them both, 'and what shall be my name? For I, too, must have a name to go among you.'

'Oh, that you shall have,' proclaimed a new, harsh voice. It was Tawno Chikno who had come among them unawares. 'Scribe you are, and lowly Scribe you shall be, until I have taught you a better, worthier trade and you have earned another name. Come, Scribe, it is time for you to learn that trade.'

So soon! Luke had imagined himself being slowly inaugurated into the gypsies' way of life, but he avowed ruefully that he should have known better. He had called on them for help and they were helping him but as with everything in this life, as Jasper was to emphasise to him later, there is always a price to pay.

He was Luke Harcourt no longer: that fine, easy young gentleman who had lived among the fleshpots all his life, accepting the service of others as his due. Instead he was Scribe, the lowliest and least accomplished of the horsemen over whom Tawno reigned—as he was soon to learn. Tawno took him by the shoulder and pushed him roughly towards the group of waiting riders, one of whom was holding a horse ready for him to mount.

Once he was in the saddle, Tawno shouted a hoarse word of command and the riders began to wheel and turn under his directions, performing intricate manoeuvres. The only way in which Anne could distinguish Luke from the others was by his clumsiness, as he tried to keep in line and do what they did.

Tawno seemed to take a delight in taunting him every time he made a mistake, and once, as he shot by him, struck Luke's horse with his whip so sharply that it reared suddenly and Luke found himself on the ground, with his horse trying to make its way into the next county.

Jasper and the rest of the gypsies laughed and cheered as Luke rose slowly to his feet to chase and try to catch his errant steed. Tawno's cries of derision accompanied him on his quest, before hot, sore and dusty, he finally cornered him. It had become very apparent to Anne that Luke had deliberately been given a mettlesome animal which he would have had difficulty in controlling even if he had ridden him before. She thought this rather unfair, and said so.

'Yes,' agreed the *chovihani*. 'You have the right of it, Stella. But consider what Tawno is doing.

He is teaching Scribe that he is no longer the lord of his world, but the least-considered performer in a troop; every one of whom is a better rider than he is.

'Only by being made aware of his shortcomings will he ever improve—and if he does not try to improve, or gives up through false pride, then he will never be a Rom, but must remain Scribe, a *gorgio* and a servant. To be a complete man he must learn true pride, and that will only come through humility and the determination to overcome one's faults.'

She looked Anne full in the eye. 'You have learned that lesson, Stella. Scribe has yet to learn it.'

Oh, Luke was already learning something valuable. If he had not actively patronised the gypsies before he came to live among them, he had seen himself during his time with them easily proving that he could live their life as well as he had lived his own. He and Anne were to be a kind of prince and princess dwelling among the lowly. Instead he was being made to understand that if he were to live among the Rom and pass as one of them, then he must be a Rom in every way which counted.

Once the group riding had ended, Tawno handed a hot and tired Luke over to his chief lieutenant to be taught the basics of what the Rom believed riding to be. His horse's saddle was removed and he was made to ride barebacked, so that he could learn to control his mount without it.

The little crowd that had been watching the fun melted away when this routine grind began. The *chovihani* touched Anne on the shoulder, saying, 'Come. You must help us to prepare the evening meal. Also, I understand from Scribe that you are a skilful sempstress. That being so, you must join Eliza, who looks after the sewing, and she will find work for you to do. No one eats who does not work, you understand. That is why Scribe must learn to be a good rider.'

Thus, when Luke had ended his first lesson, it was Anne who served him from the cauldron of hot rabbit stew which she had helped to prepare, handing him baked potatoes from the embers of the bonfire above which the cauldron had hung. He was trembling slightly from his exertions, ached all over and not even eating the hot food could restore his tired limbs.

Anne saw that he was hiding his weariness beneath his usual charming mask as he laughed and bantered with the riders who had put him through the hardest lesson of his life. She came to sit beside him on the grass, and said quietly, so that none should overhear them, 'Are you very tired, Luke? That looked like hard work.'

He shrugged his shoulders. Not even to Anne could Luke admit how difficult the last few hours had been. To do so would take the edge off his determination not to be beat. So, they thought him a soft *gorgio* did they? One who needed to be taught a stiff lesson. Well, be damned to that! If it killed him, he would learn to ride as well as they did— better, if possible.

Luke was discovering inside himself a hard core of resolution that he had not known he possessed. He had first become aware of it when Anne had spurred him on to write seriously of what he knew. Now it was telling him to prove himself a man whom the Rom could respect. It made him put an arm around Anne's shoulders and hug her reassuringly.

'You mustn't mind if I make a fool of myself at first, Anne. Nothing which is worth the doing comes easily. I shall try not to let you down.'

She rested her head on his shoulder and, remembering what the *chovihani* had said to her of the necessity for Luke to learn the harder lessons of life, said no more.

Later that night, though, when, unable to sleep, she left the tent she was sharing with the *chovihani* to walk towards the River Thames, which ran broad and silver in the moonlight not far from their camp, she passed Luke where he lay in the open, wrapped in a blanket, and heard him moaning in his sleep.

He was tossing, and trying to throw his blanket off. One hand was clenched beside his head, and she thought that he not only looked, but sounded, feverish. She went down on her hands and knees beside him, and called his name softly. 'Luke, what is it?'

He came awake immediately and grasped at the hand which she had laid on his damp brow. 'Anne! What are you doing here? Where are we?'

'At Greenwich, Luke, with the gypsies. Remember?'

His face cleared. He sat up, and said, 'Of course. But I had a bad dream. I had lost you, and Clairval was there. He was laughing.' He was obviously finding it painful to move, and said ruefully, 'So much unaccustomed exercise has done me in a little. Riding a pen is hardly a preparation for riding a horse!' A statement which had Anne laughing gently at him.

'And I am not used to paring potatoes and hauling cauldrons of stew about,' and she showed him her damaged hands. 'But if it means that we shall escape my husband, then I think that I would walk through hot coals to do so.'

Luke kissed her scarred and burned fingers. 'My

darling Stella, for I must remember to call you that, if you can turn yourself into a maid of all work, then for sure I can turn myself into one of Tawno's riders. I had a friend once who served in the cavalry during the late wars as an ordinary trooper, and he was always scornful of the gentleman riders who took their ease in Hyde Park. I am beginning to understand how he felt.'

He stifled a yawn. 'We must try to sleep and not waken the camp—but you will give me a kiss before you go?' He held out his arms to her.

'Gladly,' and for a moment she lowered herself to the grass beside him, so that they lay entwined—chastely, he under the blanket and she on top of it.

'Oh, Scribe, my Scribe, I wish so much that we might truly be husband and wife. The *chovihani* says that we must not touch one another until Jasper decides whether he is able to make us man and wife according to their rites. I do so wish that he would hurry up. I am beginning to understand what the poets meant when they spoke of lovers burning for one another.'

For a moment or two they lay in each other's arms, exchanging the most innocent of kisses. Neither of them wished to go against Jasper's order that they were not to make love until he had made his decision, but oh, it was sweet torment to know that they were restricted to the most innocent of kisses and strokings.

Presently Luke felt Anne's body change as sleep began to claim her and, agony though it was to see her leave, he sent her on her way. They must not abuse the gypsies' trust—and here was another hard lesson he was learning.

What did surprise him though was although his aching for Anne joined the pain of his overused body to torment him, it was not long before exhaustion claimed him and he also slept.

Chapter Ten

'A fortnight,' raged Clairval. 'It is a fortnight since she escaped me in Islington, and you say that you have no news of her. I am beginning to wish that I had not thrown Jenkinson off—he seems to have had more about him than you have.'

The ex-Runner, Greene, who had taken Jenkinson's place, was beginning to wish that he had never met his moody patron. Had he known the half of it, he would never have become involved with such an unreasonable monster—but so unreasonable was Clairval that he dare not resign his post. Best to wait until his capricious master tired of him and dismissed him in one of his tempers.

Whilst he made his latest report, two of Clairval's bruisers were present and stood there grinning at his discomfiture. He was saved from further reproach by a footman entering to tell m'lord that the writer, O'Hare, whom he had sent for, was waiting in the anteroom.

'Then bring him in, dolt,' Clairval snarled. Here was another underling upon whom he could vent his rage. Despite the good money he was paying O'Hare to write favourable pieces about him in the public prints, the public appeared to be singularly unimpressed by O'Hare's panegyrics.

'Well, man,' he greeted O'Hare as he entered, turning his back on his previous victim who stood there, uncertain whether it was more politic to go or to stay. 'You have another few pages on my mad wife with you, I hope, to persuade the fools who read your vapourings to turn her over to me if they come across her.'

He held out his hand, and Pat who, like Greene, was wishing that he had never become involved with such a patent madman even though the pay was good, said ruefully, 'I am sorry, m'lord, but after this one is printed I cannot place any further articles about your missing wife until I can offer some solid news. There are other, newer, scandals which editors wish to dwell on.'

Clairval's face purpled. 'What! I am paying you good money and this is all that you have to tell me? Suppose I were to give you details of where my mad wife was living before she ran away—would that interest them? I have not done so before because it is no business of the public's to be aware that the Marchioness of Clairval preferred to live in a back street in Islington among the scum rather than with her lawful husband…' He paused, his tongue having run out of its ability to keep up with his anger.

If both Pat and Greene were of the opinion that Clairval's pride of birth had overcome his good sense to the degree that it was hampering his discovery of his missing wife, neither of them dared to say so.

Pat, indeed, driven to say something, anything, to appease the monster before him, came out with a sentence whose utterance he was bitterly to regret.

'Islington is it? I know Islington well. Pray, m'lord, what part of Islington?'

'Duke Street, in a lodging house kept by her old governess, now a widow. She was taking in sewing, by Gad! A sempstress, the Marchioness of Clairval earning her living as a sempstress! That alone should convince everyone that she has taken leave of her senses.'

Pat was carelessly unwise again. 'Duke Street, Mrs Britten's? Why, my fellow writer Luke Harcourt lodges there. Come to think of it, I met him at Islington Fair with Mrs Britten and a damned pretty girl on his arm, who was also a lodger there…'

He stopped. There was a ghastly silence. Clairval's face, now almost black with an infusion of rage-fed blood, was thrust into his. He seized Pat by his cravat and began to strangle him—slowly.

'Repeat that again,' he howled, 'about Luke Harcourt and the woman he was with. How long have you known that he was a lodger at Mrs Britten's? Answer me!'

'I can't,' gasped Pat, 'until you release me.' She couldn't have been his wife...could she?

Oh, but she could. And dancing around London with that upstart Luke Harcourt, who had humiliated him so publicly! What more likely?

Clairval half-threw Pat towards his two bruisers. Greene standing stolidly by, again inwardly cursed his bad luck in becoming involved with such a dangerous madman. Clairval was now instructing his men to 'knock the truth out of this Irish scribbler who doesn't possess the wits he was born with'.

'But I don't know anything,' cried Pat, now well and truly frightened for the first time in his comfortable life. 'Only that he was squiring a girl around the Fair. He called her Anne and Mrs Cowper. He seemed sweet on her, apart from that, nothing.'

'Sweet on her, and called her Anne and Mrs Cowper—which was the name she was going under.' Clairval was foaming at the mouth, spraying spittle over Pat. 'He's almost certainly taking her to his father's home—where else could they go?'

He swung on Greene. 'Are you listening, man? Harcourt's natural father is the Earl of Lyndale, who has a seat at Haven's End in Wiltshire. What more likely than that they've disappeared in that direction? He might even have taken her to Lyndale's home in Piccadilly. Start making enquiries at once and report back to me first thing tomorrow morning. Be off with you.'

The door had scarcely closed behind Greene before Clairval gave a wolfish grin in the direction of Pat, who was being held in a cruel grip by Fernando, the larger of the two bruisers. 'Teach that fool a lesson he won't forget,' he ordered, 'and throw him into the street when you've done with him. You've had your last guinea from me, O'Hare.'

Before Pat lost consciousness under Fernando's unkind ministrations he had one last spasm of regret: that his loose tongue had put not only himself, but Luke Harcourt and the pretty woman he had been squiring at Islington Fair, at risk. Whatever the cost, he must find some way of warning him.

The Romanies had arrived at a nameless heath some forty miles out of London. Nameless to Anne, that was. Bad weather had set in before they left

Greenwich, but by the time that they had spent two days at a small horsefair at Staines it had turned again and had remained gloriously fine and sunny.

A fortnight had passed. The only drawback in using the gypsies to help him and Anne escape Luke found, was that he had to travel at their pace. But the unlikelihood that Clairval would guess what they were doing more than cancelled out the slowness of their progress.

Most of the women and some of the men were sitting outside the tents watching the riders perform. Today they were all, one after another, to gallop across the heath whilst performing the trick of which Luke had spoken to Jasper: the twist under the horse's belly. And Luke was to perform it, too.

The fortnight had seen a vast improvement in his equestrian ability, but even so Anne's heart was in her mouth, her sewing in her hand unheeded, as she watched the riders line up. Luke was to be the last one to go, followed only by Tawno, who gave each rider the signal to begin. Jasper Petulengro, as befitted the Pharaoh, was at the end of the run to salute each rider, whether successful, or unsuccessful, as he arrived.

The *chovihani* placed a calming hand on Anne's wrist. She felt her pulse—which was galloping as hard as the horses were like to do—and said, 'Fear not, I prophesy that today Scribe will gain a new name as a reward for his hard work.'

It began. The first three riders were successful, but the fourth failed to swing his body round correctly and regain his seat. His horse went careering away with him dangling upside down under its belly, before he ended on the ground. He lay quite still and a couple of the gypsies went over to him and helped him to his feet. He had broken his arm.

And he was one who had often done the trick before! Anne's fears for Luke grew, but as one rider after another reached Jasper, the trick accomplished, they diminished a little—until Tawno gave Luke the signal to begin his run.

Now he was thundering towards them, and halfway along the run she saw him prepare to turn and swivel to lie safely tucked beneath his horse's belly, only righting himself shortly before he reached Jasper.

She could not bear to watch him! Even as Luke had begun the trick Anne dropped her sewing to the ground, her head between her knees, and prayed...

For her prayer to be disturbed by applause and cries of triumph from the watching riders who had finished their run. Luke had done it, and was swinging upright again even as he reached Jasper to greet him with his right hand held high and a look of triumph on his face such as Anne had never seen before.

And then it was Tawno's turn, and he swivelled under his horse not once, but twice, to show that he was master.

Once arrived in front of Jasper he gave the signal for the troop to dismount. Then he turned to Luke to hold his hand high. 'Not Scribe,' he proclaimed, 'but Orion is your name. Hunter you shall be, and so shall the Romanies know you. You may join Stella in the heavens.'

Luke had never known such a sense of accomplishment. A fortnight's gruelling training had transformed him in both mind and body. He saw Anne coming towards him, her hands held out, her face full of joy on hearing Tawno baptise him, for baptism it was.

He caught her by the waist and swung her round and round. 'Oh, Anne, Stella, my star, did you see me?'

When she shook her head at him, saying, 'Oh, Luke, I couldn't… I didn't see a thing… I was so frightened for you,' he took that as a testimony of her love for him, and kissed her full on the lips before them all.

'Oh, Anne, you must watch me. Only then will my day be complete.'

Luke bowed to Tawno, and asked 'May I?' of his master, who gave him permission so that he remounted and galloped again in the opposite direction, this time with Anne watching. Love and triumph combined saw him perform the trick even more gracefully than before, for on his first run he had almost lost his balance as he had begun to turn under his horse.

Stars! Her eyes were stars to greet him with when he dismounted, still full of his triumph. There on the heath under Apollo's golden chariot, the sun, which was now running towards September's scents and fruitfulness, Luke and Anne embraced again.

Nothing was left of the fine lady and gentleman whom they had once been. They were as one with the Romanies who surrounded them. Orion and Stella, fallen from the heavens to spend a little time on earth before they took their place among the stars again...

Oh, it was glorious to be young and in love, to know that one's mind and body did one's bidding. One thing, and one thing only was lacking, and that was for the two bodies to become one, and surely the time for that was almost upon them before summer fled and winter arrived.

After Tawno and the horsemen had performed

a galaxy of simpler tricks and team manoeuvres in which Luke doggedly played his part, he dismissed them for the day after the rest of the Rom had applauded them for their virtuosity.

'Next week,' Tawno announced, 'when we visit Aldershot, we shall try out our new tricks—and our new rider. Orion, my brother, now that you are truly one of us, the Pharaoh—' he meant Jasper Petulengro '—wishes to speak to you concerning your woman. Go to his tent where he awaits you.'

Now what could this mean? Luke was full of excitement. That very morning Jasper had said something to him, which indicated that he approved of the fact that he and Anne had obeyed his orders and refrained from becoming lovers until he had decided whether he could give them authority to marry according to the laws of the Rom.

Luke could hardly contain himself as he unsaddled his horse, fed and watered it, and saw that it was comfortable in the pen where he and his fellow steeds were kept once their work was over. After that, he ran down to the brook at the corner where the heath met the wood, washed himself, and made sure that everything about him was proper for an audience with the king. For King Jasper was and so conducted himself and, in calling on the Rom for help Luke had given them the right to demand that he follow their way of life.

Clean, refreshed, his sweaty shirt changed for a sweet-smelling one, his boots removed and a pair of soft-soled shoes exchanged for them, Luke made his way into the presence. Tawno was already there, and a group of the older gypsies. Anne, also in clean clothing, stood to one side, the *chovihani* and a group of older women, including Tawno's wife, at her back.

Jasper was seated on a highbacked chair, almost like a throne. On seeing Luke he called, 'Come, Orion, my brother, for now you are so named, for I have a judgment to make concerning yourself and Stella. Come forward also, Stella. For your supporters, I appoint Tawno and the *chovihani* my wife—if supporters you need.'

Neither Luke nor Anne needed a second bidding. They moved forward to stand before Jasper, their supporters behind them. Jasper said in a voice as stern as any Luke had yet heard from him, ' Join your right hand to Stella's left, Orion, and swear that you will speak true. After you have finished, Stella must so swear, too. If either of you should lie, then may the great author of the Universe strike you down.'

Luke took Anne's hand and, before he could stop himself, kissed it. He had no idea of what was to come, or what further ordeals might await them both, but he was ready and willing to obey his master. George IV might sit on the throne of England, but here on the heath, the sun shining down on them, a small wind blowing, his writ no longer ran. The law of the Rom was all.

They both swore to tell true, and when they had done, Jasper said, 'Stella, our sister, it is reported that you had a husband who treated you cruelly until you fled from the terror he wrought upon you. Is this story true? Swear!'

Anne's voice was low but firm. 'I swear that this is true.'

'Stella, my sister, when did your husband last lie with you in a true fashion, as a man lies with a woman to make a child? Tell true, now.'

For a moment Anne did not answer him, but hung her head. She began to shiver, and Luke pressed her hand in sympathy to let her know that she was not alone, that his love went with her.

Finally she raised her head. 'For the last year before I fled him over six months ago, we did not lie together as man and wife, and before that he was only able to do so after inflicting great cruelties on me. At the end he wished to put me in a madhouse, to live there for the rest of my days. This I swear before you—and before God.'

Rage, red and fierce, ran through Luke. The new strength, the new fortitude which he had gained from living and working among the gypsies had also had the effect of making his desire to protect Anne so strong that he now knew that he would kill for her—or suffer for her, if that was required of him. Now it was he who shivered and Anne who pressed his hand lovingly.

'And, Orion, my brother. You knew that Stella, who wishes to be your wife, had suffered greatly at the hands of the man who called himself husband?'

'Yes, this I swear,' replied Luke firmly. 'Not as to the details, for these are for Stella to know, and no one else, but that she had been treated with great cruelty is a matter of common knowledge.'

Jasper rose from his chair, and walked to where they stood.

He placed both his hands on their clasped ones, and said in a loud voice. 'May all the Rom hear what I have to say,' for while they had been talking the whole camp, men, women and children had arrived to stand in a circle around them, 'By heath and by hearth, by my will and rule as Pharaoh, I say that Stella's marriage was, by the law of the Rom, no marriage, and is thus ended. Let all who hear me acknowledge this.' He paused, and the assembled crowd cried with one voice, 'Aye'.

'And do you, Orion and Stella, together promise that you will remain faithful to one another and the marriage bond until death shall claim you?'

Facing one another, hands still clasped, and speaking together, they both said with the utmost solemnity, 'This we swear.'

'And now hear this. By heath and by hearth, by the law of the Rom, I declare Orion and Stella to be man and wife. That none shall come between them, or part them. This is my will, that of the Pharaoh. More, their supporters, Tawno and the tribe's *chovihani* shall lead them to the spot before the brook where a broom has been placed on the ground, and as token of their becoming one, not two, they shall jump over the broom and become one forever. Tawno! Lead the way!'

It was as impressive a ceremony as either Luke or Anne had ever seen. Out in the open, walking together, still hand in hand behind Tawno and the *chovihani* they led a small procession. At the head of it several of the younger children marched, carrying boughs of beech and willow, magic symbols of the Rom's long past. Behind them streamed Jasper's entire tribe, with him bringing up the rear, alone and majestic, his wife a little before him.

Solemnly Anne and Luke jumped over the broom, but there was one final rite yet to come.

Jasper moved forward saying, 'And now the exchange of blood.' Whilst they held their hands out
towards him he made, with the utmost ceremony,
a small nick on each of their wrists with a silver
knife, and mixed together the resulting blood
which flowed from them.

'Thus I proclaim you truly one, in blood and in
love.' He swung round to face the procession, crying, 'Fiddlers, I bid you play a merry song to send
Orion and Stella happily on their marriage way. And
if Stella's one-time husband shall dare to try to come
between them, then the curse of the Rom be upon
him and may he choke on his own blood. This is the
word of me, Jasper Petulengro, your Pharaoh!'

They were married.

Anne was free of Clairval. And whether the marriage was legal or not, neither of them cared. For
were they not part of the Rom now? And even if
one day, they were to leave the Rom behind, then
what they could not leave behind was the authority which had joined them together.

Oblivious of the crowd around them, of the
music of the fiddlers, of the chatter of the monkeys
on their sticks which some of the Rom had
brought with them to see Orion and Stella married,
they embraced.

'Tonight,' cried Luke fiercely, and 'Tonight,'

echoed Anne, for there was a tent prepared for their use alone, as ordered by Jasper, now their protector as well as their leader.

Until then there was music and dancing and feasting. Nor could either of them have thought that on the day that Luke had arrived back in Islington, a train of events had been set in motion which would end with them in one another's arms, under a clear sky, about to become man and wife.

Chapter Eleven

At last they were alone. The dancing, the feasting and the drinking were over. They had been led to the tent by all the Rom, the children at the front of the procession: the same children who had earlier made wreaths of late summer daisies and had crowned Orion and Stella with them.

The noise of the camp slowly died away. Silence fell. Outside the tent as well as in. Luke had taken Anne in his arms the moment that they were alone and had laid her down on a bed of the Rom's finest blankets given to them for this night, before he carefully removed their crowns of daisies. Tomorrow they would wear them again for a brief space as witness to the marriage's consummation.

He knelt down beside Anne—to discover that she was trembling, and that slow tears were running down her face. All her gaiety of the past hours had disappeared, and Luke knew quite well what was wrong. Throughout her short married life she had experienced what should have been an act of love as an act of terror where pain was inflicted, not pleasure given.

During their marriage ceremony, and after, she had been buoyed up by the sheer delight of knowing that Luke was hers at last, but now that they were alone came the other knowledge—that being his she must give him her body, and that was sufficient to revive all her fears. Oh, she was not afraid that Luke would hurt her, she knew that he would not, but she was fearful that she might not be able to respond to him as she ought.

What if she were to turn away from him in fear when he began to make love to her, as she had tried to turn away from Clairval during those dreadful nights of torment, long endured? She had told Luke only a few days ago that she burned for him—but that was when he was forbidden to her, and lovemaking was a distant thing. Now that the moment of consummation was upon her, all her fears were revived again.

'What is it, my love?' Luke asked her tenderly, putting out a gentle finger to brush away the betraying tears.

'Oh Luke, I'm frightened. Not of you, but that

I might not be able to love you as I ought.' She shuddered beneath his ardent gaze.

Clairval! Clairval had done this to her. Luke wished on him the death to which Jasper had doomed him to for what he had already done, let alone what he might do to Anne if he were fortunate enough to recapture her.

'You know that I shall not hurt you,' he told her, without further touching her.

'Oh, yes, Luke. I know that you are not at all like *him*. It is myself I am frightened of, not you.'

'Then we shall go slowly, my darling. For much though I wish to make you my wife, I do not want you to be truly mine until we are united in shared joy. For me to do otherwise to you would make me nothing but a brute beast.'

He did not say, 'Like Clairval.' He did not need to.

Anne knew full well what he meant. She held out her arms to him, whispering, 'Lie by me, Luke. I want to feel you near me.'

So, she was welcoming him. Which was promising, but did not mean that he could fall upon her. He must do nothing to remind her of *him* and his wicked demands. Slowly, slowly, Luke lay beside her. She turned towards him, rested her head on his chest, and he put an arm under her body around her shoulders so that they lay entwined.

'There,' and his voice was so gentle that she could hardly hear it. 'That was an easy beginning, was it not? And at your invitation, I may add, Mrs Harcourt. What would you wish me to do next?'

She spoke into his chest so softly that he had to strain to hear what she said, 'You could kiss me, Luke, on the cheek. I think that I should like that. That was the first kiss you ever gave me, at Mrs Britten's. Remember?'

Remember?

Of course he remembered, and he also remembered that in a mood of joyous spontaneity she had almost given herself to him then. So yes, he would do her bidding, even though to hold her so intimately was becoming a sweet torment to him, for his body was free of his mind and wished to do more with Anne than exchange simple kisses. But, if he were to gain her confidence and bring her safely through the gates of passion into the wide lands beyond them, he must subdue himself—or be like Clairval, unconsidering of another.

'Oh, I think that I could manage that,' he said at last.

This brought a ghostly chuckle from her as he kissed the warm cheek so near to his. And having done so he added, in as light a voice as he could, 'Kisses have no meaning between true lovers unless they are exchanged. Mr Harcourt would like a similar caress from Mrs Harcourt.'

So she kissed him, mimicking him before she did so! 'Oh, I think that I could manage that!'

'The next step,' Luke announced in an important voice, as though about to embark on a sermon, 'is to kiss together. The mouth is the usual spot chosen—at least to begin with. Shall we try it?'

Her answer was to turn her face so trustingly towards his that a strong spasm of desire ran through him. He restrained himself, put his mouth to hers, in a child's kiss first, with closed lips, and then, as she did not resist him, but put up her right hand to stroke his face, he deepened and strengthened it, pushing her lips apart so that his roving tongue might enter her mouth, and caress hers.

The effect on Anne was electric: Signor Galvani's frogs all over again. A thrill of pleasure shot through her so strongly that she sat up, tore her mouth from Luke's and exclaimed breathlessly, 'Oh, Luke, whatever did you do to me?'

He lay there looking at her. Her eyes were wide, like stars, her face was flushed, her lips were swollen.

'I kissed you,' he told her, 'and kisses are supposed to be exciting and pleasurable. I take it that you were thoroughly pleasured?' Her innocence enchanted, but at the same time saddened him, because it told him of the mistreatment which she had suffered, so that the simple early pleasures of loving had passed her by.

'Shall we try it again?' he offered.

'Oh, yes, please,' breathed Anne fervently, falling back into his arms, and offering him her mouth, which he took, more urgently this time. Next he set his hands awandering around her body, so that after the first shock of discovering the delights of kissing, Anne found that being stroked whilst being kissed heightened her pleasure immensely.

So much so that she began to kiss and stroke him in return, so that *she* might give *him* delight. Which she did, for after a moment or two he gave a little groan and rolled away from her. His desire for her was so strong that for him to be stroked so intimately by her was almost enough to send him over the edge of pleasure, he had been continent for so long.

'My darling,' he told her, 'we have begun in proper form, and as a child learns to walk, step by slow step, as he advances from crawling, so shall we too, this night, advance to where we may ourselves be lovers, as well as husband and wife. And for your next lesson you must allow me to see you, all of you.'

'All of me? You would like that, Luke?' So strong was the delight that Anne was already feeling, that it had her sitting up, and beginning to pull off her dress to please him.

'Dear girl,' Luke was laughing in joy at her eagerness, 'I know that you wish to please me, but one of a man's truest delights is undressing his love for the first time—and being undressed by her.'

'It is?'

Anne's eyes were full of wonderment. She remembered Clairval tearing at her clothed body on their wedding night, and entering her, with oh, such pain, that the memory of it set her shivering again. Nevertheless, she stilled herself, and when Luke gently drew her down again, and began to remove her clothing from her, piece by piece, she felt her fears beginning to recede. So much so that she joined in the game by unbuttoning his shirt, to reveal the dark and curling hairs on his chest.

Instinctively, without thinking, she buried her face in them to smell the essential Luke, man touched with horse, and the strong yellow soap which all the Rom used, including herself.

Luke stroked her dark head, realising what a major step she had taken in the game of love. He lifted her head back to kiss her on the lips, deeper and stronger than ever, before he helped her to pull off his velveteen breeches, until at last they were naked together, and Luke could see for the first time the lovely lines of Anne's beautiful body.

Even then, although Anne drank in the strength of Luke's chest and shoulders, the flatness of his stomach, all his muscles strengthened and hardened by the past few weeks of forced exercise, she dare not look at him, nor touch him, *there*. For *there* was what Clairval had used so often to hurt her in his thwarted attempts to pleasure himself or make a child.

Luke saw her fear, and inwardly cursed Clairval yet again. He was a third presence in their marriage bed, but he was determined to exorcise his ghost, to teach Anne that love could be joy, even though his task might be long and hard. He pulled her to him and began to stroke her all over until, when he reached her breasts, the points of her desire, she gave a little cry of joy achieved. But he dare not yet go near her dark and curling fleece, which hid what might, he hoped, yet give her her truest pleasure.

So gentle was he, so sweetly loving, that Anne sighed, and felt sleep beginning to claim her as she lay so trustingly in her lover's arms.

Which would not do at all, so that Luke deepened his caresses, until all desire to sleep fled and

Anne found herself again full of strange flutterings and a strong wish to be nearer, ever nearer to the man who was loving her so considerately.

Time passed, and slowly, slowly, Luke led Anne towards the consummation which they both desired. How she came to be beneath him was a mystery. How it was that the most intimate caresses, which she had previously feared, came to be sources of such pleasure that she begged him for more…and more, Anne never knew.

Except that at some point it seemed the most natural thing in the world for her to caress Luke there, feeling him warm and velvet in her hand, so that she had no fear that inside her he would feel any different.

After such a major step, the knowledge that he would be part of her was simply an extension of the joy that love-making was already bringing to her. So much so that, when they were finally one, the ugly spectre of Clairval flew away for good and all, and she was shaking with ecstasy in Luke's arms, all fears forgotten.

At the last, ecstasy over, the tears running down Anne's face were those of joy, not pain, and she was clutching her dear love as though she never meant to let him go, crying, 'Oh, Luke, my love, my love, I had not known…'

She did not say what she had not known, but shortly after Luke had made love to her for the second time, and she was nearing the sweet sleep of its aftermath, she murmured drowsily, 'Poor Clairval…'

'Poor Clairval!' Luke jerked erect in surprise and shock at such an unlikely statement from Clairval's late victim. 'How so?'

'Because he never experienced the joy that you and I have just shared, for he thought only of himself and never of his partner.'

It was Clairval's epitaph. Their marriage might now go ahead without his shadow marring it. One final thing that Anne said before sleep claimed them both was, 'Oh, Luke, I hope that you do not think me wicked to forget the teachings of the church and enjoy my union with you when, surely, no parson would think our marriage legal.

'I remember once, I went to the Rector of Clairval church to ask him for sanctuary from Clairval's mistreatment, and he told me to be a good woman and return to him, for I must be very sinful if my husband thought it necessary to correct me so sternly!'

Luke kissed her. 'Dear Anne. He was wrong, and I know that not all parsons are like him. He was probably frightened of Clairval, too. And no, I don't think that either of us are wicked. Only the law that makes a woman like you a victim of a man like Clairval.'

After that reassurance they both slept—to wake with the dawn and love again.

The world did not cease to turn as the lovers made their slow way westwards to what they hoped would be salvation. In his rooms in London, Pat O'Hare nursed his broken wrist and his black eye and regretted his betrayal of Luke Harcourt to a man who wished him harm. He had tried to make amends by sending for his friend, George Jackson, who had stared in astonishment at Pat's battered body.

'An accident merely,' lied Pat, pre-empting George's demands for an explanation. 'As you see, I cannot write. You would do me a great favour if you would act as my secretary and write a letter to Luke Harcourt on my behalf.'

If George thought that there was more to Pat's injuries than Pat cared to confess, he did not say so. Instead, he carefully penned a cryptic letter to Luke in which Pat said that a mutual enemy, of whom Luke was aware, was on his trail, following him to the west country, intending to do him harm. A word to the wise, was his last sentence.

'Now what the devil is all this about?' wondered George aloud, for Pat to say,

'Best for you not to know. Oh, George, I've been a damned careless fool and put Luke in danger. Seal the letter for me and take it to Lyndale's place in Piccadilly. If he and the Countess have gone to Haven's End, then ask the housekeeper—or whoever you speak to—to send it on to Wiltshire immediately. I can only pray that somehow it reaches Luke before danger does.'

After George had gone, promising to do everything which was asked of him, Pat sank back, his heart a little lighter. At least he had done *something* to try to warn Luke, even if that something might be too little and too late. He tried not to think of what would happen to him if Clairval ever found out what he had done.

Clairval was on his way to Haven's End.

Like George Jackson, he had gone to Piccadilly to find that Lyndale and his wife had already left town. The housekeeper had said quite categorically, in response to his enquiries, that Mr Luke was not with them, indeed, had scarcely visited them all summer.

Too busy seducing my wife, was Clairval's inward furious response before returning to plan his journey to the west. He would travel with as much speed as possible, stopping at inns and hostelries on the way to try to discover whether the guilty pair had stayed there for the night. Finding no such evidence as he drove towards that damned swine Lyndale's place was not calculated to improve his temper, nor did it. Luke Harcourt and Anticleia, Lady Clairval, seemed to have disappeared from the face of the earth.

Clairval was not the only traveller pursuing a westward path towards Haven's End. In a private room in a set of offices in Whitehall, a Very Grand Personage indeed gave an audience to the Runner, Jenkinson. They had met before when Jenkinson had done this Grand Personage—and the State— some favours of which none but he and the Grand Personage knew.

'Well, what is it that you have discovered this time—and how much do you want for it?' demanded the Personage, who no more wished to waste words than Jenkinson did. It was a pleasure to deal with him after Clairval.

'Something which I think will please you, seeing that the party in question never votes with the government in the Lords.'

'Who is…?'

'Clairval, m'lord. The Marquess of. Ah, I see by your expression that you and he are scarcely bosom bows.'

'Indeed not,' replied the Personage frostily. 'Out with it, man. What do you know to his discredit?'

Jenkinson told him.

'Murder and planned murder, aye. That is a juicy tit-bit for an evil-minded cat to devour at leisure. I have a wish to be evil-minded where Clairval is concerned. His day of reckoning is long overdue. One more gross scandal in high life and those who plot revolution here will have a field day. You are sure that our man has committed, or intends to commit, both these crimes?'

Jenkinson nodded. 'Quite sure. I have the depositions as to the murder of his steward. Many who were frightened of him have now become willing to shop him so that they may not be the next target for his murderous temper.'

'Quite so. And his intention to murder his wife—when he catches her and imprisons her again—how do you hope to prove that?'

'Because I have depositions as to the death of his first wife, and to his declared intention before witnesses of his determination to dispose of the second—to secure her estate.'

The Grand Personage paced the room in silence,

pausing to stare at a flattering portrait of King George IV which transformed the gross elderly man he was to something like the handsome young man he had once been.

He turned to face Jenkinson. 'So! I would like this business solved without scandal—you understand me. When you catch up with him—please God before he reaches his wife—you will use your discretion as to what action to take. You understand me,' he repeated.

'I will see that you are re-instated as a Runner, given proper warrants—including a blank one—which will allow you to arrest him and take him to the nearest gaol, to be brought to London to be tried before his peers in the House of Lords—if that is what you think will answer. But I would prefer the matter settled by other means.'

He repeated the last words again, adding, 'I do not need to tell you that I want this disposed of without scandal and a great noise being made. I shall thus support whatever measure you see fit to take to ensure that end—on condition that, if you make a mistake and are caught out in it, I shall disclaim all knowledge of you if you try to involve me. On the other hand, your reward will be great if all goes well. You have my word on that—as you have had in the past.'

It would have to do. Jenkinson did not intend to be caught, and had more sense than to try to involve the Grand Personage before him if things did go wrong—which they wouldn't.

'You may depend upon me, m'lord,' he said, bowing, 'to dispose of this affair in as discreet and satisfactory a manner as possible.'

He told the Grand Personage nothing of the details of his search: that Greene, who had been dismissed by Clairval for incompetence, had told him that Clairval believed that Luke Harcourt, the natural son of Lord Lyndale, had made away with Lady Clairval and hidden her. It was assumed that he would take her to his father's home in the west country.

Greene's reward had been that Jenkinson had hired him as an aide. 'To do exactly what you're told mind, and not go off on your own. Disobey me, and I'll have your guts for garters.'

So an agreement was struck. Greene knew that Jenkinson was a swine, but he was a fair swine, unlike Clairval. He would not swindle you unless you had swindled him first. It would be a pleasure to join forces with him and try to put one over on Clairval—who deserved all the bad luck which the two Runners could arrange for him.

'Thing is, though,' said Greene, 'I couldn't find

any trace of where Harcourt and the woman had gone—and nor could my haughty m'lord. Disappeared off the face of the earth, they have, and me turned away because I'd lost their trail. Truth is, I never found it.

'But I've been thinking. Harcourt had a friend, Pat O'Hare, who was one of Clairval's toadies. He fell foul of m'lord and m'lord had him given a beating for his pains. What say we interview Master O'Hare? I'll be bound he'd tell us what he knows of Harcourt, if only to do Clairval a bad turn. After all, they must have gone somewhere.'

'True,' Jenkinson agreed. 'Always better to try something rather than nothing. At the moment we're chasing moonbeams.'

So it was that Pat O'Hare, still nursing his injuries, and a bitter hate in his heart for Clairval, was surprised to find the two Runners on his doorstep.

At first he refused to let them in. 'How the devil do I know that you're both not still working for Clairval—tell me that?'

'Working against him, more like,' grinned Jenkinson. 'He's turned us off, as he turned you off. Only he thought it best not to have us ill-treated. If you'd like to pay him back for your broken wrist, now's your only chance. Tell us what you know of Luke Harcourt. We're after Clairval, not him, but find Harcourt and sooner or later we shall find Clairval.'

'Luke's my friend,' grunted Pat, reluctantly letting them in. 'I've already done him one ill turn, I don't want to do him another.'

'Nor will you.' Jenkinson was looking about him. 'He's disappeared, and apparently the lady with him. Now, what do you know of his haunts—where might he have gone? Talk freely, you may not know that you are already aware of something which might help us, only you don't know of its importance.'

The two men grilled Pat mercilessly once he was convinced that they truly did not mean Luke harm.

He appeared to know nothing useful until Jenkinson said, desperate to try anything, 'Did you ever meet the lady?'

'Yes,' said Pat. 'Once. At Islington Fair. She was there with him. She and Luke's landlady.' He smiled reminiscently. 'I thought that they were sweet on one another then. I saw him take her over to meet the gypsies.'

'Meet the gypsies?' Jenkinson took Pat up smartly. 'Harcourt is friendly with the gypsies?'

'Yes,' said Pat, puzzled, and wondering what that had got to do with anything. 'Always has been. Writes about them. Been friendly with them since he was a little lad.'

Jenkinson jumped to his feet. 'That's it! That's how they could have disappeared off the face of the earth. There were gypsies at Greenwich Fair the week they disappeared. What's the odds he took her there, and they're travelling westward with them?'

'To Haven's End, his father, Lord Lyndale's home in Wiltshire,' Pat ventured.

'Oh, I think Master Luke's cleverer than that,' returned Jenkinson. 'He's a writer. That means he can work anywhere. He can't safely live with m'lady here, Clairval being so powerful. Nor can he marry her, either. What price he's making for a seaport? Bristol, mayhap. Somewhere where he could take ship for the Americas.'

Pat looked doubtful, but Greene, who knew Jenkinson and his successful long shots of old, said slowly, 'Aye, that makes sense. They could take off their fine lady and gent's clothes, and melt into the gypsy band… Who would think to find them there? Or identify them easily?'

Jenkinson shook the bemused Pat's hand. 'Thank you for that, sir. It can't hurt to track the gypsy band down and try to find out if they're with them. Better than running round the west country like a headless hen as Clairval is doing.'

'But why follow Luke? Why not follow Clairval if it's him you want to catch?' Pat asked, just before they left.

'Oh, the more we have on him and his villainy, before we catch him, the better,' remarked Jenkinson, looking mysterious.

It was not for such as Pat O'Hare, or even his colleague Greene, to know anything of his collaboration with the Grand Personage, and the real end of his quest.

Now that he had mastered all the equestrian tricks and become a trusted member of Tawno's troop, Luke found that he had time in the early evening to sit at leisure under the shadiest and most secluded tree he could find, and begin to write the novel that had been fermenting at the back of his mind ever since he had left London.

Anne sat by him, sewing, until both of them, tiring of their work at the same time, turned into each other's arms to celebrate as nymph and shepherd should on a bed of grass with the birds calling above them.

Still slowly the gypsies wended their way westward, stopping at fairs and horse fairs to earn their living against the coming winter when all such junketing would stop—until spring returned.

* * *

Late one afternoon after they had left a small
town not far from Salisbury, with their goal of
Bristol drawing ever nearer, Anne arrived to sit by
Luke with the strangest expression on her face. He
was sensitive to all her moods these days and said
at once, 'My love, what is it?'

'Oh, Luke, you will think me fanciful, but I have
just remembered the dream I had last night—or
rather, nightmare. And I know that it came to me
because for the last few days I have had the feeling that we are being watched and followed.'

Ever since the *chovihani* had bestowed the gifts
of empathy and prescience on Anne, she had been
subject to strange visions and what she liked to
think of as understandings. Luke had learned not
to dismiss them.

'No, I don't think that you are being fanciful.
You were right about the red-headed man you
thought was following you—he was. Tell me,
what did the dream say?'

'Nothing directly. Only I learned from it that
we *are* being followed—and by more than one
party. They are not yet near us, and I am not sure
that they know that we are with the gypsies, only
that we are travelling westwards. One of them is
the red-headed man, but it's rather strange. I have

the feeling that this time he does not mean me harm, although I cannot be sure of that. Our other follower is Clairval.'

She did not tell Luke that in her dream the vision of Clairval had been a horrible one. Not only had he been following her at some distance, but in the dream he had caught her up and, having done so, had leaned forward to clutch at her, his face evil and triumphant. But at the very moment in which he had laid his hands on her, a tide of blood had appeared from nowhere and swept him away.

Awake again, Anne could only think that she had been remembering Jasper's curse—that if Clairval tried to harm her again he would choke in his own blood. The vision had been so horrible that she had found her whole body running in sweat and she had been compelled to rise from her bed and towel herself dry. After that, she dared not sleep again, for fear that the vision might return.

Sitting by Luke, though, on a sunny afternoon, the vision seemed far away. On the other hand, her sense of being followed was so strong that she had felt compelled to warn him so that he might speak to Jasper and with his, and the Roms' help, keep watch both when they camped on the heaths and when they travelled the roads.

Luke had heard her out in silence. He was sure

that she was not telling him everything which she had experienced, but he did not badger her for further information.

He said slowly, 'If Clairval has discovered that it was I who rescued you when he came to Islington, then it is possible that he thinks that I am taking you to my father's home at Haven's End. Since we are not going there, that should sidetrack him long enough for us to get clean away. As for your red-headed man, that is a mystery. You're sure that he is following us?'

Anne nodded. 'Quite sure, but it comes to me, as from a distance, that it is Clairval he is following, not us—or rather us and Clairval, but Clairval is his true target.'

She paused, before saying, 'There is another odd thing. I see you and him together—or rather, I don't exactly see you, but I know that you and the red-headed man are strangely interlinked—and that I am not with you when you meet.'

For a moment she looked so frustrated that Luke was afraid that she might be going to cry—and that would never do. Before he could reassure her, she added a rider to what she had been saying. 'This gift makes me fearful, Luke, for it never speaks quite plainly. I have to make sense of it, and I can never know whether I have succeeded until what it tells me is upon me—and then it is often too late to do anything about it.'

Oh, but that was the trouble with magic, both black and white, was it not? Luke thought of what a greater writer than he was had once written, the devil 'palters with us in a double sense…' On the other hand, his reason told him that it was not good for mankind to know too much about its future fate.

In that case, he thought robustly, best not to know anything at all! But he could not say so to Anne, who had a burden to bear and one which she had not chosen. The *chovihani* had called it a gift, but the gift was two-edged and both gave and took away.

He put a friendly arm around Anne's shoulders, not a loving one, for Anne was not in the mood to enjoy the wilder passions. 'Let it pass,' he said. 'Do not brood, my darling. What will happen, will happen, and there's an end of it.'

But, as so often happens, life would not let them treat the matter so easily.

The next morning, Jasper came to him as he was about to mount his horse, and said curtly, 'A word, Brother Orion. Come where we may be private.'

They strode away from the rest, out of earshot. Jasper spoke bluntly and to the point. 'We are being followed—or rather, I suspect, you and Stella are being followed.'

Luke's reaction was instantaneous. 'Clairval!' he exclaimed. 'But how did he discover that we are with you?'

Jasper shook his head. 'Not Clairval. Tawno knows them. He has seen them several times over the past few days. He knows one of them, a one-time Bow Street Runner called Jenkinson. A red-haired man. Another of his kidney is with him.'

'But they are Clairval's men,' said Luke, despair in his voice. 'Jenkinson led Clairval to Anne's refuge in Islington. No doubt he is still doing Clairval's dirty work for him.'

'Not so, Orion. The *chovihani* has read him. He is after Clairval, not you, but thinks to find Clairval by waiting until he discovers you. Why, she cannot *scry*.'

By *scry* Jasper meant foretell or read the future. 'What she does know is that Clairval is not far away, and him she can read and his near future, for his wickedness is strong. He will find you, Orion, but not Stella or us. You understand what this means?'

His face was so dour, so foreboding, that Luke was filled with a nameless dread.

'You think that the *chovihani* tells true, Jasper?'

'I am sure of it. She says the omens are among

the strongest that she has ever experienced. She thinks that Stella is reading them, too, but will not face their meaning because she does not wish to.'

That would explain the distress which Anne was suffering. It was bound up with him—although he was sure that, unlike the *chovihani* whose powers were so much stronger, Anne knew none of the details of the future which she feared.

He nodded agreement. 'The only thing I understand from what you tell me is that I must leave you—and Stella—and that for her safety.'

'To act as decoy, Orion, with all that that implies. Not immediately, but in a few days when the moon is full and Clairval, and the red-headed man, are nearer to us. And, Orion, I have hard words for you. You face a testing time, and how you come through it will determine not only your fate, but Stella's. If you hold the faith, and play the man, as Tawno has taught you, then all will be well. But weaken, and even the *chovihani,* Pharaoh's wife, cannot save you.'

To leave Anne behind, to travel alone, away from the Rom to draw Clairval and the red-headed man away, so that both he and Anne might be saved, was in itself a hard task for Luke. But Jasper was hinting at something more.

'You said that I was to be tested, Jasper. In what way? I would be prepared.'

'Alas, I cannot tell you. All that the *chovihani* knows is that there will be a test and that you must pass it. She does not know its nature. Believe me, if she did, we would tell you.'

That was that. He looked away from Jasper and saw that his wife was talking to Anne most earnestly. By the expression on Anne's face, she was undoubtedly telling her of their coming parting. Oh, how hard it would be to leave her, so soon, so soon. Particularly since, for all Jasper's promises, he knew that the end which they both desired would not necessarily be ensured.

Their safety was conditional on his behaviour during a difficult and unknown test. Almost Luke wavered. But the hard core at the centre of his being, which his days with the Romanies had enlarged and strengthened, had him accepting the doom which lay before him.

From the moment he had met Anne, this time of trial and trouble had been waiting for him and he would be but a poor thing if he took the easy path because salvation lay along a difficult one.

Almost at once he began to plan what he would do, and his next words drew strong approval from Jasper.

'So be it,' he said. 'Amen. And, Jasper, if I am not to betray where I have been, I must turn myself into

Luke Harcourt, a fine young gentleman, and forget Orion who rides with Tawno and the troop.'

'Indeed and indeed. We shall advise you on
what route to take to draw them away from us.
They will be delighted once they find you, and
think that Stella cannot be far away, so you must
be far away from us.'

'And if I succeed, Jasper, and pass the test,
what then?'

'Why, fate and circumstance will tell you what
to do, Orion, and in order to prove yourself worthy, you will do it.'

Well, you could hardly get more cryptic than
that, was Luke's sardonic inward response, but it
would have to do.

Chapter Twelve

'James, I am troubled in my mind over Luke. Not only did we not see him in town this summer, but we have not heard a word from him in months. Since we arrived here I have written to him at his lodgings in Islington, but have received no answer. Such conduct is most unlike him. It is almost as though he has disappeared off the face of the earth.'

Cressy was on the terrace overlooking the park at Haven's End. James had just arrived to sit with her, after spending the morning with his agent. He frowned a little, and said, 'I agree with you, my love. Earlier, back in town, I thought that you might be repining overmuch on his absence, but this prolonged lack of news from him worries me more than a little.'

His answer relieved his wife. Cressy had begun to think that she might be making overmuch of Luke's change of habit, but if James, that model of steadiness and applied reason, was beginning to be troubled by his son's untoward behaviour, then it was likely that something might be wrong.

'I suppose,' she said slowly, 'it is feeling so helpless that exaggerates the worry. I know that he is a grown man, but he has always been so considerate of us before...'

'Over-considerate, perhaps,' added James, as his wife's voice trailed off. 'I will promise you this. If yet another month goes by without word of him, then I will travel to London and try to track him down. Will that do?'

Before Cressy could answer, the butler came through the glass doors which led to the terrace. 'There is a person to see you, m'lord. It is the Marquess of Clairval and he says that his business with you is most urgent.'

James rose, a look of surprise on his face. 'Clairval here? On urgent business with me? What the deuce can it be? Where have you put him?'

'In the drawing-room, m'lord.' He hesitated, then added, 'I should perhaps say that he appears to be in somewhat of a high temper, m'lord.' He said no more, but James knew at once that if his trusted servant felt it necessary to make such a personal remark about a superior then it would be as well to take heed of what he was being told.

He found Clairval in the drawing-room, pacing up and down like a caged tiger. He advanced on James, saying in an angry voice, 'Ah, Lyndale, at last. I have somewhat of a bone to pick with you!'

James, Lord Lyndale, had a high temper of his own, usually kept under restraint. He held himself in check with difficulty, so menacing was Clairval's manner.

'Indeed, Clairval. And what bone is that? Not politics, I hope. I thought that I had done with them when I reached Wiltshire.'

'Politics!' sneered Clairval. 'I am not interested in politics! No, I have reason to believe that you are harbouring your bastard, Luke Harcourt, and my wife, Lady Clairval, with whom he has eloped, or abducted, or run away with, call it what you will.'

'Luke! Run away with your wife!' James could hardly have been, or sounded, more flabbergasted. 'Run away with your missing wife? I was not aware that he was even acquainted with her.'

'Oh, don't try to flim-flam me, Lyndale! I know for certain that he is my wife's paramour and has made off with her. And what more likely than that he has brought her here?'

James held his temper in check with difficulty.

'Then your idea of what is more likely, Clairval, differs completely from mine. I have not seen my son for several months, and he is certainly not here, my word upon it.'

'I think nothing of any man's word, Lyndale. Least of all yours, seeing that you represent a party for which I feel no respect, and have spawned a son whose honour is as low as his birth. No! I demand that you allow me to have Haven's End searched before I accept that the guilty pair are not here.'

'Demand, Clairval? Demand? By what right do you demand anything of me, here, in my own home?'

'By the right of a man whose wife has been reft from him. Suppose it were your wife who was missing, Lyndale, what then?'

This had James reining in his fury. What could he lose—except dignity—by allowing Clairval to conduct a search? Nothing, and since he knew that Luke was not at Haven's End, then he would have the pleasure of seeing Clairval thwarted— and of demanding an apology from him.

'Very well,' he said grudgingly. 'Go ahead, but I warn you that you will find nothing—nor, I may add, has my son been here recently. I repeat, I have not seen him for some months now.'

James was quite unsurprised when the two bruisers for whom Clairval sent found nothing, whilst their master sprawled gracelessly in an armchair in James's drawing-room. Halfway through the wretched business, Cressy, warned by the house-keeper of what was going on, walked in to where James and Clairval sat, glaring at one another.

'Ah, m'lord,' she said sweetly, as Clairval rose slowly to his feet. 'I cannot say that I am hon-oured by your presence, seeing that you only re-main here because you refuse to accept my husband's word of honour. Nevertheless, you are a guest in this house. You will accept a little re-freshment, perhaps.'

She was aware of James's fury that she was of-fering Clairval anything, but Cressy had a mind of her own. She wished to see Clairval wrong-footed a little, and was, up to a point, succeeding.

'Thank you, no,' he said a little more gracefully. Only to revert to savagery again as he went on, 'Any food you could serve me would choke me— in view of the reason I have visited Haven's End at all—the misconduct of your husband's bastard.'

'See here,' began James hotly, his face like thun-der, 'you are not to speak so before my wife...' only for Cressy to interrupt him.

'Oh, do be quiet, James. M'lord Marquess is only speaking as he does to bait you. For you and I to retain our perfect manners in the face of his insults is to win a small battle. You do understand that, m'lord, I trust,' she added, turning towards Clairval, who was wishing that he could give Cressy, Lady Lyndale, a taste of the stick which he had used upon his wife before she had disappeared.

Cressy, well aware of the thoughts which were written so plainly on Clairval's face, waved a hand at Fernando and his minion, who had returned empty-handed from a lengthy search of Haven's End from cellar to attics in company with servants who constantly informed him that Master Luke had not been part of the household since early spring.

'You come empty-handed, I see,' she proclaimed brightly as Fernando shook his head at his master. 'I think that a few apologies are in order, don't you, m'lord? You can breach protocol and begin by doing so to James, since it is he whom you have insulted the most by refusing to accept his word, and then you may pass on to me.'

James was openly smiling. He knew his wife and how little the behaviour of such as Clairval disturbed her. She was the last member of a family noted for its pride and its *savoir faire* and he was amused at Clairval's inability to dent her armour. He knew that armour of old.

Clairval, unable to attack Cressy physically in

order to punish her insolence towards him, rounded on James. 'I wonder at you, Lyndale, I really do, for allowing your termagant of a wife to speak for you. She needs a strong hand to control her, I see, and I advise you to use that strong hand on her as soon as possible—unless you are unmanned quite. Of course, I shall not apologise. I have nothing to apologise for.'

James walked to the door and flung it open. 'I think, Clairval, that it is time that you left, before I order my servants to throw you out of doors. I am beginning to understand why your wife ran away from you. Good day, m'lord. You are not welcome here.'

Whether or not Clairval wished to do more than leave in impotent fury, and without having apologised, James neither knew nor cared, so long as he went.

Their unwanted guest gone, the face he turned on Cressy was a serious one. 'Clairval was wrong in assuming that Luke was here, but I fear that we may now have an explanation for his behaviour. How or why it has happened, how he met her, or what he has done with her, I do not know, but I strongly suspect that Luke *has* run off with Lady Clairval.'

'In that case,' said Cressy sadly, 'we are no wiser than we were. We have no idea of his—or their—

whereabouts. But you said one true thing, James, which makes me fear a little for them both. You said that you understood why his wife left him—as I do—for a harsher, more cruel, man I do not wish to meet. It is plain to me that he is capable of anything.

'But, oh, I do wish that we knew where Luke might be found. I am sorry that he did not see fit to come here if he needed a refuge. And I am sorrier still that the law gives a man like Clairval such complete power over his unfortunate wife.'

He put an arm around Cressy. 'I fear that Luke has made a powerful enemy. But one thing Clairval has done by his conduct towards both you and myself today: he has ensured that if Luke does bring Lady Clairval here, I shall certainly not hand her over to her husband if it prove that he has been as cruel to her as rumour says. Haven's End shall be true to its name, if a haven is what she needs.'

Cressy had never loved him so much. The sense of honour which had driven her husband all his life was as strong as ever. She had never suspected otherwise, but to witness him demonstrate it comforted her.

'I cannot believe that Luke would ever do anything wrong, and so I must believe that he thinks the lady persecuted. I am with you on this, James, if

Luke has run off with her. But, as yet, we have no confirmation of this, only Clairval's suppositions.'

'And the fact that they both seem to have disappeared at the same time. No use in worrying, my dear, but we must be ready for anything.'

Luke and Anne spent their last night together in each other's arms. Earlier, after Luke had told her that he was leaving the Romanies to draw Clairval away from her, she had protested long and tearfully that he must do no such thing. She would take her chances with him.

When he had proved adamant, saying that Jasper and the *chovihani* were agreed upon the matter, Anne had left him to go and argue with the *chovihani*. She found her sitting in the open, looking out across the heath, her eyes blank, in deep meditation.

Anne waited for her to return safely to the mundane world of every day before she spoke to her.

'I don't want Luke to leave us,' she announced bluntly, all her usual tactful charm gone. 'I don't understand why he should put himself into danger.'

'Nor do I,' agreed the *chovihani* 'except that he must. All the signs are that, by doing so, he will prevent your enemy from finding you until shortly before his doom is upon him. For him to find you earlier than that means that he will capture you and take you into eternal imprisonment and death.'

She added after a moment, 'I can tell you nothing more than that, for more than that I cannot see.'

'That is not sufficient.' Anne was firm. 'All the signs, you said. What of the tarot cards? What do they say?' She had seen the *chovihani* use the cards to tell the future more than once.

'They say the same.'

'Then show me.'

Anne's tone was peremptory, that of Lady Clairval. It was a tone which she had never used before to anyone.

The *chovihani* sighed. 'Child, child,' she said reprovingly, 'you lack trust. Neverthless, come with me, and you shall shuffle the cards and I shall read them, and if they tell a different story today, then Orion need not leave us.'

So it was agreed. The *chovihani* went to the tent which she shared with her husband, Jasper, the Pharaoh, and came out carrying a small wooden box containing a pack of tarot cards wrapped in a square of purple silk. No one but their owner was allowed to touch them, apart from the person asking a question of them, who was always known as the querent and who was allowed to shuffle them.

'One question,' said the *chovihani* firmly, 'and a horseshoe spread to answer it.'

'This is my question,' said Anne equally firmly, as she accepted the cards and began to shuffle them. 'Must Luke leave me tomorrow in order to ensure our safety?'

'That is plain enough, Stella. Now hand me back the cards and watch.'

The *chovihani* began to lay out, face down on the grass before her, seven cards in the shape of a horseshoe: the traditional pattern for answering a single question. Each card had a specific part to play in the answer after it was turned over.

Anne had already been taught how to use the cards and had decided to acquire a pack of her own. Now she watched as the *chovihani* turned the cards over, one by one, and began to read them. The last card of all was the one which would tell Anne whether or not Luke would achieve success for her if he left.

Anxiously, Anne watched as the cards began to foretell the future. Danger was all around them, they said. There had been great danger in the past, and there would be in the future. It was essential that Luke make the right choice when his testing time came, or they were doomed to be lost to one another. Death stalked the pair of them.

Finally, the *chovihani* turned over the last card of all, and Anne trembled as she did so, for on this card all her hopes for a happy future lay. It was The Sun, and it was the right way up so that Anne clapped her hands together in joy, even though it meant that Luke must leave her. A reversed card meant failure and despair, but The Sun, glowing in all its splendour, predicted a happy outcome for her and Luke.

'But only after much suffering and tribulation,' prophesied the *chovihani,* her face grave. 'But do not despair, Stella. The cards are in your favour. See, there are The Lovers, Justice, The Tower, The Hanged Man and The Chariot, and most of them are the right way up. I also see that help for you will arrive from a strange quarter—the cards rarely speak plainly to us, although their intent is plain.'

She had her answer. Luke must leave her. To gain something that one wanted, one often had to surrender something. One had to give as well as take, a lesson which the *chovihani* had hinted to her, more than once, all mankind had to learn.

Thus, when at daybreak Luke rose to go to Jasper to be transformed from Orion back into the young gentleman of fashion he had so lately been, both the lovers were submitting to the fate which the magic of the gypsies was forecasting for them.

'Happiness after sorrow,' Luke whispered to

Anne before he kissed her goodbye, 'is better than no happiness at all. I hope it will not be long before we meet again.'

He had not told her of the cruel test which Jasper had said awaited him whilst he was gone from her, although he knew that in a guarded fashion the *chovihani* had warned Anne that trials for him lay ahead before they met again.

They clung together for a long moment, unwilling to part, not even knowing whether they would ever meet again, for who could be sure that the *chovihani*'s prophecies were true ones. Until, growing impatient, Luke's horse, Cassius, one of Tawno's finer animals, gently nudged at him. He released Anne reluctantly. Tawno, who had been standing by, lent him his linked hands so that he might the more easily mount Cassius.

Once aboard him, he was again Mr Luke Harcourt, Lord Lyndale's freely acknowledged son, in a bottle-green jacket, fine linen shirt and cravat, cream breeches, highly polished boots, and a hat as unlike the battered trophies worn by Tawno and company as possible. His hair, which had been allowed to grow a little whilst he was with the Romanies, had been cut short. Only his amber eyes remained to betray that Luke was Orion—or that Orion was Luke.

His saddle bags contained food and other supplies. Jasper had given him a horse pistol, and altogether he looked well equipped to ride the autumn roads. September was king now in all its fruitful lushness.

'Northwards,' said Jasper, who had come to see him off, as had most of the camp, 'always northwards, the magic says.'

'Towards Haven's End, then,' remarked Luke, frowning.

'Aye. Haven's End is where your doom lies—and perhaps your salvation. Goodbye, young gentleman, brother Luke, no longer brother Orion. One day, perhaps, we may see Orion again. Perhaps.'

It was his farewell.

Never look back, Orpheus had been told before he returned from the Underworld. Luke was returning to the Overworld and, unlike Orpheus, he did not look over his shoulder at what he was leaving behind, precious though it was, and Jasper and the Romanies honoured him for it.

As they honoured Anne who, tearless on the outside, although crying inside, watched him until the pathway turned and he was hidden from her sight.

Chapter Thirteen

'So, where's he off to, then?' remarked Greene to Jenkinson. They had been trailing the Romanies for several days, keeping at a discreet distance. Long-sighted Jenkinson had been given a lengthy description of Luke by Pat O'Hare, who was eager to make up for his treachery towards him. Jenkinson already knew what Anne looked like from his surveillance of Mrs Britten's.

He had lain in the undergrowth the whole of the morning when Luke was preparing to leave, watching the gypsies come and go. He had recognised Anne, changed though she was, and guessed that the gypsyish-looking young fellow in a blue velveteen suit with an arm around her was the young man with whom she had run off. He was sure of it when, some time later, the same young man disappeared into a tent with the Pharaoh, only to emerge later dressed as a fine young gent.

The affecting farewells between the fine young gent and the supposed gypsy woman who was actually Lady Clairval merely served to convince Jenkinson that he had found the missing lovers. Any surmise he was making about why Luke Harcourt should resume his town clothes was confirmed for him when he rode off northwards. For whatever reason, he and the Romanies had decided that he was to act as a decoy, drawing Clairval away from his prey.

And if Clairval was after Master Luke, then to follow him would mean that the two Runners could find Clairval without them alerting the whole of the south-west as to what they were doing—which was to their—and the Grand Personage's—advantage.

'Decoy,' he said briefly to Greene. 'They're trying to draw Clairval away from her. I suppose that they hope that when they reach their destination, which by my guess is Bristol, Master Luke will try to elude Clairval and rejoin them.'

'Why Bristol?' queried Greene, a trifle aggressively. 'Since you seem able to guess so much, perhaps you can tell me that.'

'Bristol's a port where you may leave for the Americas, you gaby,' said Jenkinson unkindly.

'But he's going in the wrong direction for Bristol,' objected Greene triumphantly. 'I think he's heading for Papa's place at Haven's End.'

'That, too,' said Jenkinson cryptically, and said no more, motioning Greene to take to his horse again and follow Master Luke—at a discreet distance. Following would be easy since there were few byways in this part of the world, and if Master Luke wished to be found, as seemed likely, he would make for a posthouse on the road to the west leading to Bristol, via Bath, and try to discover whether Clairval had gone through or was expected.

It all depended on whether Clairval had already visited Haven's End and that Jenkinson did not know. He had no wish to become entangled in any way with Lord Lyndale, who had a reputation for being upright, but a bit of a tough, unless he had to. He supposed that Master Luke had no idea where Clairval was, and was trusting in luck to find him—or be found.

All unknowing that he was being carefully tracked, Luke was doing exactly what Jenkinson supposed and riding slightly northward to the turnpike to Bath. It was an even bet that Clairval might be making for Bath to hire lodgings there and use it as a centre to try to discover where his missing wife and her lover were. He might, of course, have turned back towards London, but Luke didn't think so.

Like Jenkinson, Luke wished that he knew whether Clairval had already visited Haven's End. He was still wishing it when he reached Marlborough in the early evening, and stopped at the inn there to rest his horse and himself. Ostlers rushed forward to help the fine young gentleman whom he appeared to be, and he was glad of the store of guineas which he had brought with him from London, which enabled him to throw money about with a happy abandon, even if he were travelling on horseback and without a servant.

The innkeeper was duly subservient when Luke, in lordly fashion, demanded the best room in the house.

'I don't suppose,' he remarked casually later on, when the landlord brought him a dish of roast beef to eat by the fire, for the evening had turned chilly, 'that you have seen my friend, the Marquess of Clairval, pass through lately?'

'Indeed, young sir, but we have,' answered the landlord eagerly, always ready to assist apparent wealth. 'He was here but a few days ago, and I expect him back tomorrow. He has been a-visiting at Haven's End, but he thought it unlikely that he would stay with m'lord—he being of the opposite political persuasion from m'lord Clairval, you understand.'

'Oh, aye, indeed,' returned Luke cryptically, giving nothing away. Finding Clairval so quickly was a piece of luck which he had not expected.

'I trust that you will not object to passing on to him my good wishes. I suppose that I shall miss him, unless we meet on the road tomorrow, for I am making for Haven's End myself.'

This last was, of course, untrue, since Luke had no intention of visiting his father, although he had every intention of wandering around the country in which his father's home stood, waiting for Clairval to find him—and discover that Anne was not with him. After that, he would try to convince him that he had no idea where Anne was, and that their leaving Mrs Britten's at roughly the same time was an unfortunate coincidence.

If he were successful in deceiving Clairval, he might then make for Haven's End to put Clairval even further off the scent, and persuade him that he ought to renew his search for his lost wife in London.

In the taproom at the back, with the servants and the lowly men of the road, Jenkinson and Greene ate bread and cheese for supper, and drank their ale. They, too, had made enquiries about m'lord Clairval, but more discreetly than Luke, since they did not wish to be discovered.

One of the men drinking with them had been turned off by Clairval and had secured a job as a groom at the inn. Several pints of ale, bought for him by the apparently generous Jenkinson, had him telling the two Runners as much of Clairval's business as he knew, so that, like Luke, they were made aware of m'lord's plans.

'Do we take him tomorrow, if we find him?' Greene asked. 'I know you've got a warrant to do so.'

Jenkinson shook his head. 'No. I don't want to arrest him—if I have to arrest him, that is— until he catches up with m'lady. If he does catch up with her, that is. I think that when he does, he will give us an opportunity to deal with him ourselves.'

'Meaning?'

'Don't ask, Greene. Don't ask. There's them as wants this business cleared up quietly, no questions asked then, or later. We do what we wants, when we wants. M'lord Marquess has a nasty temper, as well I know. I suspicion that that temper— if he can be provoked—may work in our favour. Until then, mum's the word.'

He said no more and, like Luke, went to bed conscious of a day's work well done.

* * *

'Haven's End, landlord,' exclaimed Clairval. 'You're sure that this flash young gentleman said that he was going to Haven's End, and that his name was Mr Luke Harcourt?'

'Aye, m'lord, that is so. Wished me to pay you his compliments, and say how sorry he was to miss you, so he did.'

'Never mind that, you fool. Was there anyone travelling with him? A lady, perhaps.'

'Nay, m'lord. He was alone, came on a good horse, so he did, left on it, said as how he was making for Haven's End.'

'And I've just come from there, after a night at a dam'd poor local inn,' swore Clairval. 'Took the main road, did he?'

'No, m'lord. The byway, the one which goes towards Haven's End direct. Your chaises might just manage it if you wish to follow him.' Although Clairval was travelling in some state, it was not as much as he was accustomed to—another cause for grievance against the upstart Harcourt and his faithless wife—and he had only two chaises with him instead of his usual large train.

He swung round, bellowing for Fernando. 'More horses for the chaises, man, and we take the byway for Haven's End. At least we're on the track of one of our quarry. But what the devil has he done with my wife? Tell me that!' he abjured the heavens, for he had no doubt that Luke Harcourt had run off with her and, where he was, m'lady Clairval could not be far away.

Luke dawdled along the byway which would ultimately lead him to his father's home in the hope that he might meet Clairval on his way back to Marlborough. He had no wish to meet him near Haven's End, for what might happen then could possibly embarrass his father.

After a time, he decided that Clairval might have returned to Marlborough by the main road, which was longer, but easier and speedier to travel on, but having settled on this route he decided to follow it. If unsuccessful, he could always return to Marlborough in the hope of finding Clairval there. Jasper had half-hinted that it would not be long before he found Clairval—or Clairval found him.

Finally, some time after noon, Luke slid from the saddle, tethered his horse to a tree, pulled the luncheon which the landlady had packed for him from his saddle bags, and sat down in the shade of some trees, well in sight of the road, to eat it.

After that he leaned against the bole of one of the trees, and rested for a little. He was missing

Anne cruelly, had slept little the night before and soon found himself drowsy. Before he fell asleep, he tried to pretend that she was resting by him, her hand in his.

He was still half-asleep when he heard Clairval arrive. He debated whether or not to leap to his feet when the chaise with Clairval's ornate coat of arms on its door came to a stop at the sight of him. He decided that a lazy surveyal of Clairval's equipage, rather than showing a great deal of excitement at his arrival, might serve to convince Clairval of his innocence.

It was not until Fernando leaped out of Clairval's chaise bellowing his name and demanding his attention that he rose to his feet and strolled slowly towards the chaise. So slowly, that by the time he had reached it, Clairval was already waiting for him, his gold-topped cane in his hand.

'Mr Harcourt, I believe,' Clairval drawled. 'I cannot say that we are well met, except, of course, for the trifling fact that now we *have* met you will do me the goodness of telling me where you have hidden my mad wife!'

'Charmed to do so,' returned Luke, giving Clairval a bow of exactly the right strength, 'if only I knew where she is—or was. I believe that you mistake your man.'

He was neither insolent nor servile, merely a young gentleman of good birth offering a man of higher rank the deference and attention which that rank deserved.

Clairval was neither deceived nor placated. 'Come, come, sir,' he said, 'do not palter with me. I am well aware that you spirited my poor mad wife away when I traced her to Islington. You will save yourself a deal of trouble if you cease your futile pretence and tell me what I need to know. The poor thing urgently needs the attention of the best mad doctor I can hire. You, being a bastard required to earn your own living, can hardly do that.'

Luke resisted the temptation to deny Anne's madness. Even as Clairval had spoken of it, he had a sudden memory of her on the heath, among the gypsies, one happy hand in his, watching the man who owned the educated pig putting it through its paces, her eyes alight with mirth.

'M'lord,' he said. 'I have told you that you are mistook. As you see, I am all alone, travelling towards my father's place at Haven's End. You will have the goodness to allow me to pass on my way. If your wife is lost, then you waste time dallying with me.'

Clairval's patience snapped. 'Damn you for an ill-gotten bastard, Master Luke Harcourt,' he roared. 'I know that you have stolen my wife, and hidden her, God knows where. I warn you, for the last time, that if you do not answer me fair straight away then it will go ill with you. I shall hand you over to Fernando and his friends so that they may beat out of you the name of the place where you have left her.'

He snapped his fingers at Fernando and at two more bruisers who had climbed out of the second chaise and were waiting for his orders.

'I do not palter with you,' he added. 'You may ask Fernando what he did to your Irish friend when I found out that he had not been telling me all he knew. And I warn you again, that was child's play to what I will have him—and his companions—do to you.'

If Luke quailed inwardly, which he did, there was no sign of it on his face. So, the monster before him had had poor Pat beaten—and doubtless it was Pat who had unwittingly betrayed him to Clairval. Jasper had said that he would face a severe test and now that test was upon him. All that concerned him was that God would grant him the power to hold true and that pain and fear did not have him blabbing of where Anne and the Romanies might be found.

No, he told himself firmly. I must behave as though what I have said is the truth. I have no idea where Anticleia, Lady Clairval is, and so I cannot help him.

Even as he thought this, he said it, at the same time looking around him. The two new bruisers were moving to cut off his escape into the wood at his rear, while Fernando was preparing to attack him from the front.

'Liar,' screamed Clairval—which was true enough, but not to the point. 'Teach him to tell the truth, Fernando.'

Luke bunched his hands into fists and tried to remember what the Romany boxers with whom he had playfully sparred, had taught him. But this was not sparring, and here were three fully trained pugilists attacking him in fierce reality, not in play.

He landed one blow to Fernando's midriff before he was seized from the rear and held by his two henchmen so that Fernando might strike him at will—which he did. Through failing consciousness and increasing pain he could see Clairval laughing at the sight of his agony. Presently, when Fernando stopped hitting him, the two lesser men held him up before Clairval so that he might question him again.

'Now, Master Luke, you know that I meant what I said. Tell me where my wife is and save yourself further punishment.'

'Go to Hell,' gasped Luke, pain riding him. 'If I knew, I would not tell you.' He could only hope that the strength of his will would stop him from confessing everything to save his ill-treated body from further pain.

'No, Master Luke. That is where you are going. Persuade him a little further, Fernando, but leave him conscious.'

This time, when Clairval ordered Fernando to stop, Luke was on his hands and knees on the ground, and Clairval had to bend down to question him again.

'Come, man, don't be a fool. Tell me what I wish to know. The trull isn't worth what you are suffering for her.'

From where he found the strength and resolution to do what he did, Luke never knew. He would have said beforehand that he could not have withstood the brutal battering he had received from Fernando and his friends without confessing everything. The training in self-denial, resolution, and the enduring of pain, which Jasper and Tawno had put him through during his time as a Romany, had strengthened his will as well as his courage.

Thus, even through the mists of pain and suffering, he lifted his head and spat full in Clairval's face.

'That's for you for the insult you have offered to a good woman,' he mumbled.

He did not know whether Clairval heard or

understood what he had said. What he did know was that, as he knelt there helpless, he suddenly saw Anne before him, the heath and the Romanies' tents behind her, her face a mask of pain— and then everything, including Anne, disappeared as he fell into a pit of blackness.

He didn't even feel the blow to the face which Clairval gave him in return, nor the further punishment which Fernando inflicted on him before he lost consciousness.

'Damn you,' shrieked Clairval at Fernando, his face scarlet with rage mixed with frustration. 'Lift him up, and bring him round so that I may question him again.'

Fernando shook his head regretfully. 'I'll not be party to murder, m'lord. He can't take much more from me without risk of his dying on me. I would never have thought that such a pampered young gent would resist me so stubborn-like, and taken such punishment without talking. I'd have given odds that he'd have blabbed everything long ago.'

In exasperation, Clairval walked over to where Luke lay unconscious on the ground and kicked him in the ribs. 'A fine botch you've made of it,' he roared. 'What in Hell's name do we do now? The bitch is still missing, and all we have for our pains is a piece of almost carrion on our hands...'

If Fernando baulked at the notion of direct murder, indirect murder seemed a little more attractive to him.

'Leave him here,' he suggested. 'Not many pass down this byway. Let Nature take its course with him. I'll shove him among the bushes, cut his horse loose and let it run free. A young gent will have disappeared—and who's to know it's anything to do with us?'

'That'll have to do,' declared Clairval morosely. 'Everything seems to go ill with me these days. The devil's in it. Shove him in the bushes then, and we'll cut line. I'll have bills posted up for m'lady's recovery. At least she's not got Master Luke protecting her now. And you're right. Who's to know we've anything to do with this?' And he gave Luke one last kick before Fernando dragged him by the heels into the undergrowth.

But they were wrong. Lying out of sight in the scrub, watching everything, wincing at each blow which Luke received, were Jenkinson and Greene, who had been following Luke after he had left the inn at Marlborough. Useless to intervene, or try to help him, for they were outnumbered. They could only wait until Clairval and his murderous party were on their way again before they emerged from the undergrowth to pull Luke free and try to revive him.

'Damn that Fernando,' muttered Jenkinson, pouring water from a bottle which had been strapped to his saddle, and which Greene fetched from where their horses were tethered in the wood, some distance away. 'I'll see him turned off for good on Tyburn Tree one of these days, but not for this poor young fellow, I hope. Give me a hand, man, I've no mind to have him die on us, a splendid witness to m'lord Marquess's cruelty as he is.'

'Can't imagine why you didn't use your warrant and arrest him on the spot, and save the poor young fellow from this,' complained Greene as he gently held Luke so that Jenkinson could wipe his bruised face.

'Use your loaf, man. What d'you think that m'lord would have done to any warrant I'd waved in his face whilst his bruisers were cuffing up this poor young feller and us here in this wilderness without any spectators? Torn it up, he would have done, *and* had them duff me up—and you—and sworn blind that *we'd* attacked *him* on the road—with our bodies to prove it. No, a mad dog is m'lord Clairval, and as a mad dog he'll have to be muzzled—and soon. But we'll pick our ground when we do it.'

In the middle of this diatribe Luke gave a groan, clutched at the lapel of Jenkinson's coat and mumbled through bruised and swollen lips, 'I didn't tell. Anne, my darling, I didn't tell him where you are.'

'No more you did,' said Jenkinson, holding the water bottle to Luke's mouth. 'And I promise you, that if it's the last thing I do, m'lord shall pay dear for this day's work.'

They tended Luke for a little while longer. He lapsed in and out of consciousness, but the periods of consciousness gradually grew longer. Jenkinson finally said to Greene as he helped Luke to sit up for the first time, 'We'll try to find help for him. That place where his father lives, Haven's End, ain't far from here.'

Luke muttered something unintelligible about Haven's End as Greene hoisted him up on Jenkinson's horse, tying him on, so that Jenkinson could walk him along the byway to a place which was truly a haven.

Earlier that day after helping the *chovihani* to teach some of the little children their letters, Anne had taken her work and sat down in the shade not far from where the older girls were busy learning a dance that they proposed to introduce into their small act.

They were carrying tambourines, which they held high above their heads, sounding them at intervals as they twisted and turned in time to a fiddler. Presently they put the tambourines down and a gypsy boy came forward carrying a silk scarf.

This was the signal for them to rehearse yet another dance, which Anne had not yet seen them perform. The girls formed a circle round the boy, who handed the scarf to a girl, who danced with it for a short time, twisting and twirling it, while the boy danced a jig before her.

After a time, she passed the scarf on to the girl on her right and the boy now danced before her. In this manner the scarf passed round the circle until it reached the first girl, who ceremoniously handed it to the boy, who bowed in turn to them all, the scarf held high, before the music stopped, and they all sank to the ground, in a grand curtsy.

Anne joined the older gypsies who had arrived to watch in clapping and applauding the children, who rose and waved to them. One of them ran to her and gave her the scarf to hold.

Even as she touched it, a wave of pain ran through Anne. The bright scene around her darkened and disappeared as the pain came again, stronger than ever. So strong was it that she sank on to her knees on the ground, her hands shielding her bent head, crying out she knew not what.

The *chovihani* who was standing by, put her arms around her and tried to comfort her. Anne lifted an agonised face and wailed, 'Oh, it's Luke! It's Luke! Someone is hurting him cruelly. Oh, it's Clairval! Oh, I cannot bear the pain.'

As she spoke the scene around her vanished completely. She was with Luke, she almost was Luke, except that at the same time she could see his agonised face and feel the blows which were being rained upon him. Then, when it became almost unbearable, the pain disappeared, and Anne fell into a dark pit of nothingness... Even as she reached the bottom she was back on the heath again, in the *chovihani*'s arms.

'Luke!' she cried. 'He's killed him! Oh, why did I let him go?'

'No,' said the *chovihani* gently. 'I saw him even as the pain stopped. He is hurt, but he is not dead. Death I would have recognised, and Death was not there. The spirits are merciful and bestowed freedom from pain on him, so that he might not be tormented further.'

But nothing that she could say consoled Anne. She still sat, crouched on the ground, sobbing for her lost love. Tawno's wife, who had left them on a nod from the *chovihani* came running back carrying a cup full of a clear liquid.

'Come,' said the *chovihani* putting the cup to Anne's lips. 'Drink of the poppy, and find rest. I can only see darkly, but what I see tells me that, for the moment, Orion has escaped his tormentor. Drink and rest, my sister. The gift I bestowed on you earlier this year is even more powerful than I intended it to be. The greater mysteries are not meant for a novice such as yourself to endure.'

Anne drank, and allowed the gypsies to lead her to the tent that she had shared with Luke, and there, his velveteen jacket clutched in her arms, sleep took her and, at the *chovihani*'s gift, all her dreams were pleasant.

What the Romanies did not tell Anne, for they did not wish to disturb her further, was that towards nightfall the horse on which Luke had been riding returned, covered with foam, with Luke's saddlebags, still unpacked...

Clairval's thoughts were not pleasant. By the time they had reached the end of the byway on which they had caught Luke and were about to turn towards Marlborough, he changed his mind and bade his coachman return to the spot where they had left him.

'I was a fool,' he told Fernando angrily, as though it were his fault. 'I should never have left him there. He would have been a valuable prize. We should have taken him with us to question him further when he recovered consciousness. The devil was in him to make him so obstinate. Who would have thought that he would take so much punishment?'

Fernando did not argue with a man who was growing more capricious by the hour. They sent the second chaise back to the inn at Marlborough to have rooms prepared for m'lord, whilst Clairval returned to pick up the injured Luke. The trouble was that, when they reached the small clearing where they had left him, they could see the marks which Fernando had made dragging him into the scrub, but there was no sign of him.

'Gone!' roared Clairval, now in a lather of rage and frustration at Fernando and life generally, when told this surprising news. 'How can he be gone? He was unconscious when we left him. Or were you mistaken?'

'I know a stunned man when I see one,' returned Fernando. 'I suppose,' he offered doubtfully, 'he might have come to and staggered away. Yes, that would be it.'

'Then the pair of you had better look for him. In the state he was in, he can't have gone far.'

But search though they might, they found no sign of the missing Luke. Fernando, on returning to tell his master the bad news, watched him turn purple with rage.

'Disappeared! How can he have disappeared? He was in no state to walk any distance.'

'A passer-by might have seen him.' Even Fernando thought this suggestion a lame one. He thought that the Marquess was about to choke on it.

'Seen him? Seen what? You left him so that he wasn't visible from the byway.'

'Well, m'lord,' the goaded Fernando replied, turning, like the proverbial worm, at last. 'What do *you* suggest?'

'Me? I pay you to think, man. But since you appear to be unable to do so, *I* think that we'll cut our losses, return to Marlborough, and make for Haven's End again on the morrow. I believe that Lord Lyndale knows a great deal more than he's telling.'

Which, like most of m'lord Marquess's suppositions was, as usual, a case of the dog barking up the wrong tree—but occasionally getting the right answer!

Unaware of what was going on behind them, Jenkinson and Greene plodded steadily towards Haven's End. The vast parkland surrounding the great house was in sight when a party from it came into view.

At the front of it was Cressy, Lady Lyndale, superbly turned out in deep blue, and wearing a man's top hat with a pale blue silk scarf swathed around it. She was driving a curricle picked out in blue and silver. Two grooms accompanied her.

Jenkinson knew the quality when he saw it. M'lady's small procession could be the salvation of Master Luke. To stop it, he put up a hand which wavered between the peremptory and the servile.

Cressy, curious at the sight of a man slumped in the saddle of a horse being led by another man, did not at first realise that the slumped man was Luke. Nevertheless, she slowed down, leaned forwards to speak to Jenkinson, and said, 'I am Lady Lyndale, at your service. Your companion appears to be injured. How may we help you?'

'By arranging, m'lady, that Mr Luke Harcourt, who is your stepson, I believe, is taken to his father's house and a doctor found for him as soon as possible. He has been most cruelly beaten.'

Cressy, her face white with shock, drove over to Luke. 'Who has been responsible for this?' she demanded fiercely, inexpressibly shocked by the sight of his bruised and swollen face and his torn clothing.

Jenkinson saw no point in evasion. 'M'lord Clairval ordered it done, m'lady.'

Cressy's hand turned into a clenched fist. 'Did he, indeed? I think that my husband will have something to say about this. Stephen,' she added, turning to the young groom who had also ridden up to inspect Luke, his face full of concern, 'you and Russell may lift Mr Luke from this gentleman's horse, and carry him into my curricle. That will get him home double quick.

'You, sir,' she said, turning to Jenkinson as the two grooms sprang to do her bidding, 'may explain to me how this terrible thing came about when we reach the house. M'lord is sitting at the Quarter Sessions today and will not reach home until tomorrow morning, so I will have to act for him.'

Luke, transferred to the curricle where he regained consciousness sufficiently to recognise Cressy, although he did not speak to her, was driven at all speed to his father's home, Greene and Jenkinson, restored to his horse, riding behind him.

Chapter Fourteen

Clairval arrived at Haven's End the next day, at almost exactly the same time as James, Lord Lyndale. James looked from his coach's window with some surprise at the sight of Clairval's chaise with its telltale coat of arms and the two smartly dressed grooms standing at the back. Fernando was already waiting on the gravel sweep, his arm out, ready to accommodate his master as he stepped from his carriage.

James raised his fine black brows. He had no wish to speak to Clairval again and could not understand what had brought him back to Haven's End. He sighed, allowed himself to be helped out of his own coach and watched Clairval advance on him, his face purple. He adopted an expression of resigned patience, which he was very far from feeling.

He was attacked without preamble by the furious man before him.

'I almost believed you the other day, Lyndale, when you assured me that you had no notion of the whereabouts of your bastard and my adulterous wife. I now have reason to know that you lied to me. I demand that you allow Fernando and his companion to search your house again.'

'Demand away, Clairval,' returned James coolly. 'I have no intention of allowing either you, or your bully boys, into my home again. You are not welcome here, sir. Pray leave. You have my word that I still have no notion where Mr Harcourt is. He is certainly not at Haven's End. You must remain content with that. I bid you good day.'

He bowed and swept on into the house. He could hear Clairval gibbering behind him, and see Cressy standing in the doorway, a wry expression on her face. She had heard every word which the two men had exchanged.

She thought that James looked his magnificent best in black. He always dressed soberly for the Assizes, both coming and going, in order to emphasise his respect for the law. Age—and a happy marriage—had served only to enhance his looks and bearing. He had scarcely reached her before Clairval was snapping at his heels again.

'See here, Lyndale. I insist that you pay heed to me.'

'Go into the house, my dear. I do not want you present whilst I dispose of this importunate fly,' James said coldly, before turning, and saying in his most scathing manner, 'Your insistence and the manner in which you express it, serve only to harden my determination to have as little as possible to do with you. I have no intention of allowing you, ever again, into my home. I despise a man who will not accept my word. You will oblige me by leaving.'

For a moment Clairval made as if to pull him back by main force—or order Fernando to do so—until he took one look at the array of footmen and lackeys who had assembled on the gravel sweep to attend James on his arrival. It was not likely that they would disobey any orders which Lyndale might give—such as bidding them to see Clairval's small party off the premises, by force, if necessary.

He contented himself with shrieking, 'This is not the end of the matter,' before he allowed Fernando to help him into the chaise. The great double doors at the front of Haven's End clanged to, and he was left to make his way down the drive, his tail between his legs.

Cressy was waiting for James in the hall. Her expression was still odd, he thought. He knew his Cressy well. There was no doubt that she was bursting to tell him something—but what?

'James,' she began a trifle breathlessly, and then, looking at the waiting servants, 'not here. In the drawing-room.'

'Very urgent, is it?'

'Very urgent,' repeated Cressy, after the drawing-room doors were closed behind them. 'Oh, James, I heard you tell Clairval that Luke is not here. It is true that you have no idea of where he is, and that was no lie, but since five o'clock yesterday he has been at Haven's End—in his old room.'

James's eyebrows arched upwards, and his mouth thinned after a fashion which Cressy had not seen since the days before their marriage when he and she had jousted verbally together.

'Luke? Here? With Lady Clairval?' He gave a half-laugh. 'So Clairval was right in his assumptions after all, and I was an unintended liar when I assured him that Luke was not here!'

Something odd about what Cressy had just said struck him. 'In his room? Why in his room, pray? Is he afraid to face me?' He started towards the door.

Cressy was after him in a flash. 'No, James. Don't fly into the boughs. Lady Clairval is not with him. He was carried here yesterday, semi-conscious, by two Bow Street Runners who had found him abandoned after Clairval had him beaten to try to make him reveal where he had hidden Lady Clairval. Doctor Spence says that his life is not in danger, but he has suffered a light fever and is in great pain. His left arm is hurt and his ribs are badly bruised.'

James's anger was now directed towards Clairval. He started for the door again, and Cressy read him rightly. She caught him by the arm.

'No, James. You are not to do anything rash, like following Clairval and calling him out. Think! Luke would not want the scandal that would follow. Nor would you.'

James gave a short laugh, and turned back. 'My dear, it is something of an event, you must allow, when it is *you* who are cautioning *me* not to be over-hasty, and not me you. Punishing Clairval must wait. Is...' he hesitated '...is Luke well enough for me to talk to him?'

'He is now, I think. But he was not last night. The two Runners are still here and wish to speak to you—but only after you have spoken to Luke. Or so the leading one of the two said. You must understand that they probably saved Luke's life. They found him hidden away, off the road in the undergrowth, where he could not easily be seen. He could have died there.'

'Luke first, then,' was James's answer to that.

He found Luke awake, lying propped up against

the pillows, his face bruised and swollen. Behind the bruises his pallor was extreme. Cressy had told James that before he had fully recovered his senses Luke had said over and over again, 'I didn't tell him, Anne. Believe me, I never told him where you are. I would die, rather.'

So far as James was concerned, what he had seen of Clairval's recent conduct appeared to bear out the supposition that he might be prepared to go as far as murder. Luke's condition was a witness to the brutality with which he had been treated. James sat down on the bed, facing his son.

Luke stared steadily at him, his face guarded. He made no effort to speak until James remarked, as casually as he could, for rage at Clairval for what he had done to Luke was consuming him, 'You have a look of having been in the wars, old fellow. Care to tell me anything about it?'

Luke shook his head. Every movement hurt. Even speech hurt. 'No. Only that Clairval tried to make me tell him where Anne—Lady Clairval—is by having his bruisers thrash me, and I wouldn't. I suppose that is why he left me for dead.'

'So you did run away with Lady Clairval.'

'I ran away with Anne, yes. To save her from him, you understand—he would kill her if he recaptured her—and because we love one another.'

Speech was painful and his voice was husky, but Luke felt that he had to make his father understand that what had been done had not been done lightly.

'Oh, Luke, she is another man's wife. And you know how the law stands between man and wife. We talked on that earlier this summer.'

Luke turned his face away from his father. He was not about to be persuaded into betraying Anne so that she might be handed back to the monster who had tried to kill her.

'I regard her as my wife, not Clairval's. It is my duty to protect her.'

He spoke to his father as though to an enemy. Before he had left Haven's End in the spring, James had told Cressy that he feared that Luke might lack steel. He had been wrong. The face that his son turned on him as he spoke was implacable. Painful though it obviously was for him to speak, Luke was ready to do so to defend the woman he loved—even from his father. Or refuse to speak, if that was necessary.

James made up his mind. 'I have only recently met Clairval, but I have seen and heard enough of him to know that any woman unfortunate enough to be his wife would be in danger of the greatest persecution.

'I am prepared to back you—and the lady—in

every possible way, legally and financially, so that she may divorce him, as the Countess of Strathmore divorced Stony Bowes in my father's day. But you must not be seen to be lovers. Only tell me where she is, and I will go and fetch her to give her sanctuary here—even if it costs me Government office. I cannot say fairer than that.'

Could he not! Luke saw Cressy's face glow with pleasure at this great concession from her husband. But Luke's face hardened still further.

He turned away again, closed his eyes, and said in a faraway voice, 'By no means. I have not the slightest intention of telling you where my dear Anne is. She has been betrayed by too many people who had previously called themselves her friends. It is not that I don't trust *you*, but I don't trust the law, and the pressures which would be put upon you. No, allow me to recover—and once I have done so, I shall leave as soon as possible, and go to her.'

He stopped. James was about to speak, to argue with him, but again Cressy acted as mediator. She shook her head, placed a finger on her lips, and put out her other hand to lie it on James's.

'Come, my dear. Let us leave Luke so that he may rest and recover himself. He is shortly due to have another draught of the poppy to give him relief from pain. Why not talk with him later when he may be feeling better?'

James looked from his wife to his son—the son who had always been a credit to him, and who, whatever else, had been prepared to protect the woman he loved at the risk of his life. The son who was so greatly changed, not merely as a consequence of the beating, but because of the new hard determination with which he had spoken, despite his pain.

'Yes,' he said. 'I will talk to the Runners. I am curious to know why they appeared to be following Luke. Or were they following Clairval? Why should they concern themselves with a quarrel between a man and his wife?'

He found Jenkinson and Greene waiting for him in his study. He recognised Jenkinson at once. He had seen him before, waiting in an anteroom, and for some reason the very oddness of seeing his fox face, his red hair and his square blunt body in the corridors of power at Whitehall had struck him forcibly.

It was plain that Jenkinson knew him. His manner was straightforward without being insolent. 'I suppose, m'lord, that you wish to learn something of how and why we came to find Mr Harcourt.'

'Indeed,' said James, 'and if it be possible, given your calling, how and why you came to be following him? Or was it m'lord Clairval who was your quarry?'

Jenkinson looked at the ceiling and then at Greene, whose honest, dull face showed how dazzled he was to be in such grand company.

'Why, as to that, m'lord, if it were possible to send my colleague here on a small errand concerning our horses, I might find it in me to be a little straighter with you in private.'

This Machiavellian answer from such a coarse-seeming brute almost had James laughing. It certainly confused Greene, who looked at Jenkinson with a dazed face. 'Eh?' he began, 'What?'

'The stables,' James said to him. 'I gather that your horses were a trifle weary when you arrived here with my son late yesterday. I should be pleased to offer you a sounder pair. You may tell my chief groom so, with my compliments.'

'Now,' said James, taking a seat behind his great desk in the window which overlooked Haven's End's park, 'you may tell me, Mr Jenkinson, exactly what your little game is, and who you are playing it with and for, and perhaps you will allow me a hand in it if I so wish—if it benefits my son, that is. You see, I am being frank with you.'

'Aye, m'lord, I quite see that. Now the way of it is this,' and confidentially, his finger beside his

nose once or twice, Mr Jenkinson began to con-
spire with James Chavasse, the Most Noble the
Earl of Lyndale, who was only too happy to con-
spire back, both of them being pragmatic men
with an eye to the main chance.

It went without saying that neither of them was
completely frank in their dealings with the other.

The Marquess of Clairval was so enraged that
his common sense, never his strongest point, had
almost deserted him.

He roared at Fernando all the way back to Marlborough. If he had not been paying Fernando right
royally to do his dirty work for him, that gentleman would have planted a facer on the Marquess's
jaw and fled the carriage. As it was, he took all that
Clairval chose to throw at him, and when he had
finally run down, merely said, 'And next, m'lord?
What do we do next?'

'Stay at Marlborough for a time,' said Clairval,
his face resuming its normal colour, a dirty yellow.

'I am convinced that Lyndale was lying and that
his bastard was hidden somewhere near Haven's
End. Where he is, my wife cannot be far away.
That being so, you and your minions can do some
reconnoitring for me. I don't think that even Lyndale has the gall to hide her at Haven's End itself,

but in Hell's name, she must be *somewhere* near here.' His voice rose dangerously, and his expression of annoyance was back again.

It was even worse when he discovered that he had to share his dinner and the inn parlour with a gentleman who had arrived during his chase after Luke, and who insisted on treating Clairval, whom he had never seen before, as an old friend.

Except that, as they sat waiting for the landlord to bring them a loaf and some cheese with which to finish the meal, the gentleman flourished a magazine at m'lord and said confidentially, 'Some fine writing about these days, m'lord. Quite extraordinary. A tale about the gypsies and their life. Written by a young gentleman of consequence, I am told, who is a friend of theirs, and has lived among them. Although he does not use his true name on the title page.'

It took Clairval the remaining shred of his temper not to inform the fool opposite that he had no use for magazines, gypsies or fine young gentlemen who wrote about them.

All that he managed was a lofty grunt, which his tormentor took as a signal to continue his virtual monologue.

'Very true, m'lord,' he said, being of the opinion that any noise made by a lord was meaningful. 'It is to be supposed that you know him. His real name is Harcourt, Luke Harcourt.' He paused to look a trifle sly, and added, 'He is by way of being a very close relative of Lord Lyndale, whose seat is nearby, I believe. As also are the gypsies. They are camped on the outskirts of Bath, I am told.'

What he believed was suddenly immaterial. On hearing the words Luke Harcourt, gypsies and Bath, m'lord the Marquess of Clairval leaned forward and virtually snatched the magazine from the intrusive gentleman's hands.

He remembered his manners at the last moment, and gabbled, 'I would be much obliged, sir, if you allowed me to examine this work at my leisure,' before he rushed to the inn's parlour door and began to bawl for Fernando, who was eating his supper in the tap room.

The intrusive gentleman stared after him. He had heard much of the reserved and haughty manners of the aristocracy, but so far Clairval had displayed little of either. He stood helplessly by as Clairval, Fernando, and his magazine all disappeared up the stairs to Clairval's bedroom.

'I have found my lost bird,' Clairval carolled exultantly at Fernando. 'What odds would you lay that she and Master Luke have been travelling with the gypsies, and that he has left her with them? That ass in the parlour said that they are camped near Bath. Tomorrow morning I shall go to Bath and enlist the services of the local magistrates and their officers in order to help me to recover her from the scum with whom she is travelling. By nightfall she shall be mine again.'

'Aye,' said Fernando. 'Tomorrow, you say? We are off to Bath tomorrow? I suppose it's as good a bet as any.'

He sounded more than a little dubious. Clairval was a man who constantly went off half-cock. He was like an unreliable cannon on a ship's gun deck, which fired its ball whether its gunner wished it to or no. On the other hand, no harm in visiting the gypsies, either.

Luke had refused to drink the poppy which Cressy had brought for him. He was still feeling bruised in every limb, but the worst of his sufferings, he hoped, were over. He wanted to be away from Haven's End, as much to save his father and his stepmother from Clairval, as to draw Clairval away from Anne. The physician had bound his ribs with stout canvas, had assured him that his left wrist was sprained, not broken, and that a few days rest—and the poppy— would improve him mightily.

By the early evening he was sitting up, looking

belligerent, and assuring a worried Cressy that he would be gone as soon as he could climb on to a horse. Like James, she saw that she was dealing with a different person from the charming, rather easy young man whom she had always known.

Luke had always been clever, but until now he had shown little of the severity, amounting to sternness, which was such a feature of his father's character. So formidable did he look that Cressy was not entirely sure that James would find the new Luke as easy to control as the old one.

'You were never a naughty boy,' she told him, mock severe herself. 'I suppose that you are making up for lost time now by refusing to take your medicine.'

She was carrying a letter which she handed to Luke, saying, 'This came some little time ago. It was marked urgent, but as we had no notion where you were, we could not forward it. I shall leave you to read it in peace.'

To Luke's surprise, the letter was from Pat O'Hare, although it was not in his hand, which Luke knew well. He read it with a wry smile on his lips. A word to the wise, indeed. Alas, Clairval had already done the damage to him that Pat had feared.

He had just finished reading the letter when

James came in. There was an air of purpose about him which his son recognised immediately. A James who had made up his mind was a formidable person indeed.

'Now what is it?' said Luke, smiling at his father for the first time. 'What new persuasions have you come to try on me, father?'

'Powerful ones,' replied James briefly, drawing up a chair. 'I have been talking to the two Runners, or rather to the chief of them, Jenkinson, who appears to be a man of sense.'

'Oh, and did the man of sense inform you how he came to be following me about the countryside? I am aware that I owe him my life, but I cannot help but wonder what I have done to deserve such attention.'

'Oh, he wasn't following you. Or rather, he was doing so, hoping that you would lead him to Clairval. Why couldn't he simply follow Clairval, one may reasonably ask? He couldn't answer that other than to say "matters of state".'

'Matters of state, eh?' Luke began to laugh, looking and sounding like his old self for the first time since he had arrived at Haven's End. He was beginning to feel a little better, no doubt about it. 'What matters of state could involve Clairval? No, don't tell me—that was another secret!'

'Indeed,' said James, laughing in his turn. 'But he did give me some information which might persuade you to change your plans a little. But first, I must ask you another question. I take it that you do not intend to live permanently with the gypsies, and if so, what was your destination? How could you hope to keep your—and the lady's whereabouts—secret?'

There was colour in Luke's cheeks for the first time. 'I suppose that I had better tell you. We were making for Bristol to take ship to the Americas, where even Clairval might have found it difficult to track us down. I was going to send you a letter shortly before we boarded, informing you of my intentions. After all, as a writer, I follow a trade which I can practise anywhere, and the Yankees like writers, or so I am told.'

James said softly, 'You love one another so much, then?'

'Like Romeo and Juliet, or Orpheus and Eurydice, yes.'

'"The world well lost for love"?'

'What world for me,' retorted Luke hardily, 'without my dear Anne in it? What world if Clairval regained her? Tell me that. Do not try to talk me out of my intentions, Father. My mind is quite made up.'

'But if Clairval were disposed of, and Anne

freed, you would not leave, I trust? There would be no need for you to cut yourself off forever from family and friends.'

'What hope of overcoming Clairval so easily? No, Anne and I must find somewhere where we can live together in peace.'

This came out with all Luke's new determination and hardihood. He was the cheerful dilettante no longer. If Lady Clairval had done this to him, thought James, then she would be a woman worth meeting.

'I think, Luke, from what the Runners have told me, that the secret of where you have hidden the lady is no secret. They seem to think that they know what you have done with her, and a secret, once breached, is a secret no longer.'

Luke threw off the bedclothes and made to rise from the bed, to leave Haven's End, to try to find her, to…

His father leaned forward and caught him by the wrist. 'No need for that. They tell me that you have left her with the gypsies. They believe that you were attempting to draw Clairval away from them and her. That you were acting as a decoy.' He could see by Luke's face that he was speaking the truth.

'How could they know? By what magic…?' He felt numb. He accepted that what his father had

just said was true: a secret, once breached, is a secret no longer.

'No magic; something your friend Pat O'Hare
told them when they interviewed him put them on
the track.'

Pat, whose letter he had just read. Pat, who had
betrayed him—and now, in a manner, had saved
him. For if the Runners had not followed the gypsies—and then him—he would have lain rotting
in the undergrowth, lost forever. Instead, they had
found him and carried him to Haven's End.

'So,' he said, 'what follows? I suppose that, if
chance could set the Runners on the right track,
then it follows that chance might aid Clairval…'

'Indeed,' nodded his father. 'How long will it be
before Clairval stops flailing about like a loose
cannon on the gun deck of a crippled battleship,
and stops to think?'

'But we may reach Bristol—and safety—before then.'

'And he will have driven you out of England.
Listen to my proposition. I am prepared to use my
standing and my wealth, to back you against Clairval. To take the lady into my care and do all that
is necessary to gain her a divorce. Jenkinson assures me that he has enough evidence of Clairval's
cruelties towards her to make that possible.

'Allow me to go to Bath tomorrow morning, for that is where Jenkinson says that the gypsies are encamped, and bring her to Haven's End, so that we may begin our campaign against him as soon as possible.'

Luke was throwing back the covers again. 'By no means. You shall not go without me, and if you insist on going to Bath, now that you know where she is, I shall go with you. For it is Anne, and Anne alone, who must make the decision regarding her future. After all, it is she who has borne the most unimaginable cruelties from him, and she who will suffer if your plan fails. That is as far as I am prepared to go to fall in with your wishes.'

He was standing up, shrugging off his nightwear, looking about for his clothes.

'You are not fit to get up now, or sit on a horse tomorrow,' protested his father.

'Nonsense. Where Anne is concerned I am fit enough for anything. A pretty fellow I should look to let a few bruises keep me from her.'

His head was swimming, but his will was strong. The glare he gave his father, who began to try to argue with him, was a powerful one. 'No, sir. I have always obeyed you in the past. I will not obey you in this. It touches both me, and the woman I love. Would you let another dictate your behaviour towards Cressy?'

That did it. James lay back in his chair and said with a resigned air, 'If you must, then, you may ride with me. But is it possible for you to ride so far? For we must ride. Jenkinson believes that time is of the essence.'

'Jenkinson? And what part do the Runners play in this, if I may be so bold as to ask?'

'They will not accompany us. They will go to Marlborough—for that was Clairval's destination yesterday, a decision made in their hearing—and they will start for there as soon as my plans are made, in order to follow him.'

'Our plans,' interjected Luke determinedly, '*our* plans, father.'

'Our plans, then,' agreed his father, coming at last to terms with a son whose will had become as stern and implacable as his own.

'And it is agreed that Anne shall decide as to our future plans, and that you will not seek to stop us if she wishes to leave for the Americas?'

'Agreed.'

Father and son faced one another on equal terms for the first time in their lives. Mutual respect now lay between them. The shadow of patronage in which Luke had always led his life had disappeared. To know that his father was with him, was his partner, and his friend was a happy feeling, which remained with Luke until he fell into a dreamless, poppyless sleep.

He could only hope that he would be strong enough by morning to allow him to ride to Bath, the gypsies—and Anne…

Chapter Fifteen

'Oh, they're beautiful, Mrs Chikno, quite beautiful! You're sure that you wish to give them to me?'

Mrs Chikno nodded shyly at Anne. 'The *chovihani* says that it is your birthday, that you have expressed a wish to possess a pack of tarot cards—and I possess two packs. This is an old one which belonged to my mother. Tawno gave me another, and it seems a shame that this should be hidden away unused. Take it with my blessing.'

Anne leaned forward and kissed Mrs Chikno on the cheek. It was her birthday and the gypsies had been bringing her small gifts all morning. They were encamped outside Bath and, in the distance, The Crescent shone white on the hillside above them.

She thought of all the grand parties and receptions to which Clairval had escorted her in the early days of their marriage. Parties attended by the whole of the fashionable world, and not once had she felt as happy and contented as she did today, sitting on the grass, her sewing in her hand among the unconsidered of the world in which she had once lived.

If only Luke were with her! The sun was shining, she was surrounded by love and friendship, her life satisfied her, but without him… Oh, without him she was only half a being. Nor did she even have the satisfaction of knowing that he was safe from harm. But no one whom Clairval thought of as an enemy was ever safe.

She bent her head and said a little prayer, asking God to send him back to her soon. There had been times when Anne's faith in God had faltered, but since she had met Luke she had begun to recover it again. Perhaps now that He had chastened her by allowing her to marry Clairval, with all the dreadful consequences which had flown from that, God would allow Luke a safe journey back to her.

She spread Mrs Chikno's cards on the grass, having asked a question of them. The answer they gave pleased her. Soon, they said, soon. Luke will return soon.

Could she believe them? She knew that the gypsies did. That they used them constantly, as they used the divinatory powers of the *chovihani*. She sighed and returned to her work. September it might be, but the summer still seemed to be with them, and a perfect peace had settled on the encampment.

Tawno and his fellow riders had gone into Bath so that the gentry might inspect their cattle and possibly buy some of them—although not the pride of Tawno's troop. These he kept for himself and his better riders.

She was almost asleep when she heard the sound of horses approaching; they were being ridden at speed. Surely it could not be Tawno, back so soon? She sat up, shaded her eyes from the sun and looked towards them. It was not Tawno. It was a large party of mounted men, followed at a distance by two chaises, which stopped on the road when the riders left it in order to gallop towards them.

'No!' cried Anne, jumping to her feet, her cry so anguished that all the Romanies nearby turned to look at her and then at the approaching horsemen. 'Oh, no! It cannot be Clairval.'

But it was.

The *chovihani* was at her side in an instant. 'What is it, child? What do you fear?' And then, looking at the approaching horsemen, asked, 'Is it your husband?'

'Yes,' said Anne, despair engulfing her.

'Come, child, quickly. Let us hide you.'

She caught Anne by the hand and ran her towards a group of women who were preparing food
outside one of the tents. She took a scarlet handkerchief from one of them, and twisted it around
Anne's head. From another she took her gold
necklaces and hung them around Anne's neck.
There was a spent fire in the grass, she bent down,
rubbed her hands in the ashes and smeared Anne's
face with them.

'Off with your shoes and stockings.' The *chovihani* stood back to admire her handiwork. 'And
now you are the very picture of a Rom. He will not
know you, I am sure, even if you stood before
him. Stay here among the women. Do nothing to
draw attention to yourself. We shall deny all
knowledge of Lady Clairval, and rightly so. You
are Stella, Orion's mate. One of us.'

'But Luke?' cried Anne. 'What of Luke? Has he
made Luke tell him where I am? Oh, what has he
done to him?' She was shaking and shivering, once
more the poor creature who had fled her prison at
Clairval Castle, no longer Luke's happy and
much-loved wife.

'Hush, child, hush. Luke would never have betrayed you. He is braver than that. No, your husband
must have found out by some ill chance. But cou-

rage, we shall not surrender you. Get you in the middle of the women and you will be as one of them.'

Whilst they had been speaking, Jasper had walked up to the leading riders to hold up a commanding hand as they sought to drive straight through the camp, disregarding women, children and the handiwork of the women spread out on the grass.

'Hold!' he shouted. 'What do you want with us?'

They stopped. Grudgingly.

The leading man dismounted. He was a portly gentleman, well turned out and he announced himself with all the customary arrogance of a minor jack-in-office.

'I am Sir Christopher Cave, magistrate, of the City of Bath, and I am come here with, and on behalf of, the Most Noble the Marquess of Clairval, to recover his wife, whom he has good reason to believe is hidden among you. These men with me are my officers.'

'So, then,' replied Jasper, equally arrogant, 'it is he with whom I will deal, and not you.'

'You mistake, you vagabond. It is I who am the law here, and m'lord Clairval has rightly called upon me to administer it.'

'No, *you* mistake. You are on the heath, and in the camp of the Romanies, and it is I who am the law. Nevertheless, I will speak to this man who has lost his wife, if he has the courage to face me and explain why and how he lost her—and why he thinks that she is here.'

Anne was near enough to them to hear what they were saying. She had also seen that several men had left the chaises parked on the road, had taken horse and were riding towards Jasper and Sir Christopher. One of them, she was sure, was Clairval.

She was not mistaken. He arrived at the gallop, surveyed the scene before him contemptuously, and barked at Sir Christopher, 'Well, man? Has he not surrendered my wife to you yet?'

'He refuses to speak to me at all, since I am not the complainant,' returned Sir Christopher, somewhat plaintively, 'although I have assured him that I am the law…'

'Well, be damned to that,' roared Clairval. 'What the devil was the use of bringing you along if you were going to bleat at every dirty gypsy who chooses to bandy words with you! Fernando,' he bellowed at that gentleman who had carefully walked his way towards the centre of interest. 'Be ready for me, should I need you.

'Now, you piece of filth,' he bellowed unpleasantly at Jasper, who was still standing, face inscrutable, staring at him. 'I am Clairval. I believe that you are hiding my adulterous and runaway wife from me. The law says that she is mine to claim, and yours to surrender. Bring her out immediately, or it will be the worse for all of you.'

He had ridden his horse in front of Sir Christopher's and rose in the saddle to stare menacingly down at Jasper, his face even more purple than usual. His anger was a living thing, hanging in the air above Jasper.

But Jasper was in no wise daunted. He did not retreat so much as a step. He merely held his ground, stared up at m'lord Marquess, and said, his voice cool, 'I assure you, m'lord, that I harbour no Lady Clairval in this camp.'

This almost brought a hysterical choked laugh from the listening Anne. For was not Jasper's apparently massive untruth, a truth? For it was not many weeks since he had divorced her from the angry man in front of him and turned her into Luke's wife.

By the laws of the Rom, that was. Not by the laws of Sir Christopher and his kind.

Clairval was no fool. He was not deceived. He raised his hand, and shouted, 'Do not palter with me, man. Give me back my wife, or it will be the worse for you.'

Jasper slowly turned around. He looked at the silent women, at the children, some of them whimpering a little as they felt the hostility which surrounded them, and then renewed his gaze on Clairval.

'Why, sir, I see no Lady Clairval among us. Nor, I think, do you.' For he was certain that the *chovihani* would have arranged matters so that Anne could not be identified.

'And what kind of an answer is that? Sir Christopher,' Clairval announced, turning his feral eyes on that shivering functionary who was rapidly seeing his authority draining away from him, usurped by Clairval. 'I shall order your constables and my men to raze this camp to the ground so that my wife may not be hidden from me, seeing that their leader—for so I suppose this clown to be—will not answer me straight and fair.'

'Oh, I only do that to those who speak to *me* straight and fair,' announced Jasper, still standing his ground despite Clairval's threats.

Clairval leaned forward, his face dark and ominous. 'Little man, little man, I do not make idle threats. That is not Clairval's way. If you do not hand my wife over, I shall destroy this encampment utterly. Tonight you will truly lay your heads on the bare earth and lament that you gave refuge to a lying bitch of an adulteress.'

He meant it. Anne, of all of them there present, knew that Clairval meant it, that he was uttering no idle threat. He would destroy the gypsies' means of living without a thought—for that had become his way.

She shuddered. There was only one thing left for her to do. She thought of the gypsies and their kindnesses to her. Of the tarot pack that Mrs Chikno had given to her that very morning, of the joy which she had felt over the past weeks since she and Luke had joined them. Of Luke's new-found strength of mind, and of body, which had been enhanced by the time he had spent with Tawno and his men. Of her own happiness.

She closed her eyes. The *chovihani* looked at her, and divined her purpose. She said softly, 'No, child, no. We shall not give way to him.'

Anne shook her head. She knew the man before them only too well. He would leave the gypsies nothing: he would destroy them utterly. And she would be the cause of it. At whatever cost, she must stop him.

She rose to her feet and walked towards him. As she passed Jasper, he too, said, 'No, Stella, no,' but she shook her head again before coming to a stop just below Clairval, where he towered above them in all his pride of caste.

He looked down at her, a trifle puzzled. Anne knew at once that what the *chovihani* had told her was true. He did not know her. He did not associate Anne's golden glory of face and figure, her lustrous black hair streaming down her back, and her proud carriage, with the hunted and beaten creature he had driven from his home by his cruelties.

'M'lord, for I cannot call you husband,' she said. His whole bulky body came to attention when she spoke, and he recognised her voice—although he did not recognise her proud defiance: that was new.

'M'lord, there is no need to threaten these good people with the loss of their homes and their livelihood. At whatever cost, I am surrendering myself to you in order to prevent that.'

His whole face changed. He threw his head back and laughed. 'So, madam, they have turned you into one of them, a randy gypsy bitch indeed, I'll be bound, as brazen as they are. I shall have the greatest pleasure in taming you. The game is won. Fernando,' he bawled, 'you may take m'lady Clairval to the chaise.'

But Fernando was not paying attention. He was watching another large party approach them, a party which was arriving unheeded since the attention of both the Romanies and their would-be invaders was concentrated on the three principals in the action: Jasper, Clairval and Anne.

The new riders were cutting off the route to

Clairval's two chaises, were galloping across the heath and were upon them, before any saw them. What new players in the game were these?

'You have not yet won, m'lord,' Fernando told Clairval, for he had recognised one of the leading riders as Luke Harcourt, last seen left for dead on the road to Haven's End.

What Fernando had not seen was that two other riders were approaching from quite the opposite direction, and were equally intent on arriving at the heart of the Romany encampment where Clairval and the Earl of Lyndale's party were now facing one another.

Luke and James had left Haven's End early that morning.

Something, he knew not what, was driving Luke on. In the night he had dreamed of Anne. She was looking even more of a Romany than she had done when he left her, and her arms were held out to him. She was pleading with him to come to her. He knew at once that she was in some kind of trouble.

The dream was so strong that when Luke had risen and walked painfully down to breakfast, he had said to James, 'Father, I know I may sound childish and odd, but I have the strongest feeling

that we ought to set out as soon as possible for
Bath. If we don't, we may be too late.'

James did not argue with him, merely ordered the
head groom to have the horses ready for them within
the next half-hour. He had decided to take along
with him a goodly contingent of Haven's End's
grooms and stable lads. Who knew what might be
needed when they caught up with Clairval?

As they pounded along the rough roads towards
Bath, Luke was so troubled by the premonition
which would not leave him, and which told him
that Anne was in real danger, that he did not feel
the full pain of his bruised body. He only had one
idea in his head: that he must reach Anne before
Clairval did. For he was sure that the danger Anne
was in came from Clairval.

Thus it was that when they galloped towards the
heath where Jasper and the Romanies were
camped, he was not surprised to see two chaises,
with Clairval's arms emblazoned on them, standing in the road which led to it.

He ground out an oath, and forgetting pain, forgetting everything, turned and shouted at his father, 'We are too late. He is here, and, oh, God, I
swear that she is surrendering herself to him!'

Father and son spurred their way forward at full
gallop across the heath to reach the spot where

Luke's dear love was on the point of accepting hideous captivity again for the sake of those who had been kind to her. Like Fernando, they did not see the two Runners approaching from the opposite direction. They were concentrating too hard on reaching Clairval and Anne before he had time to snatch her away.

On seeing them, Clairval, his expression uglier than ever, swore at Luke and James with such force that his horse became agitated, and he had difficulty controlling it.

'So, Lyndale, I see that you are a proven liar. You were concealing your rogue of a son whilst prating to me that you knew nothing of him! Well, you may leave, and take your by-blow with you. You are too late. Lady Clairval is my wife, my chattel, and she will return with me to Clairval Castle, where my physicians will decide what treatment she needs to restore her to her senses.'

Luke, who had flung himself from his horse to run to Anne, who was staring at him as though he were the god in the old Greek plays who had descended from heaven in a chariot to save the beleaguered hero and heroine, said savagely, 'No, Clairval. It is you who are too late. Anne will return with me to Haven's End. She needs no physicians, and you lie when you tell the world that she is mad—as all the good people assembled here will testify.'

There was a murmur of consent from the Romanies. Jasper Petulengro, not in the least put out by the presence of the new actors in the drama, nor intimidated by the aristocrats around him, said in his most composed voice, 'I wish to say only to you, Sir Christopher, that Stella here is as sane a lady as I have ever met. She needs no physician— only love.'

James and Clairval spoke together. James to say, 'I have decided that I shall offer Lady Clairval sanctuary and that I am prepared to help her to argue her case against you in every court in the land, if need be.'

Clairval's bellow was, '"Stella!" And who the devil is Stella? Oh, I suppose you mean my slut of a wife.'

Pandemonium suddenly reigned. Luke, angered by the slur put upon Anne, let go of her, and seized Clairval by the leg in order to pull him from the saddle. Clairval, taken by surprise, lost his balance and, before he knew it, was on the ground with Luke now attempting to grasp him by the throat. Clairval's horse, already excited as a result of his master's capricious treatment of him, threw back its head, showed its teeth and, neighing madly, galloped at speed across the heath, away from the noise of the wrangling men, to disappear from view among the trees on its boundary.

'No,' exclaimed Jasper, as Clairval and Luke rolled, fighting, on the ground before him, 'There is no need for this.' He gave an order to the Romany men about him to pull the two combatants apart.

James had also dismounted, and watched whilst Luke and Clairval were separated, both of them glaring their hate at the other. The *chovihani* had come up to support her husband. She put an arm around Anne's shoulders to comfort her.

'Truly spoken, husband,' she said, her voice mild. 'The parties are at a stand-off,' for James's small army had now arrived and was facing Clairval and Sir Christopher's followers, who had thus lost their ability to do as they wished to Anne and the Romanies without let or hindrance.

'Truly spoken, wife. It is stalemate, since I assume that neither Lord Clairval nor Lord Lyndale wishes to fight a pitched battle on the heath,' announced Jasper, putting himself on the other side of Anne.

'I remind you again,' he continued, 'my law rules here on the heath. I order that Stella, or Lady Clairval, whichever you care to call her, shall choose with whom she leaves.'

'No,' cried Clairval, who had wrenched himself free from the men who had been holding him. 'She is my wife. The law of the land is here in the person of Sir Christopher Cave, and he has already ruled that she will return with me.'

Not quite stalemate then, was Luke's wry response. He knew that any court in the land would rule that, as the case stood, Anne had no option but to return to her husband—as a moment ago she had been so prepared. Besides that, his father was a magistrate, sworn to uphold the law which Clairval was constantly invoking. Had he and Luke arrived before Clairval they could have taken Anne away and thus created a whole new situation; but they had not.

Triumph rode on Clairval's face. Improbably, given all that he was, and all that he had done, he had the moral and legal advantage—for what that was worth. For like pieces on a chessboard, pinned in an impossible position, all the actors in the drama had no immediate move which they could make to enforce their will on the others—short of a public brawl.

Except that God, or Fate, or Providence, call it what you would, had placed a pair of new pieces on to the board. The two Runners who had been sitting their horses at a little distance, unconsidered, whilst the drama was being played out, now moved into action.

Jenkinson rode forward until he was immediately before Clairval, crying, 'Hold a moment. I have a duty to perform which may settle this matter once and for all.'

'You?' snarled Clairval, his face even more scarlet with fury than before. 'What the devil are *you* doing here, interfering with me and mine? Be off with you, before I have Sir Christopher whip you from the heath.'

'Oh, I think not,' said Jenkinson, smiling, his revenge for all the humiliations he had suffered at Clairval's hands, now ready to be taken and savoured. 'Mr Luke Harcourt, I see that you are sufficiently recovered from the beating which m'lord Clairval ordered to be inflicted on you, for you to be able to ride here today to care for your lady.'

'My lady,' bellowed Clairval, 'not his.'

Jenkinson was not to be deflected. He had heard Clairval name Sir Christopher Cave, knew who he was, and now spoke commandingly to that somewhat bewildered gentleman who had come on what had seemed to be a simple errand, but had found himself in the middle of an almost feudal war.

'Sir, I take it that you are the magistrate from Bath enlisted to do this criminal's dirty work,' and he waved at Clairval. 'Take note that I, a Bow Street Runner, carrying the commission of the Home Secretary, am serving a warrant on m'lord Clairval, and his servants George Fernando and Jem Haskins, and other person, or persons unknown, for assault and battery on the person of Mr Harcourt, done in the presence of myself and my companion here,' and now he waved at Greene.

'Also take further note that it is your duty to convey m'lord Clairval to the gaol in the precincts of Bath, there to await the arrival of officers of the law from London who will convey him to the capital to stand trial for that assault before his peers in the House of Lords. His servants will be dealt with in the appropriate court.'

He paused dramatically. Clairval, now almost black in the face, swung on Sir Christopher, shouting, 'The man's mad! How dare he speak thus to me? Take heed that, if you obey him, I shall make sure that you never hold office again.'

'I have not finished,' said Jenkinson. 'Take heed of *me*, Sir Christopher, for I am now serving a warrant on m'lord Clairval, which commands you to arrest him for the murder of his steward in the county of York some time during the summer of 1826. This warrant is to be added to the one concerning Mr Luke Harcourt, and thus it is your double duty to commit him at once to prison.

'Here are the warrants, signed by the Home Secretary and duly attested and sealed. Here also is a further warrant relating to m'lord's treatment of m'lady, but that I shall not read aloud for very decency's sake. Sir, do your duty.'

Dazed, Sir Christopher took from Jenkinson the three warrants which he was holding out. During the whole of Jenkinson's announcement there had been a deathly quiet. Every eye had been upon him.

Luke, who was by Anne's side again, an arm round her, felt that he wanted to cheer as Jenkinson threw his grenades, one by one, at Clairval's feet. He could see his father smiling in relief. Anne was whispering to him, 'I don't understand, Luke. How did they find out what he had done?'

Before Luke could try to answer her, Fernando was the first to break. He began to run across the heath at top speed, only to be tripped up, and then sat upon, by several of the Romanies. Clairval, his face working, swung on that broken reed, Sir Christopher Cave, again.

'You cannot believe this piece of scum. He has no authority to demand that you arrest me, and my servants. I defy him to do so.'

Sir Christopher, who had been reading the warrants, said unhappily, 'Alas, m'lord. These documents are all in proper form, and signed by the Home Secretary as the man has said. I have no alternative but to execute them, and convey you to the gaol at Bath…'

He got no further. Clairval, his face now almost black, so suffused was it with blood, his eyes wandering, his mouth twisted, and his voice almost unintelligible, cried out in a faltering voice, 'No, you cannot…' and he threw up his arms in supplication. In his despair, he appealed to James as a fellow peer to help him, even though he had so recently treated him as an enemy.

'Lyndale, I beg of you, you must assist me…' But before James could reply, as though his mind, like his eyes, was wandering, unable to fix itself on anything, Clairval turned his distorted face on Anne again.

'It is you who have done this to me, and you…' and he pointed at Jenkinson who leaned forward in the saddle to say softly to him,

'You should have treated me fair…but you did not.'

Clairval took no heed of him. For a moment he stood silent. He was now facing Anne and Luke, his hands outstretched towards them, foam on his lips, his eyes wild, his face working. He began to walk towards them, but before he reached them he gave a great cry and pitched to the ground at their feet. To lie there, unmoving, blood running slowly from his mouth.

Jasper's curse delivered on the day of Anne and Luke's wedding had been fulfilled. He who had tried to part them had been struck down…

Chapter Sixteen

Later, much later, both Anne and Luke would look back on what had become their deliverance and wonder at what followed it. Surprisingly, in the seconds after Clairval's fall, there was a great silence before everyone began to crowd around the body to issue instructions, each according to his own nature and his official position.

James, the nearest to person to the stricken man, was the first to move towards him, only for Anne to run from Luke's side to fall on her knees beside the man who had so mistreated her, and who had intended to kill her as soon as she was in his power again.

He had been her husband, and before he had married her he had treated her kindly. Even though she knew that this had been done to deceive her, the essential goodness of Anne's nature warred with her sense of relief that her tormentor was either dead, or so injured in mind and body that he no longer presented a threat to her.

His dying eyes looked into hers. He seemed to be trying to say something to her. His mouth quivered a little before slackening. His whole body shuddered and then stilled in the finality of death.

It was over.

The long years of fear and pain were behind Anne, and now would never be renewed in a further imprisonment. Luke had bent down to lift her up, to take her away, so that Clairval might be examined in order to establish that he was really dead, although none who saw him stretched out on the grass, his face livid, could believe otherwise.

'Come away,' he said gently. 'His race is run, and so is your suffering at his hands.'

Anne clutched at him for comfort. To the surprise of both of them, tears began to run down her face. Luke wiped them away with a gentle hand, and said, 'You are surely not weeping for him?'

She shook her head. 'Oh, no. But, Luke, what a wasted life. He was never happy during the whole time I knew him. He seemed to be so for a little before we married, but afterwards, never.'

Sir Christopher Cave had dismounted and was supervising his officials. He would be responsible for reporting Clairval's death, and for all the local arrangements which would flow from it.

'God struck him down in his wickedness, m'lady, and called him to judgement,' he felt impelled to say to Anne. He had read the warrants detailing all the dead man's crimes, and had seen on Luke's face and body the marks of the brutal beating for which the dead man had been responsible. He was regretting the ease with which he had allowed Clairval to deceive him as to his true nature—but who would have thought a Marquess to be such a wretch?

'Not God,' said Jenkinson, who had also left his horse, and needed to be present when Clairval was officially reported to be dead. 'Not God, but he, himself, was responsible for his death. His rages and his foul temper brought him daily nearer to it. I have seen such a fatality from apoplexy before when a man has allowed his rage to overcome him.'

Both James and Luke looked sharply at him. Neither said anything, although both thought of the glee with which Jenkinson had produced his warrants and how his taunting words had so fuelled Clairval's anger that they had brought about the final outburst which had killed him.

Luke had a duty of gratitude to perform. He held out his hand to Jenkinson and said, 'I understand from my father that I owe my life to you and your companion—and perhaps a little to Pat O'Hare, who put you on my trail. We—that is, Anne, the Romanies and I, thought that you were following us in order to arrest me for kidnapping Lady Clairval.'

'That weren't nohow, Master Luke. Once m'lord turned me off, he was always my target. I learned too much about his wicked ways when I was working for him. It is a blessing that he was struck down when he was. A blessing, indeed. His sudden death has saved us all a deal of trouble, expense and scandal—you and the lady most of all.'

'How much did my father know of this?' asked Luke shrewdly.

'Why, as to that, not much. Enough. Naught about the warrants. As for you, Master Luke, it was a pleasure to save a man who took his punishment so bravely and never said a word, or did aught to stop it by blabbing all. You and your lady should be happy together. You make a gallant pair, for she was ready to give herself up to the monster who was after her in order to save those who had given her a refuge.'

Anne hid her face in Luke's chest on hearing Jenkinson praise her. She lifted it to say, 'I deserve no thanks for trying to help those who had sheltered me and made me happy, but it is kind of you to say so. You are the one who is to be thanked, for pursuing my husband for his crimes when many would have allowed his rank to deter them.'

'My duty too, m'lady.' Jenkinson was thinking how well everything had gone for him. So far, that was. There was still Sir Christopher to square. He took that gentleman on one side, said, a confidential expression on his face, 'Very fortunate for you, sir, that m'lord dropped dead when he did.'

'Eh, what's that, man?'

Jenkinson sighed. So the ass wanted chapter and verse, did he, before common sense struck him on the head?

'Saved you and the nobility and gentry from another nasty scandal, sir, to excite the mob and have them howling for blood and the guillotine. I'll lay odds Lord Lyndale won't want a noise made about this.'

'True, yes, very true.' Sir Christopher struggled this out unwillingly. 'But the accusations of murder, and the warrants...' His voice died away.

'Never got to serve them, sir, did you? Dead of excitement at the pleasure of finding m'lady, wasn't he, before you had time...?' He would have winked at Sir Christopher had he dared.

'Best you hand them back to me. I can restore

them to my master and tell him as how they was never properly served.'

Sir Christopher's sense of expediency warred with his sense of what were his dues to the law as a magistrate. But Jenkinson had tipped the balance for him.

'Oh, very well—but the constables…what of them?'

'You're not short of a guinea or two, are you, sir? And they are, if you follow me. Mum's the word, you know.'

Yes, Sir Christopher followed him. And so it was arranged. M'lord had been struck down even as he had found m'lady and the brouhaha on the heath had never happened. The nation's peace and civil order were preserved until another scandal came along—and Jenkinson had earned his reward…

The milling about Clairval's body had now ceased. His death was certain and Lord Lyndale, the senior magnate there, had decided that his body should be conveyed to Bath in the chaise in which he had arrived.

Jasper and the Romanies had stood silently by whilst the great men around them carried out the due processes of the law. Fernando, who was busy telling all he knew of his master's doings in an effort to save himself from prosecution for what he had done to Luke, was to be allowed to go.

'For,' said Jenkinson to Lord Lyndale and to Sir Christopher Cave, 'we none of us want what happened here today to be brought up in a court of law. The man who set all in train is dead and Fernando and his friends were but poor tools hired to do his dirty work for him. Let them go with a warning, I say. If I know aught, it'll be back to London for them all. No pickings for 'em in Bath, Sir Christopher.'

Both Luke and his father thought that it was a pleasure to watch such a master of intrigue at work. Even Anne said to Luke, 'I am glad that the foxy-faced man was on our side at the end. I don't think we should have been so lucky if my late husband had had the sense to let him keep charge of his affairs!'

A statement which convinced James that his daughter-in-law was clever as well as good. He now said quietly to Luke and Anne as they stood side by side, hand in hand, 'You will both of you, of course, wish to return to Haven's End with me. There is no bar now on Lady Clairval going wherever she wishes. Sir Christopher assures me that he will not have need of her in Bath.

'Her lawyers will have to be written to, and her

position *vis-à-vis* her personal wealth will have to be clarified, and it will be easier for her to do that from Haven's End, or even Lyndale House in Piccadilly, than from a gypsy encampment.'

Anne gave a great sigh. She was back in the busy world of consequence again, and she must leave the Arcadia in which she had so briefly lived with Luke and the Romanies. Common sense told her that her place, and Luke's, was in that world, however much she might wish to retain the freedom of the heath and the road.

So all that remained was for Luke and Anne to say goodbye to the Romanies and thank them for the sanctuary they had so freely offered. Tawno Chikno and his men had arrived back just as Clairval's body was being carried to his chaise. He had offered his opinion to Jasper that he and his men would have seen the lot of them off if he had been present when the various parties had arrived!

'Then it was as well you weren't,' was Jasper's quiet reply. 'For all's well that ends well, particularly without bloodshed.'

A statement which was echoed by his wife. The *chovihani* looked at Anne's unhappy face, and knew the reason for it.

'Child,' she said, 'you must go back to your own world, although you and Orion will always find a welcome with us should you need one. But the stars tell me that you will not, that after sailing a stormy sea you have at last reached harbour.'

'Oh, I wish that I could stay with you.' Anne's eyes were bright with unshed tears. 'I have been so happy.'

'But you have only lived the sunny days with us, my child, not the cold and storms of winter. And you were not born to this life. Remember, you take my gift with you. Use it well, for to be aware of the true nature of others when it is needful is a gift worth preserving. The gift of love you and your man already possess.'

Anne did not need to be told that with Luke's arm around her. Together they gathered up their few possessions. Mrs Chikno came to kiss her goodbye and to tell her to consult the tarot cards whenever she needed an answer to a difficult question. 'Do not quite forget us,' she finished.

'Never, never,' was Anne's passionate cry. She kissed all the little ones whom she had been teaching to read and write, and handed over her unfinished sewing to Mrs Chikno to complete it for her.

James, Lord Lyndale, watching the Romanies come, one by one, to say farewell to his son and the woman he loved, found himself strangely moved. He was a hard man in many ways, although tender to those whom he loved, but the gypsies' farewell to Anne impressed him, there was such affection in it. He had spent some time wondering what the woman was like who had obviously been such a profound influence on Luke, and now he knew that his son had chosen well.

Finally Jasper shook hands with Luke and Anne, repeating what the *chovihani* had told Luke: that they were both welcome to return to his tribe whenever they so wished.

'And do not forget the tricks which Tawno taught you,' were his final words to Luke. He had arranged that one of the gypsy wagons would drive Anne and Luke back to Bath where James, who would accompany them on horseback, would hire a chaise to take them to Haven's End.

Alone at last, in the chaise, Luke's arm around her, her head resting on his chest, Anne gave a little laugh. 'Oh, Luke, life is so strange. Do you remember what you told me about the thimble-rigger and the way he tricked us at Islington Fair? And then you said that there was a similar game called Find the Lady? Isn't that what everyone who arrived at the gypsy camp was trying to do? Find the Lady—whom you and Jasper and the rest had so cunningly hidden away? When you rode away from the camp you were diverting every-

one's attention just like the thimble-rigger did—
and in the end it saved me.'

'Yes,' replied Luke, his face thoughtful. 'I suppose that you could say that the tricks at the Fair
all have their parallels in real life—what a splendid notion for an article for Bayes! What a girl you
are, Anne. I shall never lack for ideas with you
near me,' and he rewarded her with a kiss.

Somehow, with Anne in his arms the journey to
his home seemed all too short, when previously it
had seemed too long!

James and Cressy sat on the terrace above the
park, where earlier in the spring they had entertained Luke before he had returned to London. It
was autumn now, the trees burning with red and
gold, not the delicate green of the reviving year.
No one then could have foreseen the dramatic
events which would follow, nor the fashion in
which Luke would return to Haven's End.

They were waiting for Anne and Luke to join
them for an *al fresco* meal. 'For,' as Cressy said,
'an informal setting will make matters easier for
Luke and his lady than if we assembled around a
strictly ordered dining-table.'

It was the day after they had brought Luke and
Anne back to Haven's End. Cressy had taken one

look at Anne's white face when she had walked into the huge entrance hall where a fierce dog embedded in a mosaic pavement guarded the house from danger, and said, 'My dear, I have prepared a room for you, and you may go there immediately to rest and recover. Luke, you look as though a good rest would benefit you as well. You may tell me of your adventures later.'

'I think,' said Luke, leaning forward to kiss his stepmother on the cheek, 'we ought to inform you straightaway that Anne is in no danger of being dragged back to imprisonment, so we may all rest quiet in our beds.'

'No chance of m'lord Clairval appearing to act as turnkey and gaoler, then?' asked Cressy.

'No, indeed.' It was Anne speaking, before she allowed a footman and a lady's maid to escort her to her room. 'My husband dropped dead of an apoplectic fit earlier today. I am free at last, but the manner in which I achieved my freedom was hardly one which I would have wished. I think that I always harboured the foolish hope that he might allow me to part from him voluntarily. Everything that happened today proved exactly how foolish it was.'

'Oh, you poor thing.' Cressy, always impulsive, always frank in her approach to life, put her arms around Anne and hugged her. 'And now you are here, you must try to forget all that has passed. I shall send a *tisane* to your room, and you must promise me that you will drink it. And Luke, too.'

She stood back before adding in her forthright way, 'I cannot say that I feel much sorrow over your husband's death. I met him on only a few occasions and he always felt it incumbent on him to insult me. And James, too. I suppose I shouldn't say that, one is never allowed to speak ill of the dead—a most foolish maxim in my opinion, particularly when the dead man behaved as badly as your late husband did.'

This spirited comment had all parties present suppressing a smile, and Anne, who had been a little worried about what the nature of her reception by Lady Lyndale might be, went to her room greatly relieved. Luke had told her that his stepmother was a clever lady of decided views, and was not afraid to air them. As usual, he had been speaking the truth.

James said gravely to his wife, when all the arrangements had been made for the care of the lovers, 'I'm afraid that you spoke truer than you knew of Clairval's villainy. This information is to remain private between the two of us, although I fear that it may yet become public knowledge. It seems that he murdered both his first wife and the steward who helped Anne to escape from her prison.'

'No surprise to me,' returned Cressy briskly. 'And now we must do all we can for Luke and his lady. You are agreed?'

James did not need to answer her, but he also felt that there were matters in the sorry affair in which his son had become embroiled which needed to be cleared up. Tactfully, of course.

The tact was in evidence on the next day when Anne and Luke, both looking refreshed, joined them on the terrace to eat their lunch and to sit in the sun afterwards, talking, apparently idly. Anne said little, content to leave conversation to the three others.

Luke was telling James and Cressy of their time among the gypsies. 'It was all very odd,' he said thoughtfully, after he had spoken briefly of gypsy magic and their belief in their ability to foretell the future, 'how everything worked out as the Romany fortune teller prophesied. It was enough to make one believe in them.'

'Oh, come, Luke,' said his father, that stalwart inheritor of the eighteenth-century Age of Reason with its dismissal of all things supernatural. 'Fortune tellers and prophecies, forsooth!'

Luke, now seated at Anne's feet, her hand gently stroking his head, read James's thoughts.

'Oh, I know that you are a sceptic, father, and that tales of magic and divination amuse you. But consider this. Jasper and the *chovihani,* his wife, were insistent in their demands that I leave their camp to draw Clairval away from it and Anne.

'Jasper told me that not only was I needed to be a decoy, but that whilst I was acting as one I should be required to pass a test to save both Anne and myself.'

He paused. 'I don't think that I believed him. I went—but solely to act as decoy, nothing else. But you must admit that events fell out as Jasper foretold. The consequence of my side-tracking Clairval and passing my test was that his arrival in Bath was delayed. Thus, when he finally found Anne, he did so only shortly before you and I, and the Runners arrived to spoil his plans. Had we not done so, he would have snatched Anne back again.

'And that caused the rage and fury which brought him his death.

'So, Jasper was right. I had to pass the test to save her. And he and Tawno Chikno, their equestrian *extraordinaire*, had prepared me for it by making my life as hard as they could—they thought that I was a soft cit, you see, and they were right.'

Luke smiled up at Anne again. 'Anne will tell

you that I can now perform the most remarkable feats on a horse. I could gain work at Astley's Amphitheatre tomorrow, I am sure.'

'True,' said Anne. 'He—and they—frightened me to death. The *chovihani* told me that it was necessary, but I did not know why.'

'To conquer fear,' said Luke soberly.

But Anne could see that they had not quite convinced James.

'More than that, m'lord,' she said quietly. 'When he married us, Jasper put a curse on anyone who would try to separate Luke and me. He said that they would perish by drowning in their own blood. And that was exactly what happened to my husband—as you saw.'

'Married you!'

Both Cressy and James were almost more struck by this piece of information than by Jasper's ability to foretell the future over the manner of Clairval's death. They both spoke at once. James was incredulous, and Cressy amused—although she did not allow her amusement to show.

'Well, he did divorce us first,' said Anne reasonably, her face a little pink, but 'Speak the truth and shame the devil', her father had always said. 'By Romany law, of course, which allowed him to divorce me from Clairval because of his cruelty to me. And Clairval did try to separate us, and he did die choking on his own blood.'

'Married!' pursued James. 'And you lived together as man and wife?'

He addressed this question to the air between Luke and Anne, looking at neither of them. Cressy, unknown to the other three, was giggling internally, although nothing showed. My poor conventional James! What a turn up! Nice Luke, previously as conventional as his father, living among the gypsies and marrying his runaway love! Oh, how I should have liked to have been present when he did.

'Yes,' said Luke, looking his father in the eye. 'Jasper married us as soon as he saw that we really loved one another, and that I was a fit person to look after her. He took some convincing of that, I can tell you. After all, they had given us sanctuary and we were living by their law.'

For some reason, Anne began to find this whole conversation amusing. The rules which governed the conduct of those who lived in the polite world seemed to be the silly ones, not those of the Rom. She was cautious enough not to say so, and careful not to catch Cressy's eye. She had the impression that Cressy's notions of commonsense living might be a little different from those of her husband.

'Of course,' Luke went on, 'now that Clairval is dead, Anne is free, and we are back in polite society again, we do intend to go through a formal marriage ceremony first—before we live together, that is.'

This offering was intended to placate his father, and assure him that he and Anne were serious in their love for one another, and were not engaging in a passing affair.

'No reflection on the Romanies and their marriage laws, you understand, merely an acknowledgement that our laws demand it,' he added. 'We must always remember that they helped to save Anne's life when they gave her refuge, and were willing to sacrifice themselves when Clairval arrived at their camp and demanded her back.'

'You haven't proposed to me formally since we left the gypsy camp, have you, Luke? But, seeing that I am already your wife, you hardly needed to. Of course, I shall remarry you, by English law this time—to satisfy the proprieties.'

If there was a touch of satire in this last statement, then Anne thought that she might be forgiven it. After all, the proprieties had done precious little for her whilst she had been undergoing Clairval's persecution!

'At once, if not sooner!' Luke replied, his eyes on her brimming with love. 'I shall travel to London tomorrow, haste, post haste, and obtain a special licence so that we may be married on my return. We shall attract less notice if we marry quietly, here at Haven's End.'

'She's but a new widow...' began James, and then faltered to a stop. He knew that it was his last attack on an impregnable position, and he was not sure that he wanted to win it.

'No one would expect my dear Anne to go into mourning for a husband who had repeatedly abused her and had tried to kill her. It would be eccentric in the extreme! Besides, I no longer have any respect for what our world considers *comme il faut*. It nearly condemned Anne to an early death.'

There was no denying that. Luke said into the silence of agreement, for he wished to be alone with his love a little before he left for London, 'Pray allow me, Cressy and you, sir, to take Anne on a tour of the grounds. I have told her more than once how beautiful they are.'

His father and stepmother watched them walk down the terrace steps and into the park.

'He has chosen well,' said James. 'What a fool her first husband was, to value her only for her money.'

'Neither the first nor the last,' returned Cressy. 'I am a little worried about how Luke will feel about marrying an heiress.'

'No need to worry,' said Cressy. 'Just trust Luke—and the lady. She seems to possess a deal of common sense, which is surprising in one so young.'

James nodded his agreement.

'What is it, Luke?' Anne's voice was gently probing. She knew him well enough to be aware that, happy though he was that Clairval no longer stood as a barrier between them, something was troubling him a little.

It was. Earlier that day James had said to him, apparently casually, 'Coutts tells me that for the last three quarters you have not touched the allowance which I have settled on you. May I ask why?'

'You may, sir. I had been meaning to speak to you of this: but in all the brouhaha of the affair with Clairval it had slipped my mind. I have decided that I must live on what I earn, not on you. I have depended on your kindness and your generosity for too long. I must make my own way in the world. By my writing, which, as you must be aware, has grown increasingly more successful of late. Successful enough, I believe, to enable me to keep a wife.'

'Yes.' Cressy had handed him Luke's novel to read and its power had surprised and impressed him. Everything about Luke was surprising and impressing his father these days. He was a changed man, and the change was for the better.

'The thing is,' James had said gravely, 'that I would wish you to have the money. For my sake, not yours. I am only too aware that if in the past, matters had fallen out a trifle differently, you would have been my heir. Allow me to continue your allowance—you need not touch it, you may let the capital accumulate. It will be there for you should you ever need it.'

He had given a half-laugh. 'Not that you will. You are marrying an exceedingly rich woman, have you thought of that?'

'Yes,' Luke had said, looking away from his father. 'Not until Clairval dropped dead, that is—but his death did more than simply provide me with the opportunity to marry Anne.'

His father had been able to see that Luke had been troubled, but he had not pursued the matter further. Luke had cut himself free from his dependence on Haven's End and all that it stood for, and he must allow him to go his own way, and make his own decisions…

Luke was back in the present again. He was out in the open with his love, and, perhaps symbolically, they had reached the very limits of the park and the open country was before them. Beyond the boundary fence lay coarse grassland, scrub and a dark wood. Luke flung himself on the ground, and drew Anne down beside him to kiss her.

'And that is all we may allow ourselves to do for the present,' he told her regretfully. 'For, out of respect for James and Cressy's feelings, we must behave ourselves until we are married. Romany weddings and divorces forsooth, I can hear my father saying.'

Anne rearranged her dishevelled clothing. 'It won't be long,' she said practically. 'Although I think it a great nonsense, all the same. Jasper well and truly married us, but I suppose that we need the law to secure our children's futures.'

Luke kissed her again. 'So pleased to learn that you propose a family, madam. In a sense, that is what is troubling me. You are so filthy rich, and I really don't want your money.'

'Oh, that,' said Anne dismissively. She knew that he was speaking the truth, and loved him for it.

'Yes, that.' He paused and began to laugh at the determined expression on her small face. Behind her air of demure rectitude and inborn modesty Anne possessed a spirit and determination allied to a forthrightness that had sustained her through Clairval's long persecution and its aftermath.

'You see, Luke, I have been thinking. There is

so much to do, so much to think about. I want to visit Islington to thank kind Mrs Britten and to see poor Dizzy again. I hope that he hasn't missed me too much. I enjoyed our simple life together on the road and the heath, and I want to come to live with you in your little house in Chelsea and look after you while you earn our living. You will earn our living, won't you, Luke?'

'Yes,' he said, taking her hand and kissing it. 'Now that we are not off to the Americas, I can take up Chapman's offer for another novel, and start on all the articles I have been asked to write by Bayes and the others. You don't mind being a struggling author's wife?'

'The *chovihani* and the tarot cards say that you won't struggle long. But even so, I would sooner struggle with you than live in the grandest castle. You see, I have decided that, with your agreement, my wealth must be put into trusts for our children and for the maintenance of the estate that I inherited on my father's death, keeping only a small income for us. But there is also another problem, which we shall have to solve together.'

'And that is?'

'Oh, it's the oddest thing, Luke. You see, Clairval was the last of his line, and there was no entail, so our marriage settlement said that, if he died before me without leaving an heir, it would all come to me. He did it to spite the Crown which otherwise would have taken all.

'It's a strange irony, isn't it? He never thought that I would inherit because he was so sure that once married, he would soon have an heir. Consequently, when he dropped dead, I inherited everything. So we shall need another trust—if you so agree.'

Luke looked at her in awe. 'Did you think of all that by yourself? It's a splendid way out of being too wealthy!'

Anne leaned over to kiss him on the nose. She loved him as much for his goodness as she hoped he loved her for her attempt to live an honest life. She put up her hand to stroke, as gently as she could, the bruises plain on his face, mute witnesses of his determination to protect her from harm.

'Oh, Luke, all the time that I was with the gypsies, I was thinking about what to do with my money if I ever gained my freedom from him. I didn't want it to come between us, you see.'

'Nor shall it,' returned Luke happily. 'But I am a little worried that you might regret not living the comfortable life which your wealth would give you.'

Anne was silent for a long moment.

'Never,' she said at last. 'I was married to consequence and a title. We had money and comfort in plenty, and all was dust and ashes. Oh, Luke, do but remember what the Bible says.'

She began to quote a text from it, but before she had reached the third word his voice had joined hers, and they were reciting it together.

'"Better a dinner of herbs where love is, than a stalled ox and hatred therewith".'

Whilst they were speaking, they had stood up and were face to face, hands clasped. Luke leaned forward to kiss her.

'Dear Mrs Harcourt, for you are already my wife, I love and worship you, and is it any wonder that I cannot wait for us to be alone together with none to come between us? We have earned our happiness, and we must not waste it. I loved you long before I knew who you were. It was the penniless sempstress I wanted to marry, not Lady Clairval. My love who was so happy with me in the Romany camp.'

'Dear Luke. There is something else I must tell you. I was fearful that I might be the barren one, not Clairval. But there is another reason for us to marry soon. I am already breeding, or so the *chovihani* says, and we must make our child legitimate by English, as well as by Romany, law.'

Joy on his face, as well as in his heart, Luke kissed her again. 'Our wedding night!' he exclaimed exultantly. 'Is it possible that our child was conceived on our wedding night?'

'Yes,' said Anne, 'we were doubly blessed.'

They stood for a moment, silent before they began to walk together into the future, where quiet contentment and fulfilment awaited them in the little house in Chelsea, not the alarums and excursions of the past year...

Above them, James and Cressy looked down on the lovers as they walked hand in hand across the grass towards the terrace steps.

'I wish them,' she said, 'all the happiness which you and I have achieved. I cannot wish them more. I could bestow on them no greater blessing.'

'Amen to that,' James said.

So be it, and so it was.